BODY SNATCHER

BODY SNATCHER

JUAN CARLOS ONETTI

Translated from the Spanish
by Alfred Mac Adam

pantheon books   new york

Library of Congress Cataloging-in-Publication Data

Onetti, Juan Carlos, 1909–
[Juntacadáveres. English]
Body snatcher / Juan Carlos Onetti; translated from the Spanish by Alfred MacAdam.
p.   cm.
Translation of Juntacadáveres.
I. Title.
PQ8519.O59J813   1991   863–dc20   90-53411
ISBN 0-679-40178-4

Book Design by Anne Scatto

Manufactured in the United States of America

First American Edition

FOR SUSANA SOCA

For being the most naked form
of piety I have ever known; for
her talent

BODY SNATCHER

CHAPTER I

Panting, sweating, his legs splayed to straddle the bounces of the Enduro spur line car, Snatcher walked along the aisle to join the group of three women. The train was only a few miles outside of Santa María. He smiled encouragingly into those faces swollen by boredom, flushed with heat, yawns, and wisecracks. The green from the fields next to the river leaned a weak coolness against the dusty windows.

As soon as I tell them we're pulling in, they'll start to chatter, to put on their makeup, to remember what they are; they'll get uglier and older; they'll try to look like young ladies, lowering their eyes to examine their hands. There are three of them, and it didn't even take me two weeks. Barthé's getting more than he deserves, him and the whole town, though people might laugh when they see them and keep on laughing for a few days or weeks. They're not sixteen anymore and the way they're dressed would put a chill on a billygoat. But they're okay, they're good, they're cheerful, and they know how to work.

"Not much longer now," he resigned himself to say enthusiastically. He patted María Bonita's knee and grinned at the other two, at Irene's childlike, round face and Nelly's high, straight, yellow eyebrows, which she drew each morning to complement the disinterest, the imbecility, and the nothingness expressed by her eyes.

"I thought so, it's time we were getting there," answered María Bonita. She pursed her lips toward the window and inaugurated the opening of handbags, the dance of mirrors, compacts, and lipsticks. She was right, after all. This Santa María must be a dump.

"It's true what you said," agreed Nelly, smoothing out her lipstick with a fingernail.

Irene daubed the sides of her nose with her rouge, languid, devoid of faith. She had her thick knees spread wide. Her wide-brimmed straw hat covered with frippery bent out of shape as she smashed it against the seat back. She wiped clean a semicircle of window with the back of her hand and saw a rainbow of dry pasture, plantings, and gray, green, and ocher distance simmering in the overcast afternoon.

"It doesn't matter much to me. Of course, it isn't Montevideo, but I like the country."

"You know I never lie," said María Bonita, mocking and irritated. She had finished fixing herself up and was smoking rapidly, sitting upright, calm, and confident of her secret power to dominate. *A real woman*, declared Snatcher, severely and proudly. *You don't think about shopping or parties. You stay home, work, and save your money.*

"That's why we came," confirmed Nelly. "The city is nice, but we're here on business."

"He's looking at your mouth again, pudgy," María Bonita warned.

Irene shrugged her shoulders and went on making marks on the window with her fingertip.

"I wasn't looking, I swear," protested Snatcher. He laughed along with them for a bit, to show he was one of them and then he took a look at the other passengers in the car. Nobody he knew. "On the platform, then we'll see." The Experimental School, dark and isolated in the unmoving air, came into view. A slack flag hung down, a heavily loaded truck hunkered down as it worked its way up the hill, toward Colonia. He considered lying to them about farms and crops and was on the verge of quoting figures and the names of different kinds of wheat. And even though he said nothing, even though the things he was thinking only showed in the whitish line of spit that formed on his smile, as he got up and helped the women to get their bags down, he suspected that the temptation to say stupid things came from that threat of fatigue, from that fear of failure which had been plaguing him for the past few months, ever since the day when he thought that finally the moment of setting things to rights, the moment for touching beautiful dreams had come, the moment when he accepted the doubt that perhaps it had all come too late.

The platform would be crowded, a group of men would be staring from the door of the Club, another guy would be leaning against the wall of the Plaza Hotel to watch the car carrying the three women toward the little house on the coast. These three disheartened women, ugly, made old by the trip, tricked out in the grotesque outfits they'd eagerly bought with the money he'd advanced them.

CHAPTER II

The women arrived on the five o'clock train, the first Monday of vacation. Tito and I were alone on the platform, except for two porters and the telegrapher. It was hot, humid, and overcast; I felt the hardness of the corn sacks against my ribs. Behind me: the silence of the empty streets, the deserted plaza. A swinish expectancy and an equally swinish rejection possessed the city, from the banks of the river to the fields of oats lining the rails. Expectation and rejection oozed and covered the indolent position of our bodies and the challenge we struggled to keep up—our heads held high and a fixed grin on our faces from which hung a cigarette (Tito) and a pipe (me).

"Tight as a drum," Tito had said near the balcony of the Cooperative. The patrolman, motionless and sweaty at the head of the block, framed by the solitary streets, windows, and locked doors, smiled and sized us up with his filthy adult wisdom. He watched us, certain that we would go right on walking to the station.

We were leaning on the sacks, still smoking, still saying nothing, when the smoke from the train appeared at the curve. Looking at the renewed smile on Tito's face, his open shirt, his crossed legs, the moist cigarette dangling from his lips, I saw myself. I examined my bravado, I began to doubt the sincerity of my hatred. When Tito stopped imitating me and started to repeat his father's mannerisms, I turned against him, I almost became an ally of the closed city.

"Tight as a drum," Tito's father had said the night before or at lunch, in an admiring imitation of the voice of Father Bergner, my relative, who had spoken at the League meeting on Saturday. With his hairy hand pounding the flower-patterned oilcloth that covered the table, with a mother trying to keep her kids quiet, with the hardware store assistant nodding his silent approval, prudently and respectfully, the priest leaned over his bowl of soup at the head of the table.

"We shall close the city as tight as a drum," recited the hardware store assistant. "I want my house to be closed tight as a drum."

If it were a single word, I could present it tonight or tomorrow to Julita, when she asks me, as she always does, to leave her a word that can last her all the next day, so she can let it burn down like a candle before the memory of my dead brother. *Tightasadrum* is what I'd say to her, consoling myself a little, freer of her and her vicious misfortune.

"Jorge, look but don't laugh," Tito said. He forgot that I couldn't laugh, that we had sworn to be indifferent and not to go beyond common courtesy if one of the women seemed to require it.

The only other people to get off the train besides the three women and the man were an old couple who talked with the porter and then walked along the platform. The man was wearing baggy, gaucho-style trousers and bending over because the valise was so heavy; he was shaking his hand over the yellowed head of the old lady, who was practically a dwarf. They took the path that led to the gate to the "Triumph" ranch on the other side of the tracks.

"Body Snatcher," announced Tito.

The man who had worked in my father's newspaper before taking on the women, arranged their bags on the ground, added a round cardboard box one of the three women handed him, and then dashed back to the train to help them down—unnecessarily, just barely touching the fingertips they extended toward him as they carefully stepped down without entangling themselves in their incredible skirts. Larsen, Snatcher, was wearing a new, dark suit and a black hat that shaded his eyes. He'd always worn gray in the editorial offices of EL LIBERAL, humiliated and laconic, but too ordinary, too old to have what Julita would call a secret sorrow. Anyway, he always wore gray, always kept his jacket buttoned, always kept his tie with its pearl pin knotted tight, even in summer, perched on a stool in the administrative office, his curved nose hovering over the huge account books, the inkstains, the political slogans carved into his desk, the ragged cuffs of his shirt covering half his hands, with or without a secret sorrow.

He helped the last woman down and the three of them

stood there, swollen, next to the luggage, patting themselves down and straightening their clothes. They twisted
their necks prudently to practice their expressions, uncertain, curious, on the defensive, as they walked along
the emptiness of the platform, through the discolored and
calm landscape where the old couple was disappearing
tremulously, where, beyond the Experimental School, a
ray of sunlight, one single ray, thin, hard, and too late,
beat down to illuminate the arrival of the women at Santa
María, officially declared a city a few months back.

The porters picked up the valises, the cardboard box,
a cretonne bag, and walked by us, trotting along and bent
over, pretending to work hard. One winked and showed
us a tooth. They turned right and pounded the tiles and
the dirt with the soles of their sandals. Then they went
through the little green door and set their load down in
Carlos's Ford. Carlos smoked behind the wheel, dead
serious, not helping them, not countering their wisecracks. Tito and I stopped smiling, we cast off our smiles,
painful, already rotten, smiles that might mean anything
instead of the relaxed solidarity we wanted them to express.

Snatcher walked a half-step ahead of the women, and
from his right hand hung a bouquet of rachitic red flowers. He looked at me and refused to recognize me. He
proffered the pardoning expression of a man who returns
to his native land triumphant, having dominated it, and
only barely concealed that look with a condescending,
happy grimace. He led the clicking heels of the women
along the platform and guided them with the victorious
security of his own march, with a man's confident stride.
But—invisible to me and the women—his bulging eyes
and prominent mouth, his bluish, sagging cheeks com-

posed a not insistent, affectionate, and considerate mask, the skillful insinuation that he, Larsen, Snatcher, or Body Snatcher, did not totally participate in the destiny and the condition of the trio of women he was dragging over the gray cobblestones. In the veiled afternoon air, advancing at a steady pace ahead of the patterns and colors of their silks, their hats, their accessories, their jewelry, their faces, and their bare arms, was Snatcher's face, ready to fight, to betray, to make deals. That face could just as easily signify the strength or the weakness of his business, of Snatcher himself with regard to his business.

Snatcher was slightly ahead and the women were behind him, walking abreast, in step with one another: The maternal fat one, the stupid, skinny blonde, the tallest one in the middle, all properly behind Snatcher. They all wore long dresses cinched at the waist, hats decked out with fruit, flowers, and veils, padded and undulating fabric around their hips. They did not seem to be arriving from the capital but from much further away, from years only imprecisely recalled. Now they wheeled, arm-in-arm, chattering in deliberately strident tones, a half-step behind the man in black who led them, heading toward the green fence, where the two porters were waiting and the hood of Carlos' Ford was vibrating. The tallest woman looked at me for a second when they made the quarter turn to leave the station. She smiled at me and rolled her eyes; her mouth hid behind the sheeplike profile of the skinny blonde.

"What do you think of them?" asked Tito.

We were still standing there, motionless against the sacks. We listened to the puffing of the train as it pulled out, and we witnessed the thinning out and disappearance of the sunbeam that had obliquely touched the fields near the Experimental School. Without speaking, we imagined the motion of the tremulous little black car through the streets around the plaza, up the Soria road next to the vineyards, along the carefully kept up highway to Colonia, always flanked by hostility and absence, by locked doors, by blind and darkened windows and balconies. We imagined Carlos at the wheel, falsely attentive to his driving, uninterested in what was sitting next to him and behind him. We imagined Snatcher, black, dissimulating his nervousness, with the hatbox on his knees, the white cuff of his shirt almost touching the stems of the dry flowers he held like a weapon. We imagined the women with their uniformlike dresses intended to shock Santa María, driving through pre-thunderstorm heat and obvious rejection, shaken and humiliated by the Ford's sagging springs, rolling toward the isolated house on the coast, near the jam factory and the small farms, fearing and losing hope in the face of the unanimous persistence of the closed town, sniffing the huge flowers that hang from their bosoms, the heat that rises from their unbelievable, triangular décolletés. But the solitude of the streets keeps on pouring into the Ford like the clouds of burning dust, and nothing can drown out the negatives that Santa María, sleeping and abandoned in the middle of the afternoon, keeps on repeating to them.

"What did you think of them?" Tito asked again.

"Just women," I said, disinterestedly waving a hand.

We went through the little green gate and were languidly crossing the deserted, bare plaza. I thought of Julita and I compared her with the glance, the smile of the tall woman.

"I don't like them," said Tito, "but what drives me

crazy is the idea that anybody can drive down to the coast, pay, and choose."

"Why does that bother you?" I asked so he wouldn't stop talking.

At eleven o'clock tonight, I have to get out of the garden, walk around the house, and go up to Julita's bedroom. Before, a month ago, I thought I understood something when I said to myself, "She's my sister-in-law, she was my dead brother's wife, my brother slept with her." I'll go to her and it's possible that I'll make up something about the women who arrived today, that I'll tell her I was the only person at the station, the only person in the entire city. And nothing will ever happen. Maybe she'll make me kiss my brother's picture and tell her how much I loved him, or she'll compare her love with mine, and correct me persistently and sweetly.

CHAPTER III

In the evening of that Friday on which the improbable women arrived at Santa María, Dr. Díaz Grey chose the darkest seat in the Plaza grillroom, far from the bar, which was occupied by Marcos, his pals, and some women. After the silence and the short noise made by the rain that stopped almost instantly, the dark boy slapped his glass on the linoleum.

"Like Marcos said today . . . We have to vote for ourselves, for the country."

"Right," said Marcos. "But the most important thing right now isn't politics. When the garbage starts piling up in front of your house, you've got to sweep it away. Any way you can."

From his table, Díaz Gray watched them as he drank. He saw the wide backsides of the men overflowing the barstools and the bony asses of the two women. The rain came back, timidly, its noise evening out until it became like another object added to the night. On the coast, gathered around Snatcher's wisdom, confidence, and barely concealed excitement, the women would be drinking *maté*, getting interested in things, covering up yawns, watching this first soiree in the little house burn down and fade.

Leaning back, the women with Marcos and his friends, one wearing slacks, the other a skirt and raincoat, glanced at each other and exchanged discouraged smiles. Behind the talk about fuselages, cylinder capacities, and flight ranges, they felt for an instant that they had something decisive to say to each other. They blinked, listless and sleepy, certain they'd never have to reveal their secret. They smiled again and leaned their bosoms onto the bar, the world of the men. The rain kept on falling steadily, static, as if it were a wide surface of sound. Díaz Grey imagined Snatcher, slightly drunk from celebrating, moved by revenge, by the victory he'd achieved at fifty years of age, daring, blinded by triumph and pride, impelled to reveal to the three women the secret of the business, the true, incredible motive he was obeying. Chilled and uncertain, wounded by the ride through the empty city, they would look for filthy words to impose normality on their world.

At the bar, as they did every night, the men got drunk arguing about machines and chassis designs; arm-in-arm, the women, slow and whispering, had crossed the darkened ballroom that separated the bar from the restrooms. Díaz Grey thought about the dream or insomnia of the pharmacist and town councilman Barthé, about the bedroom above the pharmacy, about that night of calm rain at the very beginning of the realization of his old, civilizing ideal: He was fat and horizontal with a feminine softness that surrounded and softened his bald head in repose next to the deep breathing of the boy who worked for him. The hour of triumph, the *yes* that had come to break twelve years of *nos*, to blot out the memory of twelve inaugural sessions of the city council, with their monotonous, predictable six votes against, reached Barthé in the cellar in his pharmacy, months back, as he, wearing a smock, was sniffing the aroma of a sack of camomile his little helper was holding open for him.

Once a year, twelve times, he'd asked permission to address the council right after the president finished his patriotic discourse, even before the applause died down. And the six pairs of eyes, always the same even if their owners changed, were already turned toward him, expectant, patient, distantly friendly. Barthé requested the project he had deposited a week earlier in the municipal office be taken under consideration. Impassive, the small round places on his face whiter than usual, his small stare disdainfully passing over the oval table and the briefcases, over the scorn which was not shown after the second year and the shock that was expressed behind his back after the first, the pharmacist pronounced the necessary words. Perhaps only for this would he have voted for the creation of a recording secretary position when the majority passed from the radicals to the conservatives: He was communicating to posterity the fact that he had been born a quarter century too early, that, firm and dispassionate, he was ready to die for his convictions.

"There is no need for me to present the project since it has already been distributed, with all supporting documents, among the gentlemen of the council."

"Then, if there are no objections . . ." the president

would say. And they voted, always six votes against Barthé's one. Then they passed on to a discussion of storm sewers and bus routes.

The pharmacist would swiftly give up any absurd, short-lived hope he might have had and give up as well his foreseeable bitterness. He would make ready to mix his sharp and caressing voice in with the others. Six negative votes, a few evasive gestures, futilely pious, a concerned admiration in the faces of those who dared to confront him. That was all, from one March to the next.

"I hope I'm not bothering you," shouted Dr. Díaz Grey, that early winter afternoon, bent over the trapdoor to the pharmacy cellar. Barthé was invisible; the doctor spoke to the yellow light that crept up the dusty wooden stairs together with the noises of the boiler that was beginning to heat up, accompanied by the melancholy smell of wetness, weeds, and cold. "I have to speak to you and it has to be now. May I come down?"

"Doctor . . ." Barthé's round head materialized, almost horizontal, smiling, among the dark areas and the places where there was a slight clarity. Barthé's open palms revealed excuses and desolation.

"Wouldn't you rather wait up there for a moment?"

"The fact is that people are waiting for me over at the clinic. I'm already late." Díaz Grey began to climb down, his hat and gloves in one hand, his raincoat sweeping the steps, all his attention focused on protecting his blue suit, which he'd just acquired. He held Barthé's bland and immobile hand in his own, observing the white, round smile, the excitement that was staining his fleshy cheeks, the blond and gray hair just under the spot where his clavicles met.

"My dear doctor . . ." He was cheerful and touched,

his head sunk into absurdity as deeply as it was sunk into the curves of fat that surrounded it. He took Díaz Grey's hat and gloves and pointed him to the center of the cellar, where, beneath the yellow light, the boy was balancing a sack on his legs as he held it open. "It's as if you had guessed the exact moment in the day when I can't see you properly. Until just a few minutes ago I was bored upstairs. There may be more sick people during the rainy season, but there are no more customers. I wanted to look over these sacks of camomile. It shouldn't be packaged if it's very fresh, and besides you have to know how to balance flowers against leaves. But now I can talk with you. Just step over here, dear, that's it." The adolescent bent over and twisted the sack. Barthé waited until Díaz Grey looked away to examine the sack quickly. "Very fresh. And with this weather . . ." Other smells welled up from the basins along the cellar wall, surrounding the smell of the camomile, and ate it away.

"Thank you, dear," said Barthé. He balanced over the sack and sank a naked arm into it. With his eyes rolled back he raised a fistful of camomile toward his face and smelled it. He tapped his nose and lips with it. The boy's narrow forehead remained bent forward. "Yes," said Barthé, "fresh, too fresh." He opened his hand over the sack. "Better close it up again. If we need any, we can always set some out to dry."

While the adolescent dragged the sack out of the light, the pharmacist straightened up and turned, his face, which showed, as intentions, happiness and Barthé's fifty years, as if both things had been hidden away there forever, as if he were showing them now as a surprise, to end the scene with the sack of camomile. He wiped the golden dust off his lips and from around his nostrils.

"All these sacks of weeds . . . It would be better out in the country, of course. But here . . . we have all of nature under one roof, doctor." He seized Díaz Grey's free hand to pat it, and once again the doctor felt him to be both intact and mutilated. "Did you need something? Can I help you in any way?"

Not brave enough to withdraw his hand, staring at the anxiety frozen on the round, white face that shone next to the naked light bulb, Díaz Grey smiled and used a low, clear voice to answer. Sitting on the floor, puttering around in the open sack he was holding with his legs, the boy watched the two men with feigned disinterest.

"No," said the doctor. "It's about you. Arcelo was in my office. He hinted at something last night at the hotel, and this afternoon he asked me to deliver a concrete proposal to you."

Barthé dropped the doctor's hand and let his short arms fall to his sides. His face was still fifty years old, but his gentle happiness wasn't: It was fifty years with the addition of austerity, obligation, indignation, and a bit of self-pity.

"Yes," he said, imitating the doctor's low tone. "He wants me to vote for the port concession."

"Excuse me," said Díaz Grey. "I'm not suggesting anything and I'm not interested in your decision. Arcelo is." He picked up his hat and gloves and began to clap them together, sorry and annoyed.

"Never," whispered Barthé.

Without having to look, Díaz Grey could see the pharmacist's small pink mouth, protruding and incorruptible.

"He told me that the port concession had nothing to do with it. Only the porter service."

"Never," puffed Barthé, smiling in his martyrdom. "It

makes money. Even if it is a bad municipal service and badly organized. But it makes money, and that money belongs to the town. And even if it weren't that way, public services should be administered by the city, socialized."

"Okay, fine. I'll tell Arcelo." But Barthé went on, intense, controlling himself, as if he were confessing secrets.

"It's only a matter of time. Today I'm only a town councilman. But we shall see. Truth is clearing a path for itself, doctor. And with the new plan for schools in our province . . ."

They fell silent, and the sound of the wind reached them, approaching from the river, confused and separated from them, like a memory, stirring up the sadness of the evening. The boy stood up and balanced the sack between his arm and shoulder. "You know all these things better than I do, doctor," begged the fat, patient, and pained face. "I don't want to lecture you."

"Well, then, I'm in a hurry. People are waiting for me at the clinic, and I have to see two patients in Colonia. I told Arcelo I'd convey his proposition. The conservatives want your vote on the porter concession. If you vote for it, they agree to approve the bordello project. Understand?"

He only wanted to see Barthé's face during the first second in which it began to deflate and lose dignity. Perhaps he watched him until the nervousness of hope became visible, until his face showed the dismay that accompanies all grand, sterile joys. His jawbone seemed to come loose from the fat and projected a rapacious, masculine gesture toward the doctor.

"Understand?" repeated Díaz Grey. "There's more.

They're offering to vote for your brothel first, whenever you say, in exchange for your word that you will vote in favor of the porter concession in the future."

From the shelf closest to the ceiling where the boy was trying to put it, the sack of camomile fell with a dry, light slap. It lay there, twisted and open, allowing a thick, green stream to pour out. Above the perfume of the camomile, with his smock waving as if the wind had entered the cellar, Barthé shook his arms and insulted the frightened boy, who was hanging onto a beam to see. Díaz Grey saw the eyes in the fat, flushed face full of tears, and listened to the tremor that forced the high, sobbing voice to take respites. The boy scuttled along the shelves and began to climb down.

"I have to be on my way."

"Doctor . . . Pardon me for what's happened." But Barthé's arms were not pointing to the drugstore cellar, the dim light, nor the stealthy movements of the boy around the sack. "Pardon me. I want to think. Anything I might say to you now . . ."

CHAPTER IV

Barthé agreed at the second interview, after refusing to see the doctor for four days and leaving the pharmacy in the hands of an employee. He disappeared, and the only message he left was: "Doctor Barthé is away on business. We think he's in Montevideo, but we don't know when he'll be back."

Halfway through the fourth day, the boy from the pharmacy climbed Díaz Grey's steps, took a seat, and waited his turn. He was hunched over, apathetic, his jaw in his hands, staring unblinkingly at the green majolica pieces on the side table. When he was called into the doctor's office, he showed his teeth and blew his nose, his eyes wandering toward the light coming through the windows and with one hand scratching around under his jacket.

"What's the matter with you?" asked Díaz Grey. "You don't look too sick."

The boy smiled again and showed his hand, which held an envelope.

"It's from Dr. Barthé, doctor. I was to hand it to you personally."

The address on the letter was *Relaxation Farm*, the property Barthé owned between Colonia and the road to Rosario. The letter had been written with very light blue ink in a small, even hand.

> Dear Citizen, Doctor, and Friend:
>
> I was unexpectedly taken ill when what was perhaps a presentiment caused me to neglect my obligations for a few days. I have come here to my humble domicile in search of rest. A very painful rheumatism attack has obliged me to bother you and to ask your help as friend and healer. I would be most thankful if you could call on me this afternoon, assuming your labors allow you the time. The bearer of this note, completely familiar with the route, will bring you in my car for your greater comfort.
>
> Your, as you well know, unconditional friend,
>
> EUCLIDES BARTHÉ

Passing through the humid, foggy afternoon, crossing solitary, confused vistas that seemed to have remained unchanged since the beginning of the bad season, that seemed to have maintained, against the work of time, the calm puddles in the potholes, the bent-over quality of the bare branches, the soft, depressing light that settled on the air and the ground, Díaz Grey drove down from Santa

María to Colonia. He traced an L-shaped pattern through paved, clean streets lined with white houses with tile roofs and on their upper floors tiny, shuttered windows that were never opened. He left the center of Colonia and followed the roads that lead to farms, carried along by the car and the silent chauffeur (his shaved neck unnecessarily bent over the wheel, his raised shoulders on guard against any attack, against any feared question), crossing the repetitive, identical scene: mud, wire fences, wooden doors framed by skeletal honeysuckle vines, the smoke from the kitchens rigid and embedded in the fog. He reached the top of the hill and on the way down he found the same landscape, now resolved and fanatical, proclaiming the appearance it had taken on since the first cold days of June: a gray, low sky, dripping, blackish trees without leaves, the dark, slippery dirt with its powerful, saddened aroma, the light like an obstacle to the intruding car, to the first, stiff steps Díaz Grey took toward the house, behind the boy's swaying back.

They were stiff with cold as they reached the imprecise entrance and walked between widely separated trees on an irregular, pretentious, unkempt lawn. They silently and slowly crossed through the space where a garden had been laid out. Then: "Doctor," said the boy, standing at attention before the pharmacist and saluting.

Some branches were smoking in the fireplace, but there was barely any difference between the temperature inside the house and the temperature outside. Barthé pretended to be surprised and his hands, one holding a slice of bread, the other a cup, froze. He was wearing a suit made of thick fabric with frogging and had a handkerchief tied around his neck.

"I'm so sorry to have dragged you out like this. . . ."
He brought the doctor to an easy chair whose feet were
licked by the smoke from the fireplace. "You might cut
some firewood out in the kitchen gallery."

"Yes," said the boy. "And as long as it's all right, I'll
change the battery too."

The cold seemed to intensify next to the crackling
branches. Hugging his knees with both hands, Díaz Grey
saw the fat man carefully move the china around and
heat the tea water. His round face was an equal blend of
concern, cunning, and a profound calm that simulated
goodwill. *It's just as if he were alone: He is the actor and
the audience, the hero and the story. But he's not crazy.
He just lets himself slip into his personal percentage of
stupidity more avidly than other people.*

As he drank the light, burning tea, the doctor listened
to Barthé allude to the brothel in the most fantastic eu-
phemisms and toy with the secret of the grave political
interview whose results or revelation could—should, necessarily—influence the future of Santa María.

"As strange as it may seem to you, doctor, speaking
seriously now . . . I did not have a ready answer. And
even if I did, how would I know if it were the appropriate
answer, the right answer? You must understand the di-
lemma in which your words left me. And I just did not
want to make up something on the spot. My sense of
responsibility after a life in which I have done nothing
to repent . . ."

With his voice like a bordello madam's, which he supported with his fleshy, hairless fingers, Barthé told of his
beautiful vision: He was a man of conscience, isolated
on a mountaintop, a man who'd labored through days of

struggle and meditation in order to wring from his judgment the scum of self-serving considerations.

Maybe he's hoping, deep down, that someone's going to put up a neon sign: Grand Bordello Barthé, or that the anonymous justice of the people will end up baptizing it with that name. And now, having come down from the mountain and the anguish, cleansed of the horror of anticipation, exhausted and calmed, he raised the translucent cup of tea with two fingers, became aware of the enormous room stuffed with knickknacks, vases, portraits, lace, engravings, ribbons, cushions, paper flowers, dust, and cold. He became aware of the meaning of the moment and of the generation that was listening to him with Díaz Grey's ears.

He was over fifty years of age, with downlike hair fluttering around the pink skin on his cranium, with a spongy, naked face, with sporadic flashes of cunning and interest under his precociously gray eyebrows. He relaxed, correct and heavy, on the chair's circular cushion, his tiny, glittering shoes primly side by side, his left hand tracing curves in the air or offering itself palm up on his thigh. Perhaps he knew what he was talking about as he began to recount his life story, as he enumerated and made light of the injustices he'd suffered, as his whining voice recounted commonplaces about capitalism and the oligarchy, agricultural cooperatives, and the English labor movement, as he revealed that all this had been if not a deliberate prologue, then at least an inevitable antecedent to the existence of a bordello in Santa María.

Listening, huddled next to the fireplace, where the armful of green branches the boy brought in had burned down, Díaz Grey tried to summarize everything the vehement, repetitive, fat man did not know about himself.

He was born here, on the coast. The river, the sand, and the countryside have isolated and nullified him for fifty years, while the mailboat maintains his illusion of being in touch with the faraway events he considers history. He isn't a person; like all the inhabitants of this side of the river, he is a certain intensity of existence that occupies, or takes the shape of his personal mania, his personal idiocy. Because around here we only differ from one another in the type of self-negation we choose or which is imposed on us. A little joke of a country, from the coast to the rails that limit Colonia, where each one of us grows up in his role and plays it badly. And that's why I, when I'm distracted, when I stop being alert and take part in it, I become Doctor Díaz Grey. I play the part of the doctor, the man of science with less questionable knowledge than the old women who preside over births, indigestion, and cases of evil eye in the shacks by the river. And that's why this poor man I'm really trying to like stopped being the authentic and always ignored Euclides Barthé many years ago. Without any concern, everybody sees him play the part of the pharmacist, the herbalist, the town councilman and now—until he dies—the prophet of Santa María's whorehouses.

Now Barthé's canarylike voice was trilling out the prelude to accepting the offer made by the right wing of the municipal administration. He announced that he, at the beginning of this winter evening, at the beginning of this soiree in the country, was going to formulate the unforgettable sentence and the unforgettable gesture with which he would accept, but only to serve higher interests, that the porters would change bosses.

Which is why I'll have to work hard and diligently, run every risk of being misunderstood in order to carry out my pact with God, according to which I should look at and get to know each and every one of these people, and know that I'm doing it, even if it's only just this once and that it will all only last an instant. Which is why I'm gluing my eyes to the fluctuating, central little hole that Euclides Barthé has in his face, and which is still shaking around frantically trying to give shape to his ideas. I ought to see what unique thing there is inside him, aside from the man who makes lemonade purges, aside from the town councilman, aside from the pharmacist's assistant who got to be the owner, the proprietor of this drafty country house with its desolate travesty of an English park; and what there is beneath his growing old and his habits, beneath his face and the mood in which I see him. He must be a eunuch. Euclides Barthé disintegrated; he was winnowed away by the years, the way things usually happen. Watching him sermonize in front of the weak fire as he recites tedious sentences, prudently shaking himself above the fragility of the chair, I can see nothing but a vague old man gone soft whose arteriosclerosis makes his hands shake and often cuts off the ends of his sentences. I'm chilled to the bone, bored, loveless. All I see is this thing much like any other thing of its age, dissolving in decrepitude, and propped up by vanity and imprecise fears.

"I understand," said Díaz Grey, standing up. "I don't know if I'll be able to see Arcelo tonight, but I definitely will tomorrow. I'll tell him that you accept. They'll vote in your bordello in the first session. Later you'll vote for the porter concession at the port, and we'll all be happy."

"They'll blacken my name even more, doctor," Barthé repeated from the fireplace. "But I'm ready."

"You'd better be. If a whorehouse is a social necessity

for Santa María, it's almost certainly going to be a money-making proposition as well."

"I wasn't thinking about that. It occurred to me that the radicals, when they see me vote for the porter concession are going to think I was paid to do it."

"Probably," agreed Díaz Grey. "Quite likely. But in a way you were paid. Not with money, of course. Call your boy, please, I have to go."

"Doctor . . ." begged Barthé with a martyr's smile. He went to the door and opened it to shout. The cold, calm, dark night came to join them in the badly lighted room.

"I don't know, doctor," said Barthé, coming closer, "how I can apologize for having forced you to make this trip and waste your time. But you understand the gravity of my decision and how necessary it is that no one suspect . . . At the same time, my rheumatism's got me down. I'll be at your office at noon—with no disguises." He tried to drag Díaz Grey's eyes toward the austere expression he'd arranged on his face—not in order to fool him but out of an automatic sense of doing the appropriate thing, the proper way to seal the meeting.

"Everything seems perfect," said Díaz Grey as he put on his gloves. "You have the strength necessary to resist slander. Santa María will have a bordello, and venereal disease will either increase or decrease. We'll be able to study the statistics."

"Did you want me, sir?" interrupted the boy from the bluish cold of the door.

"Warm up the car. The doctor is leaving. But you told me, doctor, that in other places, in London, for example . . ."

"Nobody really knows. At least I don't. There are arguments pro and contra, figures pro and contra. There should be whorehouses in hospitals, and doctors should examine every client."

"A utopian ideal. But what about the other problem? The boys, the masculine youth I mean."

"Yes, of course. And the girls down by the coast. We've already talked about all that. But what interests me now is the practical side of the thing." Sputtering, the car motor started to growl outside, augmenting and saddening the gaps in their conversation.

"It does?" helped Barthé.

"I mean . . ." A discouraged smell of country kitchen and the smell of age from the furniture and knickknacks. "You get the representatives of the people to authorize the establishment of a whorehouse. But how do you set it up? Who administers it? How do you go about doing it, renting the house, getting the women?"

"An excellent question," said the pharmacist, who almost allowed a victorious smile to play over his face. "But even when I didn't dare even to hope I thought about that. Theory and action. A necessary duality if you want to build something. Because, and you insinuated it yourself, they may approve the law and make sure it never becomes a reality. Doctor, I have the right man for the job. A person who works on the staff of EL LIBERAL. I don't remember his real name, but people call him Snatcher."

"Yes, I know him. I've seen him in the Berna. Once he turned up at my office. His name is Larsen."

Barthé shook the doctor's now gloved hand. His white, waxy face, excited and sweaty, glowed weakly as he drew near.

"And now we come to the most difficult moment of our little interview, doctor. The moment when I cannot forget I'm taking advantage of you. Can you sit down for a moment?"

"I really do have to leave," said Díaz Grey, impatiently, with a bit of hatred.

"Well, it doesn't matter. Just two words. I have to ask you to do me another favor. I don't know if you . . . I was in touch with that person about this matter. He came here a while back from Rosario and he says he's stayed around here working at the newspaper because of me. It isn't my fault. I simply told him the truth, that I was sure that the law would be approved. And you know now that I was right. He's a contemptible man, but necessary. I know he's been involved in activities of this kind elsewhere. In any case, he lives among us and earns an honest living."

"Yes, I know him. Maybe he can do it."

"He said he could. But that was a long time ago, when I was sure the party would have two council members. We had an argument: He was rude, but I remained calm and firm. I haven't spoken to him since, as you can understand." Outside, hoarse, as if the fog were suffocating it, the car horn protested. "Darn that uppity boy! Doctor and friend, would it be too much to ask you to go see that man and find out if he's still interested?"

"Don't worry. Tomorrow I'll talk to Arcelo and to him. I don't know which one is more disgusting, but Snatcher amuses me more."

From the brick façade of the house, insinuating his fat in the motionless, frozen air, the pharmacist raised his voice for the farewell:

"You, doctor, while you may not be my political coreligionary, you agree with me deep down in your heart."

Cold as he jumped into the back seat of the car, Díaz Grey forgot the trip and remembered sensations from other invisible landscapes, from other nocturnal journeys in rainy winters, other faces, other gestures, other solitude, other sudden and short beliefs. For a long time now his memory had been impersonal: It evoked beings and circumstances, meanings that were transparent to his intuition, old errors and premonitions, with the pure pleasure of giving itself over to dreams chosen because they were absurd.

CHAPTER V

I accept failure. I put on my raincoat, my beret. Standing in front of the mirror, I thank Julita for the secret—whatever secret of hers it was, the source of the one we're sharing. Before I turn out the light, I blame Julita for the poem, and I attribute to her the four verses I have just written down.

> *And I lose her, lose him, give my life.*
> *In exchange for old age and the ambitions of*
> *   others,*
> *every day older, disgustingly desiring and*
> *   strange.*
> *I should go and I won't; I should leave off and*
> *   I can't.*

Walking down the stairs, I convince myself that blame belongs to the part of Julita's stupidity that neither love nor madness can cover up, the inseparable part that does not belong to her but will die with her. What her parents, this candid, provincial air, her girl friends, and my dead brother added to her and imposed on her. And I myself with my inadequate way of loving her.

It's eleven o'clock at night. I'm walking with my eyes closed down the dark hall, anxiously listening to the rain, which has become very soft. I walk out and I hear it again in the trees in the garden. I stroll around to pass time, so I'll arrive late, so she can think she'll lose me. I'm not trying to increase her madness or her coldness. I'm afraid they'll grow too much, so much that she won't be able to stand them or explain things, to substitute this absurd nocturnal ritual in which I can be comfortable, in which I can embed myself without understanding, for something concrete and permanent.

I only want to make her aware that her existence is not indispensable for mine, that I am myself, Jorge, not her or her game. I am myself, this being, this "nice little boy" who belongs to them: sad, different, so insecure and solid in a way none of them can even suspect, so apart from and above all of them. I am this person I sympathetically and without excess love to watch live and do things. I am this person with well-mannered, inexhaustible patience for each one of the tedious, unamusing comedies they insist on tangling themselves up in so they can understand, so they can protect themselves from new ideas and a lack of confidence. I stroll through a well-tended, moist garden, I feel the rain that explains nothing on my face, I think about disconnected obscenities, I watch the glow in my parents' window. I don't want to learn how to live but to discover life in a flash once and for all. I judge with passion and shame, I can't keep myself from judging; I cough and spit toward the perfume of the flowers and the dirt, I remember the condemnation and the pride of not participating in their acts.

Finally I make up my mind and I arrive, cold and excited, at the foot of the trellis that frames Julita's window and spreads a few violet stains on the moss and filth covering the walls. I get up on tiptoe and whistle. I think she won't come down, that she's dead along with the rest, with everything that began the summer afternoon when Julita, after burying my brother in the Colonia cemetery, began to go mad, to look at me, and persecute me just so she could stand where she could see me and look from there without asking favors, without begging or curiosity or love or any purpose, just in order to look at me and pacify the fears that she supposed I had, raising her lip, showing what we force ourselves to take for a smile. I stretch again and whistle. The window darkens and opens, I recognize the tone of accusation and welcome in the question. I don't answer.

I imagine the muted noise of her slippers on the stairs, I imagine without much effort her blond hair hanging down, barely shaken by the stairs, her white face on which she has just painted the thick, square lips my brother liked to bite. She chose madness in order to go on living, and this madness requires that I not live. I have been nothing more than a variable dream since she came back from the cemetery, curled up in the easy chair, and gaily recited: "It was a marvelous funeral. We walked in the sun, the Küttels made the wreath with their own hands,

I suppose it took them all night, I thought I'd faint from happiness because of that smell of springtime when Father Bergner began to pray."

I'm thinking about the women who are probably sleeping with Snatcher in the house on the coast when Julita opens the door and the foreseeable, complaining words escape like animals toward the mud, toward the noise of the drops that fall from the trees. I try not to look at her, to make no mistakes: I still don't know who I am. I offer my cheeks and forehead, I allow my beret to be taken off and my head to be caressed. Then I begin timidly to be the one who climbs the stairs preceding the count of her own slippered feet, the murmur of her prayers. We enter the room where she slept with my brother. Julita closes the door and smiles at me. I turn around to take off my coat, so I won't see her. A disconsolate thought occurs to me: Adolescence is not a stage in my life but one of my illnesses, the vice of conformity, an incurable wound.

I hunker down next to the fire to gain some time. "Jorge," I state my name so I can feel myself and bid myself farewell. Soon, above the back of my neck, she'll begin to call me Federico or Fritz, or any of the other names he allowed her to call him. I sense the voice in which she'll say her first words, grotesque, false, pitiful, distrustful:

"Are you very tired? Sure you're not? But you're soaked. All afternoon I was thinking that your work on the farm is crazy. I put you up to it, that's true. Don't you ever look at your hands? They're all torn up, swollen, filthy with dirt. But they're hands for me, not for setting out plantings, for cows, threshing machines, and men. The last time it rained you were stuck in the mud with the car for an hour."

I'll walk around, rapidly losing my sense of shame, imitating the strides my brother would take in his boots. I'll laugh with the sarcastic, tender laugh in the key of A, I'll touch her shoulder in passing, her cheek, her solid, braided hair.

But she comes in silence and rests the tips of her fingers on my shoulders. She's about to speak. I'll have to give myself like a woman, die for a few hours so that she can have my brother again. She's going to mention Federico's name, she's going to resuscitate the confessable parts—and only those—of their lost intimacy. She relaxes her fingers and then slides her hands over my shoulders and arms. I hear her laugh, I conclude she is slowly shaking her head.

I turn my face and smile at her, just to do something, to get used to things. I get up slowly, I stretch the pain in my legs. I go to the wall, to Federico's picture next to the bed and the vase with yellow flowers in it.

"Such a miracle, my God . . ." she whispers, just loudly enough so I can hear. "I prayed so much in the beginning that this would happen. . . ."

This is her habitual tone for her big lies, for the scenes that she knows to be excessive; it's intense, possessive, almost never appropriate to the words, it sounds a millimeter above or below what they make me imagine. Everything turns out like a badly printed lithograph, where the colors have run. Everything becomes inexact and doubly incredible; I can feel free, I can disdain myself, and keep quiet. I abandon the excessively sad perfume of the yellow flowers, and when I turn, I see her just as I had imagined: With her hands behind her head she faces the fireplace with an astonished and stubborn expression, her eyes wide open; they blink without any sign of anxiety, as if they only wanted to caress and give luster to her gaze. I go to her, ask, insist, take an interest, but when she looks at me I can see, as always, hatred and fear, the only things she cannot hide from me, perhaps the only things that matter in our relationship.

"Jorge," she says, taking me by the ears to kiss me on the forehead again. "I just couldn't believe it."

She makes me sit down in the easy chair in front of the fire and crouches down at my feet, her calves under her backside. She's short, but she's thirty years old or thereabouts, and I never forgot it. Too old for me to believe in what she's trying to prove and what she wants to communicate to me this way, making herself small and submissive, touching my knees with her hard, coiled hair. I know what she's orchestrating, it's not the first time she's played the game of having Federico's child after Federico's death, but there are always new touches, she always changes the focus.

"I didn't dare believe it. Because I prayed that it would be true, and deep down I knew it was. I didn't dare to because I didn't deserve it, I don't deserve it. Understand? Only because of my love, because I love him. But I don't deserve it, I don't have any other place to turn." She raises her head and looks at me just long enough for her smile to appear and disappear. "Now he's dead. Dead. We've got to repeat the word. Before it was obscene, remember, a thousand times worse than the dirtiest word. No more. Only he's dead, he is, he's a dead man. It doesn't bother you, does it, doesn't hurt you?"

Her blond head, stretched out like a dog's head against my knees, her smile, so simple, devoid of intentions to the point of being repugnant. As far as that word is concerned, it never sounded as obscene as it does now, so foul, dry, and miserable.

"No, it doesn't hurt me," I say and I suspect everything's about to change: Something will free me from my earlier submission, something else is coming to enslave me.

"It can't hurt you. Dead. He's dead. He's your brother." Sometimes she'd look at you wondering how it would be to be Federico's brother.

I'm beginning to be afraid; an incomprehensible cowardice that floats up from my guts, from Julita's head and her voice, leaning against my body.

"Did you love him?"

"More than anyone, I can almost guarantee it."

A lie. More than love, I felt jealous of him, I admired him. Above all, I was linked to him by a challenge he knew nothing about. Nevertheless, now while I'm afraid, what I say is the truth. I click my teeth so she can hear them. With my hand in front of her eyes, I slowly clench my fist, as if something were keeping me from closing my fingers.

"More than anyone," I insist, only so the impersonal part of her stupidity will force her to think about my mother, force her to introduce a small rejection into her joy. But when she raises her head, there is only gratitude in her blue, dry, and gray eyes.

"He loved you too," she concedes, her jaw fitted over my knee.

I remember her standing stiff and straight saying good-by and thanking those who hadn't gone to the cemetery or who were coming back from it; I remember my hatred for her dry, not-bloodshot eyes, for her words and ordinary movements, which gave no one the chance to think they were less miserable than she and to placate their remorse by feeling sorry for her. I remember that expression: It seemed born from the pride of efficiency; and the other expression that wasn't on her face but stood there, stiff and straight next to her, ready to embody itself. In it I discovered an inexplicable disdain, capable of swallowing that present moment and any future time, the way the sea swallows a shipwrecked man.

"He's dead," she repeated sleepily; her neck tickled my leg. "I want to hear you say that he's dead, please. It shouldn't make you afraid or sad. It's just that . . ."

It's just that the rot and before the obscenity of agony and later the grotesque modesty of her closed face turned toward the roof beams, her nose longer, independent, her face that had been holding a single expression since dawn, an expression which erased and suppressed her, which cynically denied the entire past of her face and whose total indecency was revealed by its inhuman slowness.

"Dead, he's dead," I repeat, vain and enthusiastic, dazzled by the few remaining points of fire in the fireplace ashes.

"True, isn't it?" she whispers, laughing. "And that's why"—before leaving her mouth, her voice passes through her throat and rubs my knee—"when my baby's born I'm going to teach it to say that Federico is dead."

Just as I expected, I can stay just as I am, still, my eyes turned toward the coals, my leg still holding up the heat of her head. I prefer to take refuge in an earlier fear, one that's weaker, visited more often: Federico with an unfamiliar nose, which he was hiding from us like an unforgivable vice, lying faceup, sweating out the cadaver stench that pinned the perfume of the flowers against the walls and wood, the perfume of the flowers that formed small, sweet-smelling zones which imitated the outline of the petals.

I caress her head until she raises it; then I show her a smile, shift my legs and stand up. I walk toward the bed—my left shoulder and my experienced prudence protect me from the eyes in the photo—and I pick up my raincoat. I pause, toying with my beret.

"I won't love you less," she affirms, still sitting on the floor. "I'll never forget that you were more than good, that you were incredibly understanding for someone your age. . . ."

Sixteen, seventeen years old, I think angrily. Not old enough to visit the whorehouse. She's got her elbows propped on the chair I've just left, and the coil of hair over her right ear seems to have come undone or gotten loose, separate from her madness. The grimace of ecstasy covers her entire face except her eyes, though it may be her eyes that impose the brilliant, absurd expression on the rest and simply do not take part in yielding themselves. Those eyes are staring attentively at me, in hatred and fear. I retreat until I reach the wall, until the back of my neck touches the glass over the photograph, until I know I'm substituting my brother's eyebrows, smile, and sadness with my own. Then I speak slowly and try to make her understand by only saying her name that I want to throw her onto the bed, that I'm afraid, that neither of us would dare or even be able to give to the other the only thing that matters.

"Julita." Her eyes are open toward me, toward my anxious face and all the supplication I can show. But she only sees the little boy she needs and uses. And I have to recognize myself in her eyes, as I do in all the adult eyes I see before me, as weak, changeable, contradictory. I see myself and I accept: weak, pure, incapable of withstanding solitude, with no other destiny than that of being an element in someone else's existence. I'm sure I can walk straight across the bedroom without undo haste, from the wall where I'm leaning to the door, pass by her without touching her or speaking to her and get out of here forever.

"Federico's child . . ." She interrupts herself to make me understand that the words are insufficient, to smile at the seat of the chair; the tip of a finger no longer tries to tie down her tress. It traces its way, coming and going through the labyrinth. A little saliva shines on her lower lip and drips, unnoticed; but it doesn't diminish her beauty, the peace in her smile that whitens between the braces on the chair. But it isn't Federico's child. It's Federico. Even if it's a girl.

I nod my head; I mean some affirmative word, undoubtedly, with a tone of certainty, of disdain for every imaginable contrary supposition. But the word, like a bug caught on flypaper, remains, struggling and mute, in the mucosity of my throat. She's calmed down again. As alien to my incredulity as she is to the thread of spittle that's getting cold and stretching from her mouth to the chair seat. She recovers her empty, surprised smile.

CHAPTER VI

Also at the end of winter, during a period of rainy or foggy days, Díaz Grey asked for Mister Larsen, alias Body Snatcher, at the business office of EL LIBERAL. He was told that Mister Larsen was on vacation, but that he might be found in the boardinghouse upstairs from the Berna.

So Díaz Grey slowly walked through the soaked, windy streets, above and within the perceptible fury of the postponed spring, seeing the last leaves fall off the trees and slap into the mud, feeling the almost visible swirls of the wind as it touched his face. He walked trying not to tire himself, relatively hidden by the bad weather, examining the pain his illness had left in his chest, uselessly maintaining a cordial smile to excuse his recently purchased cane. Without recognizing who he was, he greeted a short man who waved from the door of the

Berna Restaurant and Beer Garden, turned to the left and, after finding out the room number, went up the boardinghouse stairs.

I'm here to tell him that yes, it's possible. I'd like to be able to get a look at his eyes, his degraded face, to know how much what I'm bringing is worth to him. But he'll hide his feelings. Much more if what I'm bringing him is happiness.

He looked calmly at the grime on the door, the peeling "5" on the metal plate. He held back a cough when he saw the design of the wallpaper. He thought someone had heard him, that his footsteps on the stairs and the silence when he'd stopped had provoked another silence inside the room, a suspicious, expectant silence. Then he heard someone snore and guitar music, the introduction to a tango. He raised his cane to knock, then used his fist.

"Yes. Who's there?" someone shouted from inside. The voice was nasty and sad. It erased Larsen's memory, the images the doctor had speculated with in the street and on the stairs: a short, plump, and stiff man who energetically crossed the plaza at noon on Saturdays, a head devoid of gray that hung and let hang its protruding eyes over the account books of EL LIBERAL, an aquiline, inexpressive face that leaned for hours on a hand next to the window in the Berna.

"Is 'at you, Vázquez? Just come in, it's not locked."

Pushing with his fist and his knee, holding his gloves and his cane in his other hand, Díaz Grey walked into Snatcher's room for the first time, smiling and blinking in the half-light filled with the smell of eucalyptus. Before discovering the ridiculous for himself, he saw it announced on Larsen's face, on his half-smile. He was sitting in a chair, with his hat on, his trousers rolled up and his feet lost in the steam coming off a basin of hot water with dark leaves floating in it. The phonograph, a very old one, deliberately old, with a huge horn shaped like a flower, spun and scratched, barely pushing, just enough so that the words and the music of a tango came out.

"But, doctor, good afternoon. The last person I expected to see." There was a rigidity in Snatcher's figure, the desire (and his instantaneous rejection of it) to get up, take off his hat, and smile an unctuous welcome.

"Am I bothering you?" asked the doctor. He quickly stopped worrying whether he was a bother. He looked calmly at the ridiculous sight and intuited the other man, clinging to the visible, from the sight of the confused, willful, inevitable persistence that Snatcher would have recognized as his soul.

The dim light coming from over the bed came forward. Díaz Grey held a hand up to beg pardon, exaggerating his limp to justify the cane, and nervously admired the few elements that made up this absurdity: the nasal phonograph, its horn sagging, as if it had melted, its handle next to Snatcher's hand; the light on the night table rescued the print of the Virgin and the photograph (in color) of Carlos Gardel from the shadow of the wall; the stand with the basin and the pitcher and the mirror where immobile postcards and magazine articles floated; Snatcher himself, intimidated and angry, wide, short, his hat on, his face moist from the steam.

"Sit down, doctor." And he sat down in front of Snatcher, close to him, introducing the tip of his cane into the fragrant zone where the whiteness of the steam crept upward. Spread open on the floor between them was a copy of *Crítica*, stained with water.

Snatcher accepted the surprise by pulling his hat down a bit lower and moving his feet around in the basin.

"Well, doctor, you caught me. For things that aren't too serious, I cure myself. But don't worry, I remember the sulpha you gave me, for which I thank you again. But for other things, excuse me, but I just don't believe in doctors. For a cold, what I'm doing here and some camphor. I thought it was Vázquez, you know the guy, the one in charge of advertisement. Remember?"

"I think so," Díaz Grey lied. He was sure Snatcher only wanted to take the initiative in talking, not wander from his usual world, look at him through half-closed eyes, protected by the steam. "I went down to the paper to see you, and they told me to come up here."

"Right, I'm on vacation. The perfect time to get sick." All he did was show his yellow teeth, separate, joylessly, his thin lips. "If you look in the dresser drawer, you'll find a bottle of nice, sweet wine for old ladies."

He didn't wait for Díaz Grey to refuse; he raised each foot and let the water run off, put them on the newspaper, and slapped at them with a towel. The needle rasped on the finished record.

Díaz Grey rested his hands on the handle of the cane, bent forward toward the basin and its mist, toward the long, green leaves that bobbed around in the lazy swirl, smiling and hiding the sweetness of his smile behind his knuckles, tempted by the possibility of suddenly understanding the man who puffed and snorted, bent over, parsimonious, putting on his shoes and socks.

"I've been sent here by someone you know. About a matter you also know."

"Okay," answered Snatcher, straightening up and shaking his legs to unroll his trousers. "Let's hear it."

He turned the crank on the phonograph and put the needle back on the edge of the record. "It's an old tango." He picked up the basin and pushed it under the bed.

The guitars sounded too slow and remote, a prelude to a melancholy joke, a hasty imitation of compassion. *I won't get to know him, he's on the defensive, maybe I'll find out what he's defending himself from.*

"I think there might be some grappa too, doctor," said Snatcher, coming near. He moved his chair slightly and tossed his hat onto the table before sitting down. "I was going out as soon as I finished taking my cure, you just caught me. Even though the weather wouldn't make anyone want to go out."

"Especially if the storm keeps up." He looked at the other man's round head, his thin, well-combed hair, the forelock that almost reached his eyebrow; he smiled at him frankly to gain time because he thought he recognized Snatcher's fixed gaze, his worn-out habit of running things, the nervous movement of his left shoulder and mouth. "But you were going out, and I have to see some sick people. We'd better not waste any time."

Larsen nodded and stopped looking at him. He rubbed his short, very white hands together. Pushing against his trousers and his vest, his stomach was round, independent of the rest of his body.

"Try to understand: I have nothing to do with this business. You only have to say yes or no. I'm here for Barthé."

"Barthé," Snatcher repeated, as if out of courtesy, without getting excited.

The doctor coughed and turned his head to listen to the wind; out of the phonograph's horn, the words on the record came sliding out:

You've got a main man who does you right
You're only twenty, you're outta sight.

Now Snatcher accompanied the guitars, strumming his fingers over the green, ink-stained blotter covered with cigarette burns. The bad weather outside proclaimed its joyless victory, taking over the street, stirring up the river.

"Excuse me," said the doctor brusquely. "Are you from Rosario?"

"Yeah." Snatcher stopped tapping and tugged at his collar under his chin. "I mean, when I came here I came from Rosario." He waited a moment; then he stood up and stopped the phonograph; he waited again, amusing himself by running his finger over the sinuous edge of the horn. "What's going on with Barthé?"

"It's very simple. He managed to get a majority on the city council so they'll vote the bordello in for him."

"Go on." He took a step forward, then a step back. He raised a hand to his partly open mouth; with his eyes sunk into the dusty green opening of the phonograph horn, he presented the doctor with a cheek thickened by the years, streaked violet by alcohol, tremulous. "Sorry, doctor. So he managed to get it? All these years, the same thing. I'm not interested anymore. Especially now . . ."

"This time it's for real. I know from Arcelo. I know the conservatives will vote it in. He asked me to talk with you."

"Excuse me, doctor," Snatcher repeated, pacing back and forth. "Why doesn't he come to me?"

Now Díaz Grey thought he was near to recognizing the attitude of his body, simultaneously erect and bent over, as he went back and forth between the door and the green horn, his head bent forward, his hands clasped behind his back. *I've either seen him somewhere before or read about him, maybe I ran into him some time in the capital.*

His legs spread, sardonic, letting his stomach stick out, Snatcher stopped suddenly in front of the chair where Díaz Grey was spinning his cane between his knees.

"Let's take a look," he said, again trying to smile. Diffident, artful, Díaz Grey examined the small desperation that altered and ennobled the face the man wore. *What might be the name of the fury that half opens his mouth and stretches it to one side, rhythmically, as if it were counting off the seconds that pass and wear us out with his mug? And his bulging, hyperthyroid eyes, frenetic and impotent, pretending, to no purpose, they know how dramatic and implacable the count is they're keeping— for my edification and benefit—of the contractions of his saliva-flecked lips.*

"Excuse me, but I'm not interested anymore. I've been here for three years because of this deal and for nothing else. And two or three times a year Barthé has someone tell me that the matter has been settled. Now I just laugh." He tried to. "Understand? In this disgusting town. And I went on waiting, rotting away here. I don't mind telling you because you know. And now he comes along with another message, and he's got the nerve to send you. But for me it's all over, I've had enough of Santa María."

"I understand," said Díaz Grey. He rested the cane against his shoulder and softly massaged the cold out of his knees. "I don't know what happened before; I don't have anything to do with what went on before or for that matter what's happening now. I only came to do Barthé a favor, because he asked me to do it. I thought I was doing you a favor. In any event, this time it's real. And not just because Barthé says so."

"This time? And what if I told you, doctor, that I believe you, and that because I believe that it's true, that this time, it's real, I feel like kicking the furniture to pieces, the Berna, EL LIBERAL, kicking the pharmacist's face in along with the rest of this stinking burg? Sorry. You can tell Barthé that I'm getting out. I was crazy, really crazy, all these years, and it's only now that I realize it. Now that it's real, understand?" He spoke, restraining his fury with ease or perhaps pretending to be furious, one hand under his lapel, the other in front of his face, waving his index finger at the doctor's tranquility.

"It's odd," said Díaz Grey. "But it's comprehensible." He visibly, slowly raised his shoulders. He was sure the other would go on talking even if he showed he didn't want to listen. "But this business, all of what you're saying, is between you and Barthé. I came to tell you he got a majority on the council so they'll pass the law. You're not interested, that's that. Tomorrow I tell Barthé that now you're not interested." Without moving in the chair, he dragged the cane along the flooring and shifted his gloves to his other hand.

He heard the wind stretch out in the street, he imagined it running from the coast toward the city, rising up to receive and conquer the coming night. Again he felt that the cold was settling on the thinness of his legs; he took note of the tame, almost immobile pain in his hip bones.

"But put yourself in my place," Snatcher was saying. "I know a lot about you, I know what the poor people out in the shacks say about you. You're not like the others, the ones from the club and the hotel. And because I respect you, I want to say I'm sorry if I got out of hand."

"Thank you." Now what hurt was his boredom, the pain in his bones barely titillated him. Without enthusiasm he looked at the wide, dark man, as if he were dreaming him that way, constructed out of tedium and absurdity. *There's no way out for me; and I can't remember what I hoped would interest me in all this, in this superannuated thug. I can go home, give myself a shot, listen to music, and think about Molly, about the house on the dunes, about the hotel made of wood upriver; think that it's possible I'll die before the year is out, imagine I'm God and imagine that the past and the destiny of Dr. Díaz Grey, extinguished, provincial dispenser of enemas.*

"Hold on, do me the kindness of hearing me out," the hand abandoned the protection of the lapel, and the two arms stretched out horizontally toward the doctor. "I'm leaving for good, doctor. First, I'm going back to Rosario, but I'll probably take right off for the capital. We'll never see each other again." He dropped his arms and waited for the noise of his palms hitting his hips to disappear. He went to the bureau crowned with a bowl and pitcher and came back with a bottle of port and two glasses. "Do me the kindness, even if it's just a quick drink," he begged, smiling and submissive. He sat down next to the table and filled the glasses. Díaz Grey lit a cigarette and left the pack on the green blotter.

"To your health," said Snatcher, raising his glass. Díaz Grey took a drink. "I came because Barthé had me called. I was in Rosario and, believe me, doing just fine. But some people came to talk to me. And I always like to change, to do things. I'd never done this before, see? A business that I would organize on my own from top to bottom, any way I saw fit, without anybody over me. I was full of enthusiasm when I came, and then the whole thing fell apart. I could have gone back and forgotten the whole thing. But no, I was hardheaded. Barthé said that in six months everything would be taken care of. I always thought—excuse me for saying so, because he's a friend— he was a little nuts. But he seemed serious and a man of his word. I had already chosen the house where I was going to set up, I'd already looked over the market. Lying around here somewhere is a budget and a complete plan for the business. Don't laugh, doctor. So I chose to stay here and wait. That's why I took the job at the paper. You already know the story: I keep the books for the management and could keep them for a business ten times as big. Everybody's got a secret side. You don't like the wine. Maybe you'd like some grappa instead?"

"No thanks, I'm a little sick. But keep on talking."

Now Díaz Grey listened with greater enthusiasm, thinking at the same time about the hours of insomnia that awaited him, imagining the whine the wind would make until dawn.

"Since I was twenty, I can tell you honestly, I've never worked. And then I almost got used to living another way, to living on a salary, just imagine. And every six months, especially every March, when the city council meetings would start again, someone would come from Barthé to tell me everything was set and that I should get ready. Me, a guy who's always ready. At the end of last year—and now I understand things—I found out that Barthé had fixed the voting. Another vote. But the business didn't involve me anymore. Think about it: I'd buried myself here for more than two years, living a life that makes me die laughing just to think about it. Not counting that he didn't want to see me, that we always had to communicate through third parties, as if I were a mangy dog, as if it wasn't him who wanted to set up a whorehouse in the town. And then I find out that I'm not included in the deal anymore, that he's got a deal with Tora, a nut who's got a house over in Colón. I hit the ceiling, why should I deny it? But I stayed on; I stayed on because I knew that Tora wouldn't have the guts to do anything here when I was in Santa María. Go ask her and her friends why. It all blew over. Barthé's fix was just like all the others before."

He raised his glass and smiled, distant, grotesquely smoothed by his tolerance. He swished the wine around in his mouth before he swallowed it. "And now it seems for real, so he sends you. I mean he asks you to come. Once again, the deal comes back to me. Want to know why? He talks a lot about sacrifice and progress and the people. But what happened was that Tora didn't want to pay him his cut. Oh the cut's not for him, he says. He wants to start up a newspaper and he's looking for support from this other business. Sounds okay to me, live and let live I always say. But the fact is that he's asking for a big cut, and since Tora only sees what she's got in front of her nose, she wasn't going to agree, even if I got out of the way." He emptied his glass and laughed, understandingly and mockingly. "What's in it for me? Simple: I'm always thinking, not about this year but the one after. Let me take a crack at it, and then we'll see. That's how things stand, doctor. And believe me, I'm sorry you got involved. I'm not a kid anymore, but as far as I can see, I've only changed in one way: Now I'm liable to yak a lot when I respect the person listening to me. The other day I started thinking about what I was doing in Santa María. I got a letter from a friend, and I started to think. It's a joke. But it's all over, one more week and I'm back in Rosario. And I'm sorry that it has to be now that the deal is set because I swear I was going to set up a house anyone could be proud of. I always wanted to build something like this. But what can you do? Barthé should get in touch with Tora, maybe they can make a deal."

"Right," said Díaz Grey. "I understand." He leaned on his cane to get up. "A little rheumatism," he explained with a smile.

"Even doctors get sick," Snatcher joked cautiously. Standing up, he put on his hat again and tugged at his cuffs to make them show. "Let's go out together, I was just leaving." He opened the door and came back in to put out the light over the bed. "This is a treacherous winter, especially around here, so close to the river."

They made their way down the stairs, entering the cold wind that came down the street. Díaz Grey, his eyes half-shut and his cane hanging off his arm, leaning on the railing and letting himself be led by Snatcher, once again felt, with as much intensity as he had five years back but with a tender curiosity he hadn't know before, the temptation of suicide. In the darkness, he descended toward the wind and solitude of the streets, toward habits, toward meals eaten alone, toward the repetition of gestures and phrases directed toward the maid, toward old card games which allowed him not to think about himself, face himself. *God just for an instant bent over the short case of Díaz Grey, putting up with me with His indifference, His benevolent surprise.* He was one step ahead of Snatcher, with his eyelids almost closed, with a smile of tameness, with the distracted awareness of the pain in his kidneys and the oblique pain in his chest and the little taps of his cane against his knee.

"Thank you, doctor. Again, I'm sorry," said Snatcher slowly. "Come to think of it, I just might pay a visit to Barthé."

CHAPTER VII

I was hidden behind the curtain around the little altar, motionless the whole time it took Julita to help her brother vomit in the bathroom. I listened to them talking and whispering, I heard Marcos repeat his threats against the whorehouse and the whole city, and then the noise he made stumbling down the stairs and the motor of the little red car as it headed toward the coast. Julita had been pacing around the room, before she spread the curtains, rearranged the flowers and saints, and invited me to pray.

"Poor darling," she whispered, bent over to caress me.

Taken aback and ridiculous, trying to get up off the floor without being awkward, I knew who I was and what my name would be when I was born out of the darkness.

"It's late," she said. "Let's pray."

Very slowly, visibly concerned for her body, as if she

had just discovered it or been put in charge of it, she kneeled down, her knees, one after the other, silently touching the floor.

Kneeling down, holding my beret in my hands, pretending to think about the words, I heard her use the language of the angel to greet herself, bless herself, and confirm the annunciation. I spied her closed eyes. I knew she was sure the smile that barely raised the ends of her lips expressed humility and beatitude; but for me that smile was nothing more than an insignificant sketch, an empty form she only just managed to fill with tedium and fear. Swift, instantaneous fear coursed to the curves of her mouth and leapt out at me, from the ends and the center, from the place where my widowed sister-in-law's upper lip stuck out, swelling upward like the lip of a newborn baby.

Despair, set in the center of her smile, swirling around the shallow grimace of her lips, became, once it was corrupted and swiftly transformed, fear. And the fear poured toward me like a precise restitution of my own.

"And blessed be the fruit of thy womb," Julita was saying in a rough voice.

I saw her insane and dead; her loose tress hung motionless, opaque, and wiry, like a tangle of vegetable fibers. I recognized my fear and, even if she could feel and breathe it, even if it were mixed with the fears of everyone else in the world, I would know it's mine, that it's the most painful to suffer, the only one in which I can really believe, the only one I can endure.

"Blessed be the fruit of thy womb, Jesus," Julita repeated. Blinking, she muttered with an absorbed, careful expression, and rested her hand on my shoulder to communicate the *Ite missa est* to me and to help herself up.

She brought me to the door, and when she was about to kiss me, she stepped back. I understood that for the first time I was Jorge for her, I sensed I could no longer stop being Jorge, and I blushed, intimidated, as if I were looking at a stranger.

She opened her eyes to give them to me with such fury that I was waiting for them to fall right out, waiting to hear the simultaneous slap of the two soft blue or green drops against the floor. She smiled at me with her mouth open, astoundingly wide. The two rows of teeth were solid and even, but the only thing that counted was the round, black hole, all the elements that made up the scream she was capable of making. Later, she used her mouth to breathe, lowered her eyelids, and stood there looking at me, rather taller than I am even though she'd taken off her shoes, and with an astonished, infantile smile. *I'll remember this evening, I'll go on seeing this open face, devoid of negatives, offering itself with the hollowness of its mouth and the dilation of its eyes. I'll remember it to-morrow, whenever I want, all my life.* I forced myself to swear it.

"But just try to imagine," she whispered. "A child. No one knows. You're the only one. I'll hide it as long as I can. Just imagine."

She grabbed the tips of my raincoat's collar, laughing with her weeping noise. Before she came any closer, I thought about myself, as if I could look at myself. I thought things over and calculated the height, weakness, and tranquil attitude of my body, while I leaned on one shoulder inside the door frame. I saw the angle of the beret on my head and the warm, mature, understanding expression on the face that I placed opposite her smile. I thought that my eyes expressed my having given up sufficiently, even though I would never be able to give myself up to anyone.

"Federico's child," she concluded; as if it were impossible to move her smile, she moved her head from one shoulder to the other. Insane, and I less helpless, less young than she was. But I still knew she was a woman, stronger, infinitely more ancient; complete and solitary, like an integral unit. Without pushing me, weightless, she put one cheek against my chest and laughed; when it was time for the other cheek, she was weeping. I caressed her head with a hand made awkward and false; with my other hand I squeezed the pipe inside my raincoat pocket. Behind me were the emptiness and darkness of the staircase, the progress of the night, and the negation in her silence. Rhythmically, slowly, Julita alternated the side of her head she leaned against me so that I could go on caressing her. The emptiness of the staircase, nothing more than the depopulated shadow behind me. I remembered her face from a moment ago and understood that I had seen there, deliberate, exhibited with willful exaggeration, the meaning of all human faces, the reason why they grow, act; why the bones, the skin, the muscles, the hair, and holes in faces exist: to dominate others, abolish them, be in them, and oblige them to be in us.

She kissed me again and stifled a yawn with her knuckles. Not caring about the noise and taking pleasure in pounding my heels when I was halfway down the stairs, I walked down, opened the door with my eyes closed in order to separate myself from the groaning hinges, and went out into the garden, the hot, now rainless night. There were stars and big, light, ashy clouds drifting away.

Exactly as always, the way it was each time I left Julita's rooms and set my feet on the dirt, the weeds, the short, flattened grass: I felt that everything which had just happened—she and I, the words and the situations of the secret, of the incomprehensible lie that linked us—had no more value than the combined events in a dream.

Here I was again, real and awake, noiselessly jumping over puddles, lighting the last bit of foul tobacco in the pipe, I, this person I designate by saying *this person*, the one I see move, think, get bored, fall into a depression, get out of it, abandon himself to any small, variable form of faith and get out of it.

This person who discovers the lunar glints of Marcos's little car stuffed in down among willow and pumpkin leaves in the garden. This person who approaches the window of Rita the maid and who tonight can only see— because he doesn't want to climb up, because he trembles when he imagines the moisture and the coolness of the vine against his face—the head of the girl in the candle-light, her hair going up the pillow, and Marcos's thick forearm, immobile, collapsed onto the disk of the wrist-watch where the yellowish light is reflected without tremors.

Perhaps I'm too late or it's not happened yet; but to-night it doesn't matter. What I can see and remember of the two naked bodies neither excites nor shames me.

I'm not sleepy, I don't feel like stealing food from the kitchen, going up to my room and chewing as I look over the pages I left on the table. It can't be much after mid-night; I can walk toward town and wait for Lanza in the Berna, or walk into the newspaper and answer the greet-ings given to the boss's son until I get to the cast-iron stairway that leads to the presses, go down and sit next to Lanza at the badly made table where he's probably correcting galleys.

I push open the gate and walk out to the road; but I don't really have any desire to do it, to repeat today my nocturnal comedy with old Lanza. I'm doing it anyway, my hands in the pockets of my raincoat, taking care that my shoulders remain loose, relaxed, trying to keep my arms from participating in the effort of walking, avoiding, occasionally with difficulty and alarm, the potholes full of water or angrily stepping into them. I keep my nose open to try to discern the origin (the kind of tree, or mound, or hollow, or dark lair) of every end-of-summer smell the humid night rots and sweetens. I hold my head up at that angle which indicates despair and the will to assimilate it, that exaggerated, virile, and painful angle which determines the sag of the mouth and the eyelids. I'm doing it—taking long steps along the road that goes up and down and that seems to twist continuously to the right in a spiral—because I really want to do the other thing, go upstairs to eat and sprawl, chewing, aware of the shine of grease on my lips, over the desolate stupidity of the four lines with no future, which never should have been formulated, for whose useless introduction into the world I am responsible and which I cannot excise from my memory.

Because tonight I also don't want to rub my face and hands, wet them on the vine around Rita's window just so I can see her naked against Marcos, watch them push while they try to mix together or pretend they are mixing together, watch them stop being and become, in a short, anonymous fury, like a cow, a pigeon, or a dog.

I pass in front of a curve of orange trees, I walk staring

at the dirty stains on the sheepskins hung on the wire, and when I feel I'm alone I pound my heels in along the middle of the road. Now I'm near the mill and the lights that brighten the last white clouds without touching them. Tomorrow I'll have good weather, heat, and it's almost certain I'll get together with Tito and Alejandro at the grotto. Sometimes all the things I don't want to think about because it's impossible to think about them are inside me; but usually they're behind me, like a forgettable shadow I'm not allowed to step on. They'll ask me questions when the eyes and smiles and the silence become transparent and reveal the emptiness and solitude, the separation; I'll talk to them about Rita and Marcos as if I'd seen them today, I'll shrug my shoulders and take my pipe out of my mouth so I can spit in disgust.

"But you never did it," Tito will repeat. "So you can't know."

And even though I'm sure he's never done it either, I will acknowledge, without saying it out loud, that he's right, in part. I'll feel I'm saying good-by or so long to them, that a world more impure than that of distracted friendship has trapped me and I can't, it's true, know until then.

But I'm alone. Tito, Alejandro, the German, Julita, my mother, my father, all of them have their ears to my mouth. But they can't understand that when I do it, it will have nothing to do with what they did or may do. Not in this or in anything else.

There's a cop shaking out his cape under a streetlight; one more block and I'll start to cross the plaza. Nothing important can be thought, important things should drag themselves along unconsciously with us, like a shadow. Even so, I can try, tonight, to picture Julita's child, that thing she added to her face, to her movements, that thing which will alter, a lot or a little, the air of the bedroom where we meet. On some bench in this plaza or walking under the trees, there was or will be someone who could be my friend; someone, man or woman, closer to my tastes than the people I live with. I'll never see that person, I'll never know if he or she breathed the humidity of a summer storm while crossing Santa María's plaza, idly changing, out of a sense of play and despair, the arrangement of materials that make up the world. Perhaps that person decided, on this very spot, step by step on the uneven gravel, to dedicate his life to a single purpose or, which is the same thing, to renounce all purposes. It's just as easy for me to share his faith and his slightly surprised laugh, the slightly fearful laugh with which he will accept or has already accepted his renunciation.

A child for Julita, Julita's child, which I am not, I think as I turn the corner; I belabor the absurd idea as I fill my pipe by the light of the spherical lamps outside EL LIBERAL, next to the bronze plaque that commemorates the fact that it was my grandfather who founded the newspaper. Besides the date and the sentence with two adjectives, there is on the plaque the figure of an oil lamp and the profile of a woman. I walk up the marble stairs, cross the gray light of the vestibule without being seen, and walk down the twisted iron stairs that lead to the presses.

Old man Lanza has his head resting on a fist and raises his lip to moisten his sparse, gray, sunken moustache. Against the edge of the table a hand waves away the cigarette smoke, which is half ash.

"Hello, hello," he says, shaking himself, waking up, clearing his throat. He's happy to see me. Touching his shoulder and the tips of his fingers I realize I love him more than I thought. His shirt collar and cuffs are filthy, as are his hands. His hands are swollen, hairy, spotted, almost devoid of nails, the veins on their backs prominent; they did things, they moved between themselves, and they wore out.

"How long has it been, for heaven's sake, that you haven't had a thought for the poor of the earth. Have a seat. We can still get a coffee and a drink. Especially if you were the one to order it. How's the poetry going? Still with Juan Ramón Jiménez and his personal spelling style? It stopped raining, didn't it? I've been thinking about you, about what we talked over the last time you were here. I rummaged through my few personal effects and found a little book that comes right to the point of our discussion. I didn't bring it, but I can have it sent over. Here comes the guy; order some coffee—do me a favor."

I know that he never thinks about the fact that I'm the boss's son. He'd be polite with any boy my age. He doesn't think he's helping me, unlike the others. I amuse him, give him a chance to remember out loud. His eyes are shining, he makes fun without being bitter, he's intelligent, and in the way he massages his smile with his fingers I confirm the fact that he's clever and alert.

"And that thug of a brother-in-law or brother of your sister-in-law, how's he doing?" he asks to locate me in a terrain where my adolescence can be comfortable and spontaneous.

"Marcos? Still a thug, still drunk." I take off my beret as we stare at each other laughing.

"It's sad, but I don't believe in him, not even as a drunk. I don't believe in drunks with excuses."

Suddenly I do what I was sure I wouldn't do. I take out the pages folded in two with the poems typed out on them and toss them across the table.

"Take them with you and later tell me what you think."

It doesn't matter to me whether he reads them or not. I'm not interested in what anyone has to say about the five poems. They're bad and good for me. Whatever they might be for someone else is meaningless.

We drink our coffee, and Lanza kids around with the boy who brings him the galleys. He looks old, he's an old man. For years, everything he's done has been separate from the man he once was, just as the echo of a bell is from the moment it was rung and from the bell itself. With a good-natured face, almost with love, he looks over my poems. He moves his glasses before the first poem, the worst of the five, and puts the pages away. He alludes to Juan Ramón Jiménez again, and we make jokes and smoke, separated by the narrow, stained, cold table. Even though the old man doesn't know it, we are balancing our mouths on the edge of my despair, where it's possible that he, dead, plays at understanding me, with this person who will never exist.

With no rebellion, merely with a sensation of fatigue that drags along and keeps all the fatigue of the day's work together, I think that I walked the road to town with the same resolute steps my brother would have taken and that I've also stolen from Federico the rapid, confident movement with which I took out and tossed the five pages with the little poems onto the table.

"So the women have arrived," says Lanza with an exaggerated wink. "Well, after all, we boys have a right to have fun, what the hell."

He wasn't thinking about me when he said it, he isn't trying to direct me or dirty me, maybe he doesn't know that the house where they've set up the bordello belongs to my father, that my father rented it to the guy they call Snatcher.

"I saw them at the train station," I concur with the calm, countrified voice of Federico, with his polite, abstracted smile.

CHAPTER VIII

Two days after Dr. Díaz Grey hobbled his way up the boardinghouse steps, Larsen paid a visit to the pharmacist. He audaciously began the interview with the most difficult of his tricks. He dispassionately described the rage Barthé's earlier maneuvers with Tora caused him and then leaned toward the other man with his eyes half-shut, making a cold, dead gesture, pinning him there for many seconds. Anything might have happened then, anything might have been expected: from a heart attack to the hasty joy of the last judgment. Without alluding to any specific threat, his face and his silence expressed all of them. Then he stepped back with a definitive movement as a smile of relief spread over the stupidity of his cheeks.

"Now you need me. Now settle things with Tora."

Barthé folded his round hands over his chest. They

were standing in a corner of the pharmacy, in the shadow of the cash register and the big bottles filled with colored liquids, where the pharmacist had placed a school desk: He called it his office. He looked indifferently at Snatcher, showing no more sadness than what he felt for wasting time. The bucolic scent of the open sacks of herbs wafted up from the open cellar.

"I'm sorry Dr. Díaz Grey isn't with us," said Snatcher.

"So am I," agreed Barthé. The weather hadn't gotten any better over the past few days; a dark, wet nightfall flattened against the dirty windows. "He's ill."

"I know he's sick," Snatcher interrupted, irritated by the pharmacist's meekness, by his soft, infantile skin, by the unalterable anxiety of his round mouth, by those hands resting on his chest, as if on a child. "I know. Rheumatism. Doctor and all, he still doesn't know how to cure himself. It's none of my business. And none of yours."

"He gets it every year, every winter. A week, ten days."

"It's none of my business. You two are the doctors." Snatcher lit a cigarette and held the light next to the diamond he wore on his pinky. The pharmacist went on looking at the panes of glass in the windows and the display cases.

"All right," he murmured. "You know that my negotiations with that woman are finished."

"Hold on," Snatcher protested. "I meant what I said. I really would like to have the doctor here as a witness. You, with all due respect, don't know who I am."

"It's possible," Barthé agreed. "It's hard to get to know people, and we haven't had much contact." His voice sounded high-pitched to him, invariably stubborn. "Why do you need witnesses? I never went back on the deal, it was always quite clear. That woman made me an offer, and I turned it down."

"A mistake," said Snatcher, now adopting an advisory tone. "Because now I'm of no use to you. The deal doesn't interest me anymore. I waited a year and some months, until the day I woke up and asked myself what I was doing in this town. Me. Think about that." He took off his hat and tilted his head over so Barthé could see in the light of dusk the gray hairs over his ear and the youthful, cynical smile he could still make.

"Really . . . " said the pharmacist. It was impossible to know if he were objecting or agreeing.

A dark, pot-bellied woman dragged a melancholy zone of bad weather in with her. She leaned on the counter and, without any sign of impatience, tapped a coin against one of the glass jars.

"Me," repeated Snatcher, surprised, bragging. "But you can't understand why I spent all this time in Santa María. Not even the doctor can—completely. Some things happen so a few people can understand them, other things happen so a few others will understand them. At the beginning, I had my hopes, and I went on thinking I was only staying on in order to hope. But when I realized . . ." He put on his hat with a rapid, exaggerated thump of rage. "Just imagine. This dump they've started calling a city. When I woke up, as I was saying, I discovered that I'd stopped hoping a long time before, that for months the deal had stopped being of any interest to me."

"You'd be the best judge of that," said Barthé without interrupting him, actually helping him to go on. With his fat body hunched over, and rubbing his soft biceps, he showed that it was late and cold. Now his face was in the shadow, like a simple whiteness, like a pale volume offered to the fingers that tried to give it form. He was also showing the infinite patience of an obsession which had become a habit, a destiny. Snatcher understood that in one short look.

"Of course I am!" exclaimed Snatcher, placing a loose fist on the desk. He stared at his fist in sympathy and curiosity.

A yard away from them, the woman left her final, flirtatious, inviting laugh to Barthé's employee and walked out, sashaying along the counter. When she left, she allowed a little piece of the humid, now windless, dripping, and silent night to be seen. The clerk put out one light and walked out on the softness of his sandals to lower one of the pharmacy's metal gates.

Barthé was also watching the neglected fist Snatcher had placed on the desk as if it were just a thing, separate from himself: the folds under the thumb, the unconsciously obscene gesture that raised one of the fingers. Body Snatcher's head, its baldness hidden by the hat, was quite close to his own: Snatcher's bulging eyes, his conquered nose prophesying defeat, the periodic, almost imperceptible contraction of his mouth toward his right cheek. Then the pharmacist guessed or supposed a form of brotherliness in the other man, a vocation or mania, the need to fight for a cause without having real faith in it and without considering it an end in itself.

"I know things you can't know," said Snatcher with distracted aggressiveness. "You've got to live some things to know them."

The pharmacist narrowed his eyes, and his pink little mouth stretched slightly to smile. *He thinks living is the other thing and only that. He would never understand the meaning of my money, my prudence, my lack of anecdotes to tell.*

"I can't tell you why I stayed on," Snatcher repeated. "With people like this for all this time, without doing anything, without hoping for anything. Do you understand? I thought that I'd be able to have my own business and run it as I saw fit, without anyone else poking his nose into it. I was sure that with you it was all going to be possible. A solid concession, and I could choose everything, the furniture, the women, the schedule, the style. Even the perfumes, the rouge, the face powder, I thought; I would have bought them all from you, of course. I would select them all myself. It wasn't meant to be. Well, patience is a virtue."

The clerk walked by, sleeves rolled up and slow, sweeping; he stopped to cough and the noise in the empty drugstore startled Snatcher and the pharmacist. The cough, dry and aggressive at the beginning, later moist and almost confidential because of the phlegm the clerk spit onto the trash, informed them that the interview was coming to an end. Snatcher clenched his fist, softly punched the desk, and then, relaxing the fist, brought it to his chest.

"Patience is a virtue."

Then, with very little effort, without the perceptible superiority that pity permits, the pharmacist smiled again and for an instant abandoned himself to comparing his impossibility with women and the relationship with women that had been Snatcher's entire life, with that obvious dependence which it was indispensable to take into account if anyone wanted to understand something of the sarcastic man wearing a hat who was hesitatingly searching for a way of saying good-by, one that would work to the advantage of both his vanity and his interests.

"Dear friend," the pharmacist finally said, "if you've hoped for such a long time uselessly . . ." He didn't want to look at Snatcher; he stretched out a hand to play with the pencil tied to the desk by a dirty string. "It can now be done."

"Now," Snatcher chorused, trying to laugh. *He's got to start believing all that garbage at some point*, thought Barthé. *Here he is, an old man, he's the one who's hysterical, beating around the bush just so he can say yes. Just like a woman.*

"The conditions remain the same," the pharmacist recited, staring at the half pencil he'd grabbed up. There were others in the grade-school-sized desk, more in the pocket of his tunic. "I don't care about the profits from the exploitation of the business. I only want five hundred pesos a month to defray the expenses of the weekly paper." He fell silent and looked at the teeth marks in the pencil, which he'd lifted up amid the silence.

"Yeah?" Snatcher said to himself. "Okay, and what about the start-up money, the organizational expenses? The rent, transportation, furniture: all that comes before anyone earns a cent. After all, I hope you don't think I'm going to take out a women-wanted ad in EL LIBERAL or in your little paper."

The pharmacist separated his fingers and let the pencil fall and bounce on the desk. He sighed, leaning back in the chair, and once again placed his rounded hands on his chest.

"Not a cent," he said amiably, as if he were offering something. "I won't have anything to do with that garbage. You do things as you see fit. And you give me five hundred a month beginning when you open up."

Snatcher examined Barthé's drowsy face for a while. He again leaned over with his expression of indifferent menace, but he instantly straightened up. "All right," he said, getting to his feet. "Now it's your turn to deal. But first I want to see them approve the law. There are lots of interests against it." He smiled, protectively and mysteriously.

"That was never any of your affair," Barthé answered.

Snatcher merely raised a hand in farewell. He grumblingly bent over to get through the little door in the metal gate, which Barthé's assistant held open for him.

That night at the newspaper he requested ten days off without pay to go to the capital and consult a doctor. "Not that there aren't any around here. There are, and good ones. But what I need is a specialist." He had a ticket on the morning train in his pocket. But as he drank his last beer in the Berna before going up to bed, standing at the bar next to Vázquez, from the newspaper, Snatcher discovered that it would be very hard for him to leave Santa María unless he achieved, for himself, a kind of confused justification.

Perhaps, hunched over the account books in the upstairs office at the newspaper, or alone in his room over the Berna, or alone or leaning easily against Vázquez's admiration standing at the bar in the Berna, he'd gotten too used to hoping for the moment of triumph. It was as if he himself and all his motives had metamorphosed into that hope and now it would be impossible to get beyond it.

Gloomy, a bit disconcerted, without the audacity necessary to be bored next to Snatcher, Vázquez smoothed his moustache with two fingers. He knew nothing about why Snatcher was making this trip, and he maintained himself resolved and small in the face of the silent concern of his friend, his hat resting on his right eyebrow, the large black knot in his tie slipping its corners under the collar, his stained fingers moving back and forth over the smoothness of his moustache. *There must be something I forgot. Nothing I have to do, for certain. As soon as I remember, things will be fine. Maybe I'm getting old.* He smiled. Then Vázquez rested his fingers against his nose and breathed surprisedly, as if he didn't know that mix of nicotine, sweat, printer's ink, and cologne by heart.

"Remember María Bonita?" Snatcher asked.

"Yes, of course. I know which one you mean." Calmer, he swallowed some beer and recited: "The one from Rosario and the capital, the one who got you out of jail, the one who left and came back, the one who threw the doll down on the table in the café. María Bonita. How could I forget?"

"That's the one all right," said Snatcher, opening his hand over Vázquez's narrow, bony shoulder. He gestured to the bartender to bring more beer. "I was thinking, and it occurred to me that this make-believe life as book-keeper at the paper is wearing me out. That's why I remembered her."

"Wearing you out how?" Vázquez protested. "Of course it is true you never led this kind of life."

"I did when I was very young," Snatcher corrected him. "And I did a little bit in Rosario, but just to get out of sight for a while. There was a time when people took it seriously. But this is different. It's been about two years. Eight hours a day by the clock and never making any trouble. And it was María Bonita herself who told me once that it was dangerous. Besides, I'm not a kid anymore."

They drank and stood silently leaning against the bar, elbow to elbow, united by the past and the mysteries of sympathy. Staring at the winter landscapes in the enormous photographs that interrupted the walls of the restaurant like windows, Snatcher thought that the memory of María Bonita had no special meaning, that even evoking the woman and the time surrounding her in nostalgia, he couldn't overcome his own awareness of the failure which had begun to anguish him. It wasn't here where he could find the thing he had to meditate on before getting on the train to the capital. So he tossed some money onto the bar, gave Vázquez's faithful shoulder a long squeeze and walked out.

He knew he'd never fall asleep. Already on the stairs he was remembering the antagonistic face with which Barthé had insisted and refused. There, in that white face, at the moment of humiliation—which he had accepted— was the source of this weakness he felt now, of this indifference that distanced him from the future and from himself. He undressed, leaving a light on: propped up against the pillow, running his hand over the hair on his chest, distractedly sucking the little medal he wore around his neck, he stared at the half-light, the familiar forms of the furniture, waited for the dawn, demanding his own presence, wanting to examine himself, separate and other, demanding the name of the act or thought he knew to be absolutely essential to reconcile himself.

CHAPTER IX

During distant months, anchored in Rosario, Larsen had been lost, giving himself over to inertia and the passing of time without visible struggles. That was the state he was in, fat and unconcerned, when he was told that Tora wanted to sell her house, carry it like a suitcase to some other city.

She'll want a fortune for it, he thought, staring indifferently at his informant.

He wasn't doing badly; he could live decorously, have two or three suits a year made, comply with the daily rite of the barbershop, and invite his friends to at least one dinner a week. But he was sure that even if he could double the number of bodies under contract at present and make them work dawn-to-dawn, that not even then, not even by multiplying the profits by ten, would he be able to get together enough money to pay Tora the price of her key.

He knew the house and would have liked it if he could have used it as a customer. But he was forced to look at things with a critical eye; he was as bound to trip over its defects as he was bound to trip over badly arranged furniture. With his hat on his head, a distinction insisted on by Tora, his hands in his pockets, sitting unrelaxedly on one buttock, as if to establish the lack of intimacy, he took bitter and proud note of each of the hundred differences that separated Tora's house from the one he had imagined. Now, perhaps, that house was definitively unattainable, but it lived, solid, a gold mine when he compared it with this one.

But life hadn't come to an end, and it would always be interesting to know the figure Tora was asking. He visited her again; he waited without even a glance at the girls, who were smoking and talking about dresses and movies in the tile-covered patio, talking about gold-plate, about shades of purple that turned black in the attenuated light. He waited for Tora to come downstairs. *Why does she have this place lit up like a wake when the patio is so small no one can really use it? It would be a good idea to get rid of that partition and put in small tables and divans with a big lazy Susan for a table. Since she sells drinks, instead of having them brought in from the kitchen, why not put a little bar right in here, with a Victrola and records. The women or she herself could take care of it.*

Tora came down wearing a long, black dress, smiling at him from the banister, swaying back and forth and vigorous. The woman's clothes and the jewels on her breast and her well-manicured fingers made him remember that the next day was a holiday and that an official train from the capital was coming to carry out an inauguration.

"But why didn't they send you right up?" she asked as she stopped, first him and then the girls, who smiled, shrugging their shoulders, briefly grief-stricken. *Too much powder, too much makeup, all three of them have the same hairdo.* Tora opened the door to her office, scratched at the wall until she found the light switch, and ushered him in. She put a bottle of cherry liqueur and a single glass on the table.

"I won't waste your time," said Snatcher, settling himself on one of the tiny chairs made of pink wood and presenting the woman with his profile.

"Excuse me for coming over on a night like this, a work night."

"No big deal, son, it's still early. You know that in summertime there are no early birds."

She drawled her *r*'s a bit, had bleached her black Indian hair blonde, and her heavy, cruel face tried to camouflage itself in an immobile aspect of patience and fatigue. Within the swollen flesh of her face, her eyes narrowed to see better and then blinked to conceal the effort.

"Didn't you tell me on the telephone you had something important to discuss, son? Go ahead, have a drink. I can't; liver's acting up. We all get old. How's Ercilia? Okay? Things are better this way. She was a good girl when she wasn't acting nuts. No, I won't have any. It's my liver and my girls. I swear this life . . . Not even their mothers would have the patience, son. But what are you going to do, I was young once myself."

She smoked, using a long cigarette holder decorated with silver ivy, making regular movements, excessively revealing her false teeth whenever the holder approached her mouth, exhaling the smoke with a gesture of yielding and disgust on her thick lips when the holder, which she slowly removed from her mouth, hung vertically from her fingers.

"How right you are," said Snatcher, advancing a sympathetic smile toward the Bolivian bracelet, tinkling innocently, which at that moment she was bringing near to her black silk dress. "It's a battle."

Soon you'll want people to call you madame. Her allusions to how young her girls were and to her past relationship with Ercilia, one of the bodies in his own mortuary, seemed deliberate to him, made to point out differences of condition and to evoke the bent, deformed bodies, the frayed, grotesque faces, even the very sicknesses that afflicted the four obscene remains of women that he shepherded, intuitively helping them with slaps and minuscule infamies, with long, often-repeated monologues that promised happiness, or at least, peace on earth to all the whores of goodwill who accepted supporting him.

"I'm here to talk about cash," said Snatcher. He heard the doorbell ring and the whispering, the silence—so familiar to him, so unmistakable—of the girls getting up to greet the customers. "People tell me you want to sell. How much do you want—total?" Her smile ended and went into retreat, driving away a severe, definitive expression from the collision of the holder and her dentures.

"Sell? I'd have to be nuts. Nobody's going to pay me what this thing's worth, what it cost me to get it on its feet." The nodding of her head, her smile, the cigarette holder stopped in midair along with the smoke of the almost-finished cigarette: It revealed no mockery, pity,

or incredulity. Tora merely wanted to express the satisfaction of a triumph that could be shared without envy.

"Then I'm mistaken," Snatcher excused himself. "I
was told that you were selling out and moving to Santa
María."

"Who said that?"

"That's what people are saying."

"They know more than I do, son," she complained
resignedly. She moistened her fingernails with her
tongue and pulled the butt out of the holder.

"For a million, who knows what I'd do. . ." She leaned
forward to laugh and slapped the air with her open hand.
The doorbell rang again, and from the patio came the
insincere noise of voices greeting each other.

"Looks like you've got company," said Snatcher. He
got up and raised the glass to empty it. "If you have to
go to work . . ."

"No, my boy. The girls know how to work. Later on,
when the place is filled up, sure. Or if something out of
the ordinary were to happen. But for now they can get
along without me." She spoke with some haste, with the
tone of an impersonal complaint, as if being believed
weren't at risk, or being heard. As she went on grumbling,
having recovered her French pronunciation of r's, she
went about inserting another cigarette in the holder and
filling the glass Snatcher had abandoned. "That's no reason for you to leave, my boy. If you've got something else
to do, well that's another matter. So they say I'm selling
out and going to Santa María? To do what? To work on
the harvest or to die of hunger?"

"I don't know," said Snatcher, sitting down again on
one buttock. "They said you were selling out and I came
to find out how much you'd want—cash."

"It would have to be cash, my boy. If I decide to sell
. . . Well, you know the house and know what it's worth
as a business. It's sure cost me enough to get it to where
it is; only I can know how much it cost me. But for me
to sell—it'd have to be to some nut, son, someone who'd
give me in cash double what the place's worth. That's
the only way. . . ."

Snatcher sweetened his tongue with the liqueur and
lit a cigarette. He was certain Tora wouldn't bargain; she
simply—and she was right—didn't believe in him, thinking the idea that he could buy her out absurd. She suspected he'd come to get a price out of her so he could
offer it to others and get himself a commission. Everything was proper: She was not going to quote any figures,
and he had only come to hear figures, just to be able to
use them to measure the distance and the impossible
number of years to live that separated him from one of
his dreams. But he decided to stay for no good reason,
because he was comfortable in profile to the desk, with
one buttock on a shaky little chair, or because he had
nothing better to do until his predinner cocktail or because he wanted to be near her a few minutes more, near
someone who, unjustly, had succeeded in a business almost identical to the one he coveted in his hopeless anguish, his parody. He decided to stay a while, listen to
her and stare at her, while the doorbell rang and rang
and the girls made their heels echo in the patio, distributing greetings in voices that had begun to grow hoarse.

He never managed to hear the figure he was looking
for, but, sitting uncomfortably on the velvet-covered
chair, he did manage to hear cynical and false comments
amid the noise of the comings and goings in the patio,
noise that fortified Tora's detached superiority. Excited,

he drank the last sweet drink on guard against himself, while Tora put the bottle back into the low, black, bombé commode.

He got up to say good-by, calculating that every ring of the doorbell meant a minimum of ten pesos for Tora. Evoking the smiles, stares, and tricks of the trade his four bodies tricked out in party dresses were probably acting out in dark, badly ventilated cabarets, bodies he would have to see, perhaps caress, in any case listen to between midnight and dawn, just to earn—because it was the night before a holiday—a maximum of forty pesos, once the meals and eventual drunkenness were discounted.

At noon the next day he awoke in his boardinghouse room and lit the first cigarette of the day. It was a holiday, so three radios mixed their songs beyond the door, while outside the balcony blackened by the curtain, fireworks exploded at regular intervals in the center of town. Next to him, one of the four women, naked, snored, her anonymous head covered by hair resting on his arm, on the short sleeve of his undershirt.

He thought again about Tora and Santa María, remembering his youth, when he'd sworn solitary vows in faded neighborhood cafés, discovering, proving, with shock and fear, with perplexed pride, that he was different, irreconcilable with the victorious and paltry fate wished and prophesied for him by his friends and his first shocked women.

That noon, while the body on duty, hideous, fat, short, with stains of sleep and makeup on her sagging, beaten face manipulated her cigarette and vermouth with rapid gestures, bothered him so she could tell the frightening and simple dream she'd just had, Snatcher added up all the money he'd saved and the jewels he had left. He put a price on the jewels and, cautiously, greedily came up with a round figure. It was enough.

"I think it's from eggs, darling," said the skeleton, now sitting on the bed, tapping her elbows and knees with her fingers and the glass she held between her open leg-bones, excluding her age, stupidity, and worn-out life.

"You feel like eggs?" asked the magnanimous Snatcher, touching the green loudspeaker on the phonograph he'd decided not to sell. He suspected that he no longer had anything to do with the obese, barely greenish, stinking corpse, this presence.

"Go on," she said, laughing, bent over the edge of the bed. "I mean that I have eggs before I go to sleep and probably that's what makes me dream."

"I didn't understand you, sorry," said Snatcher. "You're probably right, though."

"But some dreams really do mean something," the thing murmured. She took a drink, then dropped her cigarette into the glass.

Hairy, wearing the brown T-shirt whose bottom twisted up near his belly button, running his finger over the flowerlike shape of the green loudspeaker on the phonograph, Snatcher wavered between pity and disgust. It always happens this way with the dead ones. He took a step and watched with curiosity the hand he advanced to touch the reddish, burnt, dry, still-perfumed hair of the cadaver seated awkwardly on the bed.

"Don't get carried away by dreams," he advised, caressing the body. With a movement of his tongue, he dropped his cigarette into the glass held up by the enormous, tightly squeezed thighs of the whitish, tranquil fat woman. "With dreams you just never know. Sometimes they try to tell you everything backwards. But as long as I love you, why are you going to worry about them, tell me?"

The cadaver raised its head and tried to smile. Larsen was thinking about a rich, white, fortunate city next to a river. He missed its imagined, special air, as if he'd been born there and was finally facing the chance to go back. He looked at the corpse, which was standing up, its smile wider without flesh, its small skull shining, the empty glass sunken into the hole in its stomach. Forgiving and generous, he breathed in the putrefaction in the few remaining bits of cartilage and examined what it had in common with the other bodies, which perhaps had also just awakened and which, very soon, would begin to telephone him.

Snatcher spent two days in Santa María and went back to Rosario to sell whatever he could, pack up his phonograph and lie to friends and women, saying he was going north for two weeks or a month. During one after-dinner chat or another, he imagined selling the dead women he was abandoning, dreamed, between amusements and smiles, that he exchanged Ercilia and the other three corpses for simple favors, shots of rum, or friendly pats on the back.

But there was nothing for him in Santa María, nothing more than the probability of defeating Tora and an absurd promise guaranteed by the pharmacist Barthé. But various forms of youth awaited him, stable and his for the taking, in the town or city. He spoke with Barthé in the back room, noting how over the course of an hour distrust, disdain, and passion animated his white, round, hairless face, threatening to tear open the bloody little

B o d y   S n a t c h e r

mouth that seemed smeared with the grease in his double chin.

For an hour he helped the pharmacist talk, allowed himself to be fascinated by the temptation to measure that form of madness against his own. He believed in the bordello Barthé was offering—not in Barthé, Tora, or humanity—and he dedicated himself to organizing it, to projecting the arrangement of its furniture, and the psychology, the age, the racial antecedents of the women he would have to put under contract. He got a job in the business office of El Liberal and systematically, without pleasure, got to know the town and its inhabitants, regaling the men with the twisted smile of his youth, seeking out clients for the hypothetical future, and trying to figure out what atmosphere, what style of place, what prices, what size women they would prefer.

And when Barthé obtained the conservative votes for his project and the danger of competition from Tora was eliminated, when the pharmacist in the back room exaggerated his joy and carefully explained why it was inopportune to talk about contracts, he, Snatcher, beneath the trickery, the reticence, the self-control that pride and experience recommended, felt he was ready to run to the capital, find María Bonita, and carry out with her a dream he'd never confessed to her.

He was old, incredulous, sentimental; founding the brothel now was, essentially, like getting married *in articulo mortis*, like believing in ghosts, acting like God.

CHAPTER X

From Tuesday to Friday, the house with the blue shutters closed at two in the morning. Then María Bonita made herself up again, put on her shiny black silk dress and the high heels she'd worn at the beginning of the after-noon to receive guests. She entered the vestibule smiling, with a freshly lit cigarette smoking in the long holder she'd learned to use like a fan. Sometimes all she had to do was appear and make some slow, courteous remarks, a yawn mixed with laughter for the men—who wanted to stay and couldn't, who stared with gross envy from the little tables in the covered patio at the doors of the three unmultipliable bedrooms—to stand up, pay, and drink their last drink standing up, generally to the health of the corpulent woman who was throwing them out.

María Bonita locked and bolted the door. And while the old, half-asleep maid went around wiping ashes,

moisture, and slime off the tables, picking up empty cigarette packs, María Bonita, whether or not there was a
man waiting for her in her bedroom, poured all the left-
over grappa and rum into a tall glass, sat down for five
minutes on a window ledge, looked over her silk stockings, knocked the ash off her cigarette on one of the bars
over the window, and amid the smells she brought with
her and those of the invisible summer night, always undefined, barely allusive, gave herself over to her game of
make-believe worries and memories.

It was her one moment of happiness during the work
day, her compensation for every unpleasantness, for the
lightning flashes of awareness that she was bored and
that time was flying by. She was smoking and drinking
and believed she was alone, at last, once every twenty-
four hours. She thought she could find herself again and
tolerate herself in those furtive encounters at the window
with the bars on it: above the mature night and its air,
above the absence of men, above the noise of the old
woman's broom on the reddish tiles, above the convincing
phrases and snores that reached her from the bedrooms.
She played at supposing the existence of a barely aged
María Bonita, calm, constructed out of acts of goodness
and comprehending renunciations, with clothes and
manners born to be copied, with a sensation of life that
did not conflict with other lives or have any need to mix
with them.

She closed the window and made the centimeter of
cigarette fall into the bottom of the glass she handed to
the old woman. Whether or not there was a man waiting
for her in bed, she would see herself by surprise first in
the bedroom mirror. With an always fleeting curiosity,
she would try to discover the hard decisiveness and fa-

tigue that defined her. Later she would examine, as she restored her lipstick, as she listened to the silence or some masculine voice behind her, the face of María Bonita, the subtle wrinkles with no history that only seemed to represent the fatigues of the day.

She could no longer recognize herself completely. She would stare at the shine, the softness, the lines of shadow, and conclude that in reality she had no face, that the only thing she could use to distinguish herself was a fluctuating excitation devoid of motive or hope; that and her big eyes surrounded by blackness, where old yellow fibers languished. Her mouth was still fresh, still far away from the growing fatness under her chin, from the horseshoe-shaped bit that separated her chin from her neck. The world was over until tomorrow; she was going to sleep, or to work a few more minutes before going to sleep.

The house closed at two, but on Saturday nights closing time depended on the number and the enthusiasm of the guests. Mondays they opened just at nightfall, when the sun stopped heating up the blue shutters and the dried earth in the flower pots filled with dead geraniums.

Monday was the day, the afternoon, when the women went out. After the first week, María Bonita had foresworn the privilege of strolling through Santa María, spending money in the shops, and sitting at a table in a poor café just to be served. She had seen and heard the town's disdain, spontaneous, without aggressiveness, like a change in the weather that included all of them, men and women, the house fronts and the slope of the streets.

She'd seen the blushes, the awkwardly averted eyes, the blank looks of the men who'd been with her, or at least in the house, the night before; she didn't want to go out again, not out of fear but simply because she imagined that Irene and Nelly brought her absence with them in their walks through the town, her will not to go, her equivalent disdain. She stayed in the house and, later, during the siesta, Snatcher would appear. They would drink *maté* in the bedroom and talk, with long pauses, about business, each one trying to appear tougher and more selfish than the other, since from the start they had declared to each other that they were only trying to get money to help each other, María Bonita helping Snatcher, and he helping her.

In the half-light turned to stripes by the shutter, under the large color print of Saint Jude Thaddeus and the flowers changed weekly, the "do-you-remember's" were repeated, shocked, happy, diversely significant. They lied and forgot, or helped each other to lie and to forget; as occasionally happens with the dead, the past cleansed itself of impurities, renounced circumstances and motives, and occupied, docile and flourishing, the warm air of the bedroom, sonorous, like a history book, like a legend of courage, wisdom, and sacrifice.

Sometimes, like ghosts, they made love again in the darkness and labored at it for the sake of pleasure, without egoism or haste, certain that the mirror next to the bed made their bodies twenty years younger by copying them, and that from the very marrow of their bones to their skin, dignity grew impetuously, a virtue that each one thought and designated with different, unformulated words.

At the same time, Nelly, the blonde, and Irene, the fat one, joined at the hands and elbows, had just finished walking up the steep street that led to the plaza. Commenting on the heat with sighs and tiny, astonished giggles, they wiggled their way under the intermittent shade of the trees.

A bit insecure, Irene occasionally leaned on the pink parasol she never dared to open; holding their heads excessively high, conscious of themselves as if they were things, from their complicated hairdos to their silver and gold shoes, they went striding along the diagonal path across the plaza. They would stop with languid brusqueness in front of store windows and, without listening to each other, exchange words only remotely related to their motives.

They bought a few things, almost never what they'd come for, without arguing over prices, without paying any attention to the rudeness or the faces of the salesmen. As if they were blind, they were isolated from the irritation their ankle-length summer dresses aroused, from the hatred stirred up by their measured, slightly inexpressive, singsong voices.

In fact—they felt it from time to time during their stroll, like the smell of the perfumes and talcum powder with which they'd completed their postsiesta bath—what they were dragging through the town was fear, the sensation of not having any right to walk on those sidewalks, to sink their hands into the piles of silk and wool on the counters. They knew it without knowing it fully, which is why they never named it.

Each Monday they scrambled up the streets under the sun, fatigue and sweat undoing their recently made up faces. Distressed, they looked out for easy paths and kept an eye on the size of the moist shadows growing larger around their armpits. They advanced toward the weekly humiliation because it contained the pleasure of their feeling alive and important, the hitherto unknown gift of provoking, without words or looks, a collective condemnation; they sank in it—slow, barely smiling, barely kind and cowardly, the smiles of tightly pressed lips—because they could not have tolerated the meaning of a Monday afternoon spent in the house, because, despite everything, they were too young to know exile and injustice.

After doing their shopping and poking their noses in here and there, they walked down toward the avenue next to the river. And amid the hard, dark silhouettes of the settler families, not many of whom were present on Mondays; amid the patience of the fishermen, extended and immobile over the dock wall; amid the recently laid out rhomboid flower beds, where rachitic young trees struggled to live; amid the decline of the afternoon and the provincial sadness then settling on Santa María, their brightly colored dresses traced a path along the promenade like a contradiction in terms planned out over a long time, like a naive provocation. They whispered nonsense so they could enjoy the abandon that allowed them to whisper nonsense; they annoyed and caressed each other by bumping shoulders.

Their faces, fully made up, fatigued and hardened by now, still keeping up a double expression of humility and indifference, were dazzled by the reflections of the last light of the afternoon on the oars of the rowboats out on the river and tried to discern personal features in the small busts wearing white T-shirts that moved rhythmically without showing any effort.

Irene and Nelly ended their Monday walk in a cool, almost always empty riverside café; they piled their packages and purses on a chair and chatted about the prices they'd paid, venturing guesses about María Bonita's reaction to their purchases. The Monday waiter was an old man who wore a blond toupee, slow and overworked, who detached himself from the chorus of jokes at the bar to come over and serve them. For no good reason, he always changed the pile of packages on the chair, and, staring at the rag he dragged over the table, he divided between the two women his good-natured, joyless smile and the unmistakable silence with which he greeted them.

They ate cookies they'd moistened in tea with cream; they put the soaps and perfumes they'd bought under their noses, and compared their aroma with memories. Touching each other's arms, breasts, and necks, they planned the dresses they would have made with the fabrics wrapped up in the packages.

The sun sank toward the river and they, smoking, followed it from the window of the still unlit café, where the men from the cannery had begun to gather. Opposite the sunset, the two women ruminated a sweet, light sadness they attributed to mistaken origins, as they indecisively contemplated the burning ends of their lipstick-stained cigarettes. They were near the end of their day off, and now their sense of obligation and custom grew, exciting them.

Fear had made them walk through Santa María without looking at its inhabitants. They had only seen hands and pieces of legs, a humanity without eyes that could be forgotten instantly. So when they got back, loaded down and disguising their haste as they crossed the plaza where the reddish globes of the streetlights arose, they brought with them toward the house the image, as incredible as a dream of a town without people, of businesses that functioned without employees, of empty, swift

buses that opened their way along empty streets by honk-
ing their horns. A few idle insults which had come from
no mouth still resounded in their ears; the fat woman
and the blonde came breathlessly down the darkened
street, each one thinking about herself, each accusing
herself without undo severity, thinking about curses
which had fallen from heaven, attributing familiar voices
to the offensive words.

From the blue door of the house, under the streetlight,
arm-in-arm and arguing over the weight of the packages,
they turned around for a second to look at the blackness
that began to touch the farmland, the tree trunks, the
sandy earth; they greeted the end of their Monday holiday, went into the house, crossed the patio where two
or three prostrate men were waiting with their legs
stretched out and resting on the reddish tiles. Snatcher
had disappeared. With an urgent, theatrical tone, María
Bonita clapped her hands, smiled at the men, picked up
the packages, and shouted: "Girls. Change; we've got
guests."

Except for the two women's slow trip that lasted two
or three hours on Monday afternoons, the only relationship the town had with the house by the coast was that
established by furtive, nocturnal males. And just days
after the arrival of the women, the comments, the jokes
made by sweaty men drinking beer in sidewalk cafés, and
the whispers of young girls on the boulevard or in salons
with pianos and slipcovered furniture all ceased.

It was a November full of jasmines: Women with baskets on their heads and barefoot, dirty, whining kids
would try to sell them for a peso a branch. By nightfall
they would settle for just about anything, and the thick
flowers, brown stains growing at the edge of their petals,

would remain in town, and in Colonia, above the tomb-stones and biographical syntheses in the two cemeteries, on the church altar, in living rooms, dining rooms, and bedrooms. Some were taken for walks, in hands, on bos-oms, on heads, all along the promenade next to the river on Sunday afternoons; others, or the same ones, rotted in the plaza, trampled under the heat, refreshed by the drizzle.

The aroma of the jasmines invaded Santa María with its excitation devoid of objective, with its apocryphal evo-cations; it came daily, like a low, long white wave, and very quickly covered any traces of the arrival of the three women and the opening of the coastal bordello. Everyone had to open his nose and close his eyes to breathe in the scent of wisdom and falsity that came from the farms; everyone sniffed the jasmines in secret or on the sly and proved the existence of pardons for each injustice, in-tuiting that each true desire engenders a promise to carry it out. The reality of the women priced at ten pesos, the memory of the house painted blue that rose on the easy slope of the river coast foundered in the white intensity of the perfume.

The bordello had been commented on as an obscene joke. Like all jokes that last too long, it now only provoked a will to oblivion, an exaggerated ignorance, short smiles on the faces of the men who from the shops that sur-rounded the plaza saw, especially on Saturday nights, groups on foot or in automobiles heading toward the isolated place where the house was.

November filled up with trivial surprises because of the overabundance of jasmines, but by the time it was half over it had become a normal, recognizable Novem-ber, with prices and figures related to the harvest, with renewed discussions about bridges, roads, and transport charges, with news of weddings and deaths. But when Snatcher swaggered back to town, to the Berna or the miserable cafés near the promenade, with his hands in his pockets—caressing his pistol with the same distracted devotion he used to caress the medal hanging around his neck—from the just-closed house, having given his last, mechanical kiss to María Bonita, he made a point of discovering in the streetlights, in the last, solitary light in some window, in the rapid greetings from people he knew hostility and threats, still-green conspiracies.

And when he was having his last drink at the bar in the Berna, alone or profiled against Vázquez's silent admiration, he was forced to recognize that enthusiasm and apprehension each occupied half his soul. *It was a stroke of genius to set the price at ten pesos from the beginning; the ones who haven't come yet will. In two months it won't matter to them any more than a visit to the doctor or the barber. There's something going against me, something they don't talk about, something they probably don't even think about, just yet. It's all legal. I have a decree from the Town Council. I never really got to like this town, those old ladies who go to early Mass, the Italians from Colonia. mulattos and Italians, and not a one of them has time to live because they're always watching everybody else live. I don't know if it would be better to bring another woman, not blonde, not skinny, not fat, not brunette. I just don't know.*

He finished his drink and walked out of the Berna without worrying about whether the boss was smiling at him or not, alone, heavy and disdainful, to the right of Vázquez, who always walked with him for the half block and who sometimes went with him up to his room.

Before going to bed he counted his money and noted the sum in a little book. Proud, defiant, shaking with confidence, disdainful, without being offensive, of the gloomy, incomprehensible Snatcher of six months back, he paced his room and once in a while used a wooden needle to listen to a tango while he drank a grappa, ritually seated at the table, wiping his mouth with a finger after each swallow, surrounded by acquiescent ghosts it wasn't worthwhile to individualize.

Withered, with its neck broken over its green leaves, the jasmine María Bonita had given him was agonizing on the blotter stained with ink and cigarette burns. When he would wake up at midday, Snatcher would blink at the light coming through the window and suppose it to have special qualities, shades, aggressions, and reserves that kept it from being confused with the noon light anywhere else in the world.

I am in Santa María, he grumbled in his thoughts as he groped for his first cigarette. Scratching his head, he set about recognizing, also as different and unmistakable, the noises that reached him from the street and from the other rooms in the boardinghouse. The light over the house on the coast, on the small mountains, the beach, and the river was, at any time, a light that could not be located in any memory. In reality, this noise, the velocity of life the sun represented, the voices, the motors in the street, and the racket in the boardinghouse, were all foreign, incomprehensible in their essence.

"Fucked up town, town full of rats," Snatcher murmured as he sat down on the bed to put on his slippers. It infuriated and disconcerted him not to find, midday after midday, any concrete target for his hate.

CHAPTER XI

*S*tanding at the perimeter of the plaza, Díaz Grey turned around to look toward the river, certain he wouldn't be able to see anything, nothing more than an attenuated glow, a curved light in the sky, a geographical indication.

Without its usual escort of motor scooters, Marcos's little red car was parked in front of the Plaza Hotel. Díaz Grey walked in through the bar door, and the bartender smiled a hello to him, pausing to look at him with his hand around a bottle. Leaning on the bar, facing the entrance, with his knee against Ana María's corduroy trousers, drunk, with one hand clinging to the lapel of a too-well-dressed man, Marcos was laughing. It was a laugh he invented to help himself, and he forced it to fill his mouth and cover his entire face, on top of the shine of his sweat. He laughed softly, without stopping, without meaning anything, as if he felt hidden by the laugh, and was afraid of using it up too soon.

At the bar, there were only Marcos, Ana María, and the man wearing the new suit. She and Marcos were perched on stools; the man was standing, nodding courteously, his hair slicked back, his hat in his hand. There were three tall glasses in front of them. The bartender came back with the bottle, his face still turned toward the doctor. Ana María, bored, neutral, taking her cigarette out of her mouth and blowing smoke through her nose, swiveled around to look. Behind the rise of the smoke was Marcos's ruddy face, his obedient laugh. *He was talking about me or something I'm involved in.* Díaz Grey looked at the table next to the column where he sat every afternoon. He leaned on his cane and bowed while taking off his hat. His hands resting on the shelf, his back against the mirror, the bartender looked at Marcos's profile and instantly turned his face toward the doctor. Now he was disinterested, trying to camouflage himself with the bottles, barely linked to the others by curiosity. Díaz Grey met Marcos's eyes and smiled. Slowly, more lame than ever, he approached the bar, dragged a stool next to the woman and sat down. Separated from the floor, his hands on his cane covered by his hat, he felt in peace and resolute.

"A San Martín."

"A dry one, coming up, doctor," nodded the bartender.

Despite the heat, Ana María was wearing a sweater that covered half her neck, as well as an unbuttoned flannel jacket. She was surrounded by a sweet, stupid, and insistent perfume, a morning scent.

"Very dry, doctor," said the bartender, putting the

glass on the bar. He looked at him and smiled: Now he had nothing to do with the other three, and was offering the doctor his limitless complicity.

"Thanks." Díaz Grey drank half the drink and nodded. The bartender smiled again and ran a napkin over the bar. Suddenly, simultaneously, Díaz Grey noticed and remembered the silence of the others. Marcos had stopped laughing, the man was taking small sips of his drink, Ana María was smoking in front of the mirror, using the smoke to conceal herself or to blur her reflection. She blinked and exhaled again.

Immobile and silent, rigid against me, quiet against me. And a perfume like some short sentence whispered in secret to make it seem important.

"Let's have another," said Marcos. "Another round."

He again laughed slowly, very carefully, as if he wanted to give the laugh a certain form.

"A drink for everyone, Hansen. It doesn't matter to anyone. I'm not talking about the ones who are happy because they've brought women for hire from the capital. I'm not talking about the riffraff. I'm thinking about decent people, or people we think are decent. It doesn't matter to anyone, it seems natural to everybody."

"I understand," the man standing said softly. He smiled at the rest of the drink in his glass. "But I already told you, Marcos. You've got to separate the moral issue from the legal issue."

"Is that so?" asked Marcos, his arm stretched out, waiting for the bartender to fill his glass. "Really? But I don't give a damn for the legal part of all this crap. Tell the governor. Tell him that in Santa María there's more than one man who isn't going to put up with it. All this legal maneuvering, it's what Jews do."

Hansen laughed, turning toward Ana María. She'd lit another cigarette and watched the smoke rise in the mirror, mixed with reflections and bottles, next to the bartender's white shoulder.

"We aren't going to put up with it. You can count on it, Hansen. This isn't just talk."

"I understand," said Hansen, sucking little sips out of his glass. "But that wasn't what we were talking about. As far as I can see, there's nothing to be said about it."

Díaz Grey turned to look at him through the perfume. His face didn't look as if it belonged to a Hansen. His hair glistened, combed straight back, like a chunk of dark wood. His moustache was thin, dark brown; his teeth very white, on display; his small forehead flat, sweaty.

"Legal or not, who cares?" laughed Marcos. "If we have it, it's because it's legal. I know that. But it's a trick. You're a lawyer, you know you can always pull a fast one. It's an old game the Jews play."

"But there are no Jews in this business."

"There are always Jews in every business. You know that as well as I do. At the bottom of any rotten business there's always a Jew. The pimp who fronts for it, Body Snatcher, I'm sure he's a Jew. Don't worry, I don't care if people hear me." He raised one hand, and with the other lifted his glass to drink. Then he put it down on the bar without letting go of it, sliding it over the stain of moisture. With her cigarette hanging out of her mouth, Ana María looked at herself in the mirror, her face cut off, interrupted by a line of smoke.

"That's not the point, Marcos," Hansen insinuated without a hope.

"That is the point. And now I'll prove it to you. First, that Snatcher is a Jew. Second, that the concession may be perfectly legal, but it's just a trick, an indecent trick. Suppose they pass a law that you've got to spit in your mother's face, you wouldn't stand for it. You wouldn't check to see if it's legal or not. You just wouldn't put up with it, that's all. That's where I stand. And if Snatcher isn't a Jew, listen, it doesn't really matter. The Jews aren't the worst. A Jew is a Jew, and we all know they'd do anything for money. The worst are the others. The ones who play the game without being Jews. The ones who go on being friends with Barthé and Snatcher and all that garbage we've got to sweep out of the city."

"You . . . ," began Hansen, still smiling. He looked at Ana María, the bartender, and took a big swallow. "You haven't stated the case properly. I respect your personal feelings, Marcos, even though I think you're exaggerating. I mean that from my point of view . . . But let's not argue anymore."

"Okay," said Marcos, "let's drop it. But you tell the governor that we aren't going to stand for it. Legal or not, we're going to get rid of the little house, the women, all that garbage. And we're going to get rid of the ones we thought were decent, the ones who came to be someone in Santa María and now would rather have the bordello."

"Come on, Marcos," said Hansen, raising his shoulder and his glass.

"All of them. Maybe they get a cut; maybe they can't get women any other way. We're going to get rid of all Barthé's friends. Tell that to the governor."

Díaz Grey ordered another drink and smiled back at the bartender. *He's talking for me, he wants to provoke me, but only to have the pleasure of arguing with me. Before the whorehouse, he'd come here every night with this woman and his friends and talk about motors, about different kinds of cars, about pistons and crankshafts. He'd get drunk or already be drunk when he got here, he'd abuse Ana María, blush with excitement; he'd always look over at my table between topics to measure me, disdain me, excuse himself. But in his heart he was bored. Now he thinks he's sure, he thinks that the holy war against the brothel can justify him, make him think he's completely alive.*

He'd turn up in his little red car, followed by the cars or motorbikes of his parasitic friends; I'd be drinking at my table, and sometimes I listened to him; he'd turn around to smile at me, hating me because I was different and had the courage to be alone. Now he thinks he can treat me as an equal, he imagines that the bordello, the house on the coast, María Bonita, Barthé, and Snatcher constitute a conflict, a huge theme that divides us because it interests both of us. He must think it drives us both wild. But he's just a poor guy, and all the others are just poor men and women. I can no longer be pushed by their motives, all their convictions, all the different kinds of faith these pathetic people have and that sentence them to death; also, I'm not interested in the things that objectively, socially should interest me.

I don't understand, this I do recognize, that image of myself sitting up against the bar in a Santa María hotel with my cane and hat between my legs; but, and that's just it, understanding it doesn't matter to me. Now, when life does interest me, when I am curious, when I like acting without worrying about success, I like taking part in it, impersonally, without any egoism.

"We've got to clean house," said Marcos. "Divide people into friends and enemies. The whorehouse gang on one side, decent people on the other."

"Light up another cigarette," said Díaz Grey to Ana María. He stared into her face in the mirror.

"Me? No thanks, doctor. I don't feel like smoking any more." She was white with fear, but she didn't look at Marcos.

"I liked your face in the mirror; the smoke made it unrecognizable. But it doesn't matter; what I liked best was your expression as you stared, the attention with which you examined your face."

Now she did look at Marcos, and then she smiled, bobbing her head. She rummaged around between her jacket and her sweater and then put a pack of cigarettes on the bar.

"Tell us what you were thinking while you were smoking and looking at yourself in the mirror. I just had to ask you that question, which I know you won't answer. So tell me instead about your perfume; I'm sure I know it, but I can't seem to place it."

Ana María laughed so she would lift her head, carefully place it between Marcos and the doctor. She lit her cigarette with Hansen's lighter.

"How can I answer a question like that? But seriously, I do smoke too much. Sometimes I get so hoarse I can't even talk. I must be sick. What do you think?"

Even if we're beyond or above all this, separated from it, it's only possible to act and talk as if we're in it and tied to it. Truth would be silence, complete quietude.

"Some people just don't realize," said Marcos. "They're not Jews, probably not even riffraff, but they just don't realize what's happening."

"Are you sure the train comes at midnight?" Hansen asked. "It might be better to eat now. They didn't have the car ready for me on time."

"That looks good," murmured the doctor. "Your face and the smoke in the mirror."

"Come on, doctor, keep quiet, and don't laugh," said Ana María, trying to put her eyes in the smoke she exhaled.

"Tell me about that perfume, talk to me about your hoarseness and your sore throat."

"Let's get going," said Marcos. "One more drink. Some people will be going forever, I swear."

"*Souvenir d'amour*," answered Ana María, looking at her mouth in the mirror. "*Souvenir*. Do you like it? My throat doesn't hurt; sometimes I get hoarse, that's all."

"It's nothing, I'm sure there's nothing wrong with you. But come by the office whenever you want. *Souvenir*. No, I don't think I do know it."

"They're going, even if I have to clean the place out by myself," said Marcos, not smiling and showing his teeth, which were whiter than the skin on the side of his nose. His sweat was shining, as if on purpose, like an expression.

"There are lots of perfumes like it, doctor," said Ana María.

"I don't think you're sick. If you were, you'd have fever. It's probably from smoking so much. But you never know. There are people who all their lives think they're healthy and suddenly . . ."

"You must know a thousand of them." She was nervous, looking old. She supposed that her chatter and her bobbing body on the stool were enough or might be enough to separate Marcos from the doctor, so that neither would hear, see, or find out about the presence of the other.

"I'm going," said Hansen.

"Well, I'm staying," answered Marcos. "I've got a lot to do tonight."

"But you were going to drive him to the station, Marcos honey."

"I can still drive him. There's time, time for lots of things."

"It doesn't matter," said Hansen. "I'll get a cab in the plaza. Good night, ma'am. You know now, that if you get over there next week . . ."

He nodded his farewell again before putting on his hat. He passed in front of Díaz Grey, with a friendly, sarcastic smile.

"Let him go," Marcos commented. He had his mouth open against the glass without drinking. His wide back was exaggeratedly bent over, showing that together with Hansen he'd been abandoned by everyone, but that he could stand it.

Ana María rapidly turned around to talk to the doctor, but she could only smile. She parted her lips as if it were difficult or painful to separate them, and for a moment she showed her smile to Díaz Gray.

She looks old and desperate; under the fear she's got right now there's another, permanent, interminable. Soon she'll turn into fear, that's all she'll be.

She fanned herself with the lapels of her flannel jacket and stopped smiling. She lit a cigarette in the mouth of her face in the mirror; then she put out the cigarette in a moist saucer.

"Yes sir," Marcos said to his glass.

It may be that she can't stand it any more, that this might be the precise moment in which she can't stand any more, we always think a moment like that will come; maybe she'll start screaming out of fear after looking at her face in the mirror. She might scream when she discovers fear outside herself; maybe she'll scream because of what fear has done to her.

Ana María examined the rise and fall of a sudden desire to vomit; she imagined the rest of the night with Marcos, the likelihood she'd get a beating, the possible reasons for that impulse, now frequent, which forced her to provoke Marcos's slaps. Slaps meant an end, a pause, an obliteration; the substitution of herself, of the entire world for crying and compassion for herself. Slaps meant the short liberty of hatred, they promised an ephemeral, partial return of tenderness: her tremulous mouth, open, blocked by Marcos's shoulder as he slept. The tears and deep breathing would extend in the darkness over the man's skin, his smell, his temperature. Softly, the pity ceased to be directed toward herself and descended from her bosom, the memories it was sheltering, and began to cover, like a blanket, like a perfect caress, the heavy body of the man and his meaning.

With disgust and without hope, she tried to evoke the smell that came at certain hours from the hotel kitchen. She tried to discover what time or event had been marked by oil or spices.

"Yes sir," Marcos repeated, slowly straightening himself up above his empty glass. The bartender was not behind the bar; someone spun the hotel's revolving door, and the three of them listened to a phrase, a car horn, the hammered silence of the summer night.

She heard Marcos snort, felt the rage, which was pushing the deliberate unhappiness inside the man, grow and reach its peak: *It's better he hit me later on and not this poor man now.* There in the mirror, playing at not being in between the two men and their antagonism, she mixed a certain pride, a certain fine and melancholy distinction she derived from the sentence "I saw my mother die like a dog," mixed that with the memory of a thin, dark, now anonymous adolescent who invited her to drink vodka and cocaine in the Trocadero over in Rosario.

Marcos grumbled something, and the doctor laughed weakly, clapping his hands to call the bartender. The corduroy slacks, the unbuttoned flannel jacket were indeed on the stool. For as long as she could, she held herself in the mirror, her face thin, shadows under her eyes, in need of makeup, mixing her face with that of her dying mother, cut off by the hard hair falling over the forehead of the boy from Rosario. All of it, including her, so long ago; all of it almost completely transformed into lies; the three faces were infinitely less real than the exalted despair, ignorance, and avidity they symbolized in a disorderly way.

"Let him go and all the rest with him," said Marcos. "I'm not going, I'm staying, and I'm staying until the end."

He turned toward Ana María's back, and in front of the woman's body—she was rigid on the stool, still immersed in the mirror but aware now of the game, incapable of losing herself—showed the doctor a smile that was half ashamed and half insolent. Díaz Grey put some money between his glass and Ana María's ashtray and called the bartender again.

"That's not enough," Marcos announced. She began to blink, to move her mouth, to leave the mirror. "That's not enough. I'm staying. Maybe the show begins tonight; maybe it ends." Despite his small eyes, quite close to the shine of the sweat and the pallor and the contractions of his nose, Marcos's face constructed a serene, sweet, and stubborn expression.

"Don't call the bartender, doctor. Wait a minute. If he comes, order another round. But don't pay yet. I'm not leaving, did you hear me, Ana María?"

Ana María nodded, leaning back, tapping her ring against the edge of the bar; she was trying to leave the two men alone.

"All of them are leaving. I don't mean from here or the city. They're all leaving things, see? Try to understand me. All the guys were like me, we grew up the same, we did and thought the same. Now only I'm the way I was before. And why? Not because I'm better than they are; what's happening is that I'm not afraid and I'm not looking for new things. Neither one."

Now he hit the bar with his fist, measured, without conviction; his voice very drunk, in a confidential, sad tone. *Maybe he isn't definitively brutish; an unexpected complication. Now I'll have to separate, recognize, and respect what there is in this brute that is intelligent, and what there is that is error.*

"I don't mean they're cowards, that way, in front of another man or in the face of danger. You understand. Understand, please," he squeezed his chest with his open hand. "See? It isn't fear. They're all my kind, they grew up with me. But they don't want trouble, they changed; they'll put up with anything as long as it doesn't interfere with them. As long as it isn't personal, I mean. So I'm alone. Look at Hansen. He was like me, we went to school together. Now he's secretary to the governor and could put a stop to that filth if he felt like it. But he's got to think about the elections and all that. He plays both sides against the middle. But you can't do that, I'm telling them you can't do that. You're wrong too, but I respect you, and I want to talk to you when I'm not drunk. I'm going to come over to your office and we'll talk. I'm not saying you're going to agree with me, but at least you'll understand."

He got down off his stool and was vacillating in front of the face of the bartender, who had just reappeared. Then he shook his head: "No. And don't charge the doctor. This is all on me."

With a sigh, shaking her shoulders to help herself, Ana María stretched her legs and jumped to the floor. Díaz Grey turned to say good-by to them from the door. Marcos was holding onto the woman by one arm while he let his head droop over the glass the bartender was filling.

He's afraid too, thought Díaz Grey as he crossed the street. *United by fear, it would be as melodramatic as being united by guilt or remorse but much truer. Maybe he'll beat her up when they get to the Phalanstery. I'd like to know if they swap beds with the other Brothers or if they used to. But this doesn't only apply to them; all couples, all friendships are motivated by fear. Now I have, I transport, I'm in the process of organizing, I shall divulge, the theory of fear. I can have dinner over in the Berna, although it's probably true there are leftovers at home.*

He traced out a U walking in and out of the flower beds; he remembered his leg and again limped toward the shadow. *Not indubitable but much more convincing than Marxism or Freudianism, my theory of fear determining the history and psychology of mankind.*

In the darkness, he tripped over a bench under a tree; he sat down and put his cane between his knees. He was tired, as usual, but not bored, and not interested either. A car passed, enraged, invisible, next to the dock; for a second the noise agitated the smell of the grass, of the cone-shaped plants in the beds. It was as if someone else were using his body abandoned on the bench to look at the night and to smell it, listen to it enthusiastically, to improvise divagations about the destinies and motives of ghosts.

Knowing who I am. Nothing, zero, an irrevocable company, a presence for others. For myself, nothing. Forty years old, a lost life: a manner of speaking because I can't imagine it won. A few memories which are not necessarily my own. No ambition located beyond tomorrow. There are sentiments of love, solidarity with landscapes, lights, animals, skies, vegetables, children, people who suffer, acts of kindness, young, charming women. Perhaps it's more appropriate not to speak of sentiments but of tender impulses, brief ones, satisfied by themselves. Even though I've been called to write the theory of fear, I am not afraid; and without fear there are no passions and action becomes absurd. This man who is sitting on this bench: no one, for me. With regard to others, those who see me cure people, make them suffer, hand them bills, those who are obliged to think of me as a small god who can inflict pain on them or relieve it, who can or will be able to kill them or help them live, equally nothing.

Solitary in the Santa María plaza, shortly after turning forty on a night in that summer in which the city filled with jasmines. It was around the time of the coup d'etat. He could deliver a baby, join broken bones, diagnose a cancer, clean wounds, prescribe painkillers or morphine. He had his body bent over in the direction of the river, and he scratched the ground with the tip of his cane. He was surrounded by people who were sleeping or staying up in the city and on the farms; he was surrounded by the human race, which was distributing itself, with its miseries, its always impure, rachitic grandeurs, in various climates and edifices; above his hat, an impressive sector of the universe was shining and trembling.

It was nothing more than saliva filling his mouth, the need to reach the platter with cold meat and brown potatoes. He had just intuited the theory of fear; that night he swore he would finish it, to prove that each person is the sensation and the instant, that the apparent continuity is overseen by pressures, by inertias, by the weakness and cowardice that make us unworthy of freedom. *Man is dissipation*, he postulated, *and the fear of dissipation.*

Living next to the river has the advantage that in summer the nights are bearable, often too cool. Near the corner of the plaza, four methodical feet flattened the gravel and stopped. Silence; he stood up and began to walk timidly, limping badly, one shoulder twisted, sniffing, with repugnance, the perfume of the jasmines, withered, moist, and rotten, the vendors had tossed next to the trash barrel. The man and woman at the corner of the plaza turned and began to approach him, retracing their steps without speaking, repeating with their four feet the noise of destruction on the gravel path. They were arm-in-arm, his hand hung over the woman's white, bare elbow; tenacious and distracted, she tapped her skirt with a little branch, which she sometimes used to scratch the bark of the trees standing erect at the edge of the plaza.

We're going to pass by each other, we're going to stop to let each other pass; I am going to be infected with whatever they're carrying, with what is walking along, un-

named, with the two of them, with, at least, the melancholy certainty that I'll probably never really know who they are, the certainty that it really doesn't matter to me. I can turn around and go to the Berna; I can let them pass by without looking at them and go to bed without eating. Under the streetlight, the woman's hair shines and then stops shining; I don't know her, I remember the golden glow, the narrow and confused band of light that surrounded her head. He too is very young and walks slumped over, with an air of pigheadedness, of being absent and being sorry for himself. I walk more slowly, I pause, leaning on my cane.

"Good evening, doctor," she says; he looks at me and mutters something. I take off my hat without recognizing her; maybe she's Otero's older daughter, Otero, the owner of a fleet of trucks and an ulcer. She had a false, high voice, she carries her jasmine branch pinned to her shoulder.

Naturally it's of no importance and, besides, it can't be proved; but when I cross the street to enter the house—now my leg really hurts and I limp and lean on the stick without exaggerating too much, and the suffering that is reborn in my knee comforts me, like company—while I pull the key ring out of my trouser pocket, I affirm with nods of my head my conviction that of all the possible Díaz Greys, the most desirable, the most convenient, the one least harassed by sensations of failure, renunciation, and mutilation, is that unknown Díaz Grey capable of conquering another air.

Instead of the perfume of the yellow, trampled jasmines, which the wind carries from the river, which will float forever, immobile in the shadow of my stairs, a smell composed and breathed in mid-afternoon in a café in a crowded city I have never seen. The most Díaz Grey of all Díaz

Greys is seated at a table, alone, not waiting for anyone. It's not a familiar café, not very luxurious, not very poor, with windows facing a wide, badly washed avenue.

Díaz Grey is smoking, with his body relaxed, a trifle sweaty, cool, and warm from that light humidity characteristic of walks taken at the end of spring; he rests his cigarette on the edge of a cup to knock off the ash. Someone is sweeping up and scattering sawdust behind the bar; they've left the lavatory doors open and a smell of sex, ammonia, and dead snails rubs against the floor, against the smell of the wet sawdust. From the window comes the smell of gasoline from the street and the smell of newly printed newspapers; there is also a woman's perfume, intense, soft, with an intention that doesn't manage to focus itself.

Naturally, nothing of all this means anything or has any importance; in any case, I cautiously walk up the stairs in shadows with a slack envy of the supposed Díaz Grey, with my eyes closed and my nose nervous, trying to collect and breathe in the different aromas that make up the smell he needs.

CHAPTER XII

I remember just as if I could see myself, a kid just like you maybe even with a beret like that pulled down to my ears," says Lanza; he breathes through his mouth and leaves it open so I can see he's smiling, see how many teeth he's missing, and how smoking has stained the ones he's got left; it bothers me, no one's got any right to look that old. "Maybe not quite as clever, the beret not as much on one side and not pulled forward as far. Of course I wore it in winter. But it's not important. I see myself that way—now we get to what really matters—certain that there was no way I wasn't going to write a work of genius. And not a work in the sense that . . ." He moves a hand to mark out a circumference in the air, but stops when he makes a rhombus and raises the mug of beer. He takes a swallow and wipes off his moustache with his fingers. "It had to be a book. But a book that would say all that had to be said. So literature, philosophy, theology, psychology, and many other things would be dead. I can't remember it all. Perhaps, naturally, a certain little girl was involved. And it was nothing; I believed it was the desire for glory, in the worst case, admitting with humility that it had nothing to do with predestination or messianic urges. But it also had nothing to do with any desire to assert myself, to grow, to take myself seriously. Because despite everything, right, when you're that age we need people to help us, we need people to take us seriously."

He smiled without rancor; even though it's hard for me to do it, I nod my head, but I make him understand with my eyes and a movement of my hand that there are things he hasn't even dreamed of, about which we will never be able to understand each other. My eyes tell him that this lack of communication saddens me.

"It may be, but I'll tell you again that I know my style is still unformed."

I raise my beer so he doesn't see my shame, and I know he'd think it ridiculous from what I've said if I were to take myself seriously, if my age weren't in itself an absolute form of the ridiculous. The Nazi behind the bar scratches an armpit and chats with the waiter; they look toward my table. Women had come in, maybe the waiters want to ask me to take off my beret. Body Snatcher is sitting in back with the guy who handles the distribution of the newspaper. I'm not going to take off my beret; I'm going to tell the boss that if Body Snatcher can set foot in the Berna, then I can too. I call the waiter and order another beer, a pack of cigarettes. Julita put a hundred pesos in my hand; she walked me down to the garden gate, kissed me on the lips as she put the money in my

hand, and then pushed me out. She said something before she locked up. Lanza saw me look at Snatcher,
turned toward him, and now he's winking at me.

"How," he said unwillingly, "can people put up with
the fact that the devil himself comes to drink and stuff
his guts in this citadel of the good cause? We're going
to be smelling sulphur. Unless your relative Marcos turns
up. a crusading knight, rescuer of the holy sepulcher, and
makes us smell blood and spilled beer."

I love him without tenderness. Even the filthy lenses
in his glasses, his frayed cuffs, his greasy tie, help me
respect him infinitely more than I do my father. He's old,
and I'm less than young. The difference between us isn't
a matter of time but of race, language, customs, morals,
and traditions. An old man isn't someone who was once
young, but someone different, with no connection to his
own adolescence, another man. We have nothing to say
to each other, but here we are, drinking beer and saying
things to each other.

"But let's not forget the other one," he goes on, "let's
not forget Father Bergner, your anointed relation."

"Know something?" I interrupt him, instantly ceasing
to look at him, "The priest is one of the few intelligent
people I know. And anyway, he's no relative of mine.
He's the uncle of my brother's widow, Marcos's uncle."

"Quite right. I knew he was that kind of relative, by
marriage. But he's a real character, Father Bergner.
Once, I remember, and your father will remember this
too, he came to EL LIBERAL to protest—in a manner of
speaking, I mean, because people like that only really
protest *in extremis*—or ask us that when we alluded to
him in the future in the paper that we wouldn't call him
clergyman but priest. I liked that."

He's old but he's cleverer and more on the up and up than anyone. Not when he talks: Then it all dies. Listening to him is like reading. The Nazi looks over at me again, and the group with women also turns toward my table. If they ask me to take off my beret, I'll pay and leave. I can't use Body Snatcher's presence as an argument, I can't wave the bourgeois flag against Body Snatcher, the antibourgeois in person, a symbol, something true, concrete, a past besides. But each rebellious position also has its own articles of faith, its prejudices, its bourgeoisie. Again I think about Julita. In despair and astonishment, I know that it won't be possible for me to free myself from thinking about her all night. So I offer Lanza a light and insist:

"Bergner, the priest—since that's how he prefers it— is one of the few intelligent people in Santa Maria."

"*Ora pro nobis*," intoned Lanza. "No doubt about it. And I can say that for two reasons: first because of the geographic limitation you stated and second because on Sunday I went to listen to him. It was a terrific sermon, no joke."

All it would take would be a new suit, a shave, a haircut, and a moustache trim, clean glasses, and new teeth for that mouth out of which bits of the peanuts he's trying to chew are falling.

"And don't think . . . ," he goes on talking, ". . . must be an old superstition, but now it's a fact and not so much a superstition. In Spain, especially in the Spain of the poor, we had to grow up thinking the idea of culture and the idea of the Church were one thing. It was the priests who knew Latin, history, or geography. What the hell, they were the only ones who knew how to read and write. And even though I ran into the dumbest priests in Spain—

which is saying something—I learned something. Later on, of course, came philosophy and theology and philology, you know, things compared to which chess is nothing. So what I have, and I don't mind confessing it, is an admiration, a habit of admiring people who've lived their lives reading. Despite everything, of course, for better and for worse."

I say I understand, that what he says is true, in a weak, womanish or childish voice, because I'm nervous and I'm beginning to get sad. I signal for another beer and walk across the room to the lavatory. I pass next to Body Snatcher, and he starts talking with the newspaper sales guy so he won't have to look at me, to keep me from being able to pretend I don't see him. I go, urinate, come back, always thinking about Body Snatcher, so I won't have to think about anything else, about something thinking itself inside me, independent of whether I want to think it or not. When I sit down, I smile at Body Snatcher, I wave my smile twice, but he doesn't see me.

"And what I was saying before you went to the john reminds me of something that came up before," says Lanza.

I wait, without confidence, to hear something that will provoke me and drag me along; I smile at him encouragingly while he opens his mouth against the cool beer.

"I mean the work of genius, the unique, decisive book. You, of course, need poetry, so your book has to be a book of poems. But I, even though I wrote poems, because I wasn't a poet in the same way I'm not anything else, I dreamed of a book in prose, a novel maybe, who knows, although I tend to think it was a different genre, something absolutely new. A book of verses, now that I think of it—and we can argue the point—can never be definitive in the way that interests us; it's always a beginning, a road that opens."

I distractedly ask why and instantly feel myself tremble; I wake up for fury and screaming.

"Well," he says, laughing, "because it's interminable, because it doesn't exist, because poetry is made, let's say, with what we lack, with what we don't have."

"So's all the rest," I get excited and pound the table with my mug, "the thousands of books that have been written were also made with what we lack." I incite him with a gesture to go on talking, not to pay attention to me, and my momentary enthusiasm dissipates as I discover a bump on his forehead he tries to cover up with his hair.

It doesn't matter to me to make a gesture of defeat because it was, is, understood that the truth belongs to him rather than to me in matters of that sort. We argue out of his goodness, for his and my pleasure. I stop listening to him, I observe the growth above his eyebrow, where the hair on his forehead dips, I follow the movement of his hand and its prominent veins over the table, back-and-forth, as if he were smoothing or cleaning something.

At the back table, Body Snatcher is smoking in profile, twiddling his thumbs in front of his glass and the sleepy silence of the newspaper guy, his black hat tilted over his nose. There are other men here with their hats on; the owner and the men who have the women with them weren't looking at me because of my beret. The old hand stops, starts moving again, now vertically, making tiny slaps. "Make you happier," was what Julita said as she was pushing me into the garden. It's time for me to go to bed; for Lanza too.

"Not now," he whispers, with the best smile of the evening, staring at his slapping hand; his nails are black but not chewed up, wide, square, short; like the rest of him, they have that essential, distracted dignity despite everything else.

"Now, on the other hand," he goes on conversing, "I only wish I could write a book, it would be a novel made from beginning to end out of commonplaces. It comes from having to correct galleys at the paper. . . ."

It's exactly this: *She put the bank note in my hand while she kissed me; as she closed my hand and pushed me outside, she said that I should try to be happy with that money since she couldn't make me happy in another way. So I was immobile and alone in the garden, next to the locked door—a hot, humid wind, the ambition of the trees against the white, thin clouds that ran over the moon— making the bank note crackle between my fingers, mixing that crackle with my memory, the probable intention behind what she said, until I came to believe that the words were there, written on the paper, surrounded, protected, and rotting in the sweat of my hand.*

"But it's not only that, my dear friend. I'd like to go back, if you don't mind, to that anxiety about the definitive and universal thing from which you suffer or which I seem to detect in you. We never cleared it up. In any case, I had it when I was your age and for a long time after. A book that by the power of its genius and originality would say everything for everyone. It would send literature, the novel, psychology, etcetera right to hell. Once the book was written, they'd have to make up something new, some other game. Well, what with one thing and another in life, I never wrote that book. Now I've come up with another one that might be its equivalent.

What I was telling you about, the novel composed totally of commonplaces. Instead of a genial originality, what we could call the genius of common sense."

"I understand. Have you started writing it?" I ask with a smile, cautiously. Lanza copies my prudence and raises his glass. Making a grimace of expectation, leaning on the table, he slowly gets up. He always sits on one buttock. "I too must evacuate," he says. "If the Aryan beast comes by, please ask him for a pack of my cigarettes." I see him make his way, limping slightly, nodding his head as he passes Body Snatcher's table.

Later, on the road, I actually believed for a while that everything had happened just like that, that she had said she wanted to make me happy in another way while she kissed me. The kiss was no different from those she always gave me on the forehead, except that I could imagine having felt, like a quick imprint, the whole outline of her mouth. There was light in Rita's room, but I didn't see Marcos's car anywhere.

I ask for the cigarettes and order another beer. I stare at Body Snatcher's quietude and unsuccessfully try to figure out what he's like, invent his past, suppose it was with the oldest woman in the house on the coast, María Bonita. The house he rented from my father. Nothing, no appeal works; I know I'm going to die young, naive, ignorant, without understanding. The life that matters belongs to the grownups and has nothing at all to do with me. If I occasionally manage to circulate in that life without discomfort, almost convincingly, it's only by persistence, memory, imitation, by copying attitudes whose profound sense I just can't fathom. It wasn't when she was kissing me. I only want things, concrete, absurd new things that will make me different. I want people to look at me, I want to be a scandal, I want to make it impossible for people to confuse me with themselves, to take me for or think of me as their equal. I'm not interested in a past, and the future is always alien territory. It has to be now, always now, and right away. I only like words when they turn into things; all these words that belong to old man Lanza, all Father Bergner's words, all the words that belong to my school, friends, almost all the words I hear are as bland as spit, they fall, they shine, they dry up, and they cease to exist. I also say them, I wear myself down using them. The spit that belongs to other people and my own is only good for wasting myself away. They waste my time; my time in solitude and silence, it doesn't exist, it doesn't wear out.

But besides, aside from, and assuming I could accept this game, this life they've invented, I would also like to have a past like an empty space and fill it with some moment from my childhood in the country; with that Father, that Mother that have no relation with those I have now, with Federico and a horse, the smell of dead animals, my envy and pride watching Federico. That crust of earth for my past, that love for the country I conceal and which no one suspects. Then—besides and aside from again—I'd be able to dedicate a night to place there, now, as if making those things come to life there as I ordered them, a Julita who'd wake me up and kiss me in the morning after I'd returned from a trip to the capital; a Julita who'd look at me and not stop looking at me as she begins to go insane after returning from burying my brother; a Julita who'd transform me into Federico, a Julita who'd knead the legend of the child and again deposit me, Jorge, next to her. I'd put only a few Julitas in my past; and it would be impossible for me to get any of them to be larger, or to approach me more than this one who over the past few nights has begun to know that the child and the madness are leaving her, abandoning her, like light bleeding or emanations that fled from her, incessantly, without undo haste, from the tips of her fingers, from her toes, from her bosom, from the hair she's stopped combing. It's through those places that women ought to lose their hope.

Some night next week, she's going to find herself un-inhabited and alone, and have to recognize herself; it won't do her any good to call me Freddy or to burn the facecloths in the fireplace.

That time, as soon as I walked in, she ran to sit in front of the fire, her face red and dripping sweat, she put her jacket over her shoulder and trembled. She hummed, and I was watching, alternately, the fibers of cloth and cotton which were left twisting in the coals and her smile, suddenly fixed, where she was declaring the ecstasy proper to pregnancy.

I know all this; I also imagine the uselessness of re-peating phrases and attitudes in bed before going to sleep; I see her delineate the movement with which she carries a kiss on her fingers to her stomach. And those things are not going to happen in an acceptable past which I can populate as I see fit. They will be—or their consequences will be—before me, against me, trying stubbornly, mechanically, to drag me to the center of her anguish, to that moist, bad-smelling, frozen profundity where the adults who were damned have to live. Lucid once again, she will have to give up delays and subterfuges, she'll have to admit to herself and recognize herself, and I only concede her as preparation the hours or minutes in which she'll be beating (not violently) her head against a brick in the fireplace, against the wall where Federico's picture hangs, against

the door through which I enter at eleven at night. A widow
for only a few months, thirty years of age.

She'll be like me, we'll walk the same ground; for her
as for me, the word death will mean filth and misery; she'll
discover that life did not want to stop, that her anecdote
of failure and mourning only helped to feed life and push
it forward. I came puffing along the road, with the memory
of the kiss and the phrase, with the contact of the money
on my fingers, thinking about Federico and about the neg-
ativity, indifference, and aversion in the faces of the dead.
It isn't we but they who say that time is up. Face up,
shamelessly showing that surprising nose, Federico was re-
peating to me that what had really died was my time with
him, something that was mine, an unchangeable part, for-
ever alien to explanations, untouchable for the good in-
tention of remorse.

"Didn't you see him come in?" Lanza asks as he sits
down again; he supports himself by leaning both hands
on the table and lowers himself as if the seat were bristling
with pieces of glass. "Your brother-in-law Marcos and
Dr. Díaz Grey went back to the private rooms."

He took too long; he's pale and rhythmically twitches
his moustache to the right. He must have had a stomach
attack; now I remember—he's got a liver problem and
shouldn't drink alcohol.

"I hope we don't have an epic scene," he finished
settling himself in the chair; his voice is soft and tremulous, as if he'd thrown up. Now he's trying to smile at
me. Through the fog of his glasses I see his immobile
eyes, attentive, watching over the bad state of his guts.
"I stopped to chat with our local hero, the one with more
bodies to his credit than the French Revolution."

"The beer's hot," I cut him off. "Are you feeling okay?"

"What does it matter," he sighs, leaning against the backrest. His fingers play with the hair that covers the bump on his forehead. "Ask for two more if you think these have either gone up or down in temperature."

His forehead is suddenly covered with sweat; he pants, and for a second looks at me as if he were begging. He lights a cigarette, and I look away. I hear him laugh and cough, slap the table with a hand that smells of soap.

"Listen here," he begins. "I wanted to recommend the priest Bergner's sermons to you."

I pass him one of the beers they've just brought us, and he starts to talk rapidly, he's excited, charming, as if he wanted to distract me from something.

"What a shame you didn't genuflect on Sunday. But all is not lost; this is going to be a Sunday crusade until the end of time, that is, until they close up the bordello. But seriously, your relative, the one you apostatized and denied not three times but once—and for all—Father Bergner, is a real character. And he's got a point, he must be intelligent. Although, since we're used to associating intelligence with other kinds of things . . . The man must be six feet tall."

"Almost," I say. I'm wondering what Lanza would talk about with Body Snatcher, what could Marcos and Dr. Díaz Grey be doing in the Berna together when they barely say hello to each other.

I want to leave, but I just can't seem to say so. At the end of every night comes disenchantment, no one can give me anything, and no one's interested in what I can give. I carefully separate the money in my pocket. I catch the one-hundred-peso note between my fingers. I look around for the waiter but don't find him. He must be in the private room.

I brusquely lean over the table and ask: "Do you know what my father's political position is?"

I do it to make fun, not of Lanza, but of someone. Lanza won't dare tell me what he thinks, won't mention the house on the beach my father rented to Snatcher or Barthé, will not refer to the recent moralistic editorials in EL LIBERAL.

"There's no way for me to know. We hardly ever see each other, and when we do we have no time to talk politics."

Now I discover that when I leaned over the table I wanted to say: I need a woman, the only thing that matters to me is a woman.

"Your father was always a Radical," Lanza goes on docilely, like a nursemaid. "Of course, in recent years, seeing what was going on . . ."

He can see Father, and I can't, even though I imagine him, smiling, but with a shadow of concern on his brow. I can see him and hear him comment on news reports, aware of the attention and respect of the dozen poor men who straighten their shoulders to listen. That should be enough for Lanza to disdain him. But Father isn't his father, and Lanza isn't sixteen years old and obliged to feel tenderness for him, listening to him brag and lie for hours, repeating himself, lying and bragging with his hand on my head or shoulder. I can't stand Mother's happy eyes as she watches us. Sometimes the pity and disgust are born from the story of what he might have done; other times from the story of what it's still possible to do. "I'm not afraid of anything the future holds for me. I could lose everything, as long as they let me keep my typewriter. You understand me," Father finished, pointing to me. I was mad with rage, but I would have started crying for him.

I call over the waiter to pay him. He stops and smiles toward the bar. The Nazi makes his mouth into a circle and moves his head just once before bending over to hit the spigot. "Everything's paid for," says the waiter.

A thing like that does me good, clears me up.

"No, it wasn't me," says Lanza. "I would have paid my half with pleasure as usual. It must have been your brother-in-law."

I didn't want it to be Marcos who paid. I don't ask the waiter anything in order not to find out because that would nullify the miracle. Marcos comes out of the private room and stops next to Body Snatcher's table. Behind him, blond and bent over with his hair shining, and wearing a new blue suit, Dr. Díaz Grey smiles, raises his cane, and touches his shoulder. Leaning back in my chair without letting go of the one-hundred-peso note, I see Marcos coming over, gigantic, drunk, his face covered with sweat and his chest as well, which I can see because his green shirt is unbuttoned to the waist. He leans on the table without bending over, looks at Lanza without saying hello, looks at me again with a vague insinuation of complicity in his smile, in his tiny teeth.

"What are you doing here at this time of night?" I understand once again that everything is impossible. I think, sadly, instantaneously, that everything could be easy and that the easiness, once accepted, would transform the world.

"Nothing." I'm sixteen. Lanza shows me his small

blue eyes, which are almost blind as he cleans his lenses with a stained, striped handkerchief.

"Nothing," Marcos repeats. His nostrils are white, his mouth is half-open, and he isn't smiling. "It's time you were asleep. There's enough filth in this town without kids like you . . ."

It wasn't Marcos who paid the bill. It could only have been Body Snatcher. Barely leaning on his cane, Díaz Grey smiles at me with wan tenderness.

"Let's go. I'll take you home," says Marcos. Tonight I remember all the nights I was with Julita, and I remember that Julita is his sister. I think about Marcos's body, naked in Rita's bed, I think about Federico, my brother, and about Julita. Also in bed, under the photograph where we've knelt so often to pray.

"Are you getting up or not?" asks Marcos, softly, bending over. He stands up and shows a handful of money, tries to find the waiter's face. There's something that seems to link me to him definitively, something that establishes this intimacy in which I sense him to be inadequate to my hatred.

"It's all paid for," I say without moving. "I'm not leaving yet. If you want to go with me, sit down and wait for me."

Impassive, I look again at the musty fondness in Díaz Grey's eyes. Marcos hides his money and fills his lungs with air. Without looking at him, he shows his profile to the doctor.

"What did I tell you," he murmurs as he turns around. "He's on my side."

He softly slaps my cheek and leaves some money on the table. I thank him and recall Díaz Grey's eyes. As I put the money in my pocket, I examine Body Snatcher's immobility now that he's sitting alone at the table close to the wall.

"Time to go," says Lanza. I don't want to look at the movements he makes to disconnect his buttock from the chair. It occurs to me that a special, helpful curse, a minor form of bewitchment has fallen over Santa María, over all of us. It provokes us and puts us to the test. I say again to myself, almost weeping, that I need a woman. Out on the cool, windy street, harmonizing my steps with Lanza's limp, I shake my head to deny Julita, Rita, and the three women in the house on the coast, the house Father rented them.

Because although now I suddenly know and am sure of the destiny Julita wanted to impose on the one-hundred-peso note she put in my hand, I understand that I should postpone it, that I just don't have the nerve to walk downhill from the plaza to the blue windows of the brothel and knock twice at the door, which is also blue—if that is the ritual.

CHAPTER XIII

*S*ome months had passed since the arrival of the women. Both those among us who had walked down to the house and those among us who hadn't, those who were indifferent and those who weren't, simply shrugged their shoulders and accepted their remaining forever. Those of us who would knock at the thick door of the house on the coast, sunken behind its white, wrinkled wall, with its balconies, wrought-iron window gratings, and its sky-blue shutters, gave our consent, our welcome, with the almost always defiant banging of our knuckles on the wood. Those of us who did not go down that twisty, dusty road confessed our acceptance by no longer talking about the bordello, preferring to return to the old, probably eternal subjects of discussion in Santa María: crops, prices, politics, the progress of Colonia.

It seemed that everyone, all of us, had accepted it, and

that the whorehouse had come to blend in with all the other things that made up the structure of the city: the promenade, the fruit and vegetable stands that covered the plaza on Sunday morning, the lines of buses that connected the city with Colonia and the growing neighborhood around the cannery. It's true that the priest Bergner managed to include allusions to rains of fire and statues of salt in all his sermons, but we thought he was simply doing his duty for the benefit of our wives and children.

So, after the flap and scandal, after the novelty of the gossip that reached us from the coast wore out, we were convinced that the whorehouse was ours and ancient. Slowly but surely, we learned to refer to it without smiling. We once again said hello to Barthé and bought medicine and perfume from him, thinking it an absurd bother to have to cross the street to avoid Snatcher or to walk out of the Berna whenever he walked in.

We were habituated and indifferent, talking about the government subsidies for wheat and corn, and then the anonymous letters began to appear. There were printed models, especially at the beginning and the end; they were like the handbills given out at political rallies or strikes, printed on ordinary paper, with misaligned, broken letters that suggested haste and secrecy. The others, the more numerous and more effective and disconcerting, were written in blue ink by several hands. They were in the kind of tall, angular letters of the Sacré Coeur penmanship style taught to the girls in the Catholic High School.

The anonymous letters which today we can declare legitimate, printed or handwritten, were combative, direct, violent, and at times personal. They were never insulting. I'm talking about the legitimate anonymous letters, and by legitimate I mean the vast majority of them, those that had no other origin than the crusade against the bordello. Although it must be said that they were cruel enough to include physical or personal details about the person to whom they were sent. Also because when the wave of hate covered the city, when there was frenzy in every eye, every crack, every solitude, in every single one of the acts of the citizens of Santa María or the Swiss in Colonia, there then began to circulate apocryphal anonymous letters, provoked by old rancors and unrelated to the existence or use of the bordello.

The great organized hatred, focused on the little house on the coast and what it symbolized, exploded on those who visited it and their families as well as on those who passively tolerated, happy about it or not, the business that went on behind the blue shutters. It aroused the nervousness of diverse haters, renewed old feuds, supplied a means for relieving rage and taking partial revenge. Nothing of this concerns us today: not the tricks in wills, adultery, enumeration of common vices.

None of the spurious anonymous letters had the qualities of fanaticism, absurdity, and astonishing stolidity that characterized the real ones, traits that have made them so valuable for those who chose to keep them after reading them. Deprived by time of being real anecdotes and of containing transitory passions, disembodied, the legitimate anonymous letters now exhibit their essence, unmistakable and as hard as a skeleton. The diligent fingers of the girls who wrote out the thin letters, the *n*'s that can be confused with *u*'s, reveal only now the indifferent purity, the deliberate blindness of those who

wanted to save Santa María while they dictated the apocalyptic or ironic and familiar sentences.

At the beginning, the printed anonymous letters, the
ominous, sarcastic circulars, tried to relate every disaster,
every death, every loss to the presence of María Bonita
on the coast. They had a tone of admonition, a deceptive
objectivity, a reticence that sounded like a prologue.
From this first period, which barely lasted two weeks, Dr.
Díaz Grey has one that says: "Joining sides with the devil
and the Jews may seem like good business. But Divine
Protection flees us. Just think about those who drowned
in the Rinconada. Meditate and Wake up." It's certain
that this was the second anonymous letter, a variant on
the most uninhibited, most impassioned one, which we
take to be the first: "Why have a church when we have
a bordello? Why have a home when women can be hired
for ten pesos? When someone loses his sense of decency,
it's only proper that he also lose Divine Protection. Those
who drowned in the Rinconada began the series of
disasters."

Several days passed between letters, and this hiatus
was not filled with another local disaster; this may explain
the hesitancy revealed in the second anonymous letter,
despite its emphatic measured tone.

But very soon the battle began. On the Sunday of the
Feast of Saint Eulalia, the priest Bergner stood motionless for a long period before beginning the sermon, his
arms hanging at his sides, his large, athletic body erect
but weighed down, casting his eyes, as if searching for
someone, over the faces of those who filled the church.
The altar boys flanked him, their small heads bent forward, their hands clasped over their bellies, sure that the

words which would be resounding would have more importance than the Mass itself.

For a few moments, silence emanated from the priest and spread through the temple. On its way toward the pulpit it absorbed the nervousness and apprehension of the faithful.

"My children," said the priest as if he were answering avid questions, a request for consolation he could not attend to. Again he generated silence; he smiled, pained and comforted. His palms rubbed the cloth on the pulpit, grasped the wood. Softly, speaking to himself, he recalled the visible passion of the life of Saint Eulalia without allusions to the expected theme, as if he were restricting himself to repeating an old, pallid story separated from the city and its guilt.

A sensation of relief and disenchantment went through the assembled heads, swelled in the ogives, spread to the candles and flowers on the altars. The priest spoke slowly: His wide shoulders were hunched together, and he was held up by his bent hands, which, extended forward, seemed to be of an imposing and astonishing magnitude. There seemed to be an incredible distance between them and the pale suffering in his face. Laboriously, he straightened his body, and lifted his hands with a smile of melancholy and mockery.

"I must interrupt the life of the saint at this critical point because none of us is worthy of participating in it, not even in this way—not even through the misery of my words are we worthy of participating in her martyrdom, her heroism, and in her reward. I want to be just. This church was built by your piety and generosity. This church was built, brick by brick, with your money, with the money of Santa María's faithful. I have never called upon your piety in vain. When I arrived here—many of you should remember—we celebrated Mass in a church that wasn't more than a shed. I asked for a church, and I got one. I asked for contributions to the High School, and each year we send many thousands of pesos to the High School. Each time I asked, each thing I asked in the name of the Lord, I received. Santa María, poor and small, funds three scholarships for three future priests. The good I've managed to do was not my own good; unworthy, I have distributed among you the goods of Christ. I am in debt to you; you gave the church, the contributions, the scholarships; you've given thousands of offerings every time it was necessary to help. And I haven't given anything because what I distributed was not mine. I am in debt to all those I baptized, to all those who wanted to speak to me about their struggles and weaknesses. I am in debt to your parents, to those who received the last rites from me and who now look down on us and suffer for our sins. I thank you and ask forgiveness."

Again he stood back from the pulpit, his arms hanging, his head twisted, his enormous torso bent forward, as if it were on the point of swaying and falling, as if the solidity, the energy, the health of his wide body were threatened by a sudden malady for which there was no cure.

"I thank you just as a lay person would thank you for gifts he didn't deserve. Now, today, we are face to face and equal. From this sacred height, usurping it, a sinner speaks with sinners. I am not your priest, not the priest of Santa María. Because the devil came among us and was welcomed; you welcomed him, and I did not know how to stop it."

CHAPTER XIV

From the first moment, from the very day when the town council sanctioned the bordello, Snatcher thought about María Bonita, and decided that going to the capital to find and convince her to come back with him was indispensable. This would be the chance of a lifetime for him, but only with María Bonita could he take advantage of it without waste, without deformations. But when he returned to the capital—Barthé refused to advance him any money—he instantly lost the enthusiasm he'd anticipated having, the desire for revenge, the energy of his swaggering gait. The city belonged to other men, the powdered faces in the cafés resembled none of his memories, spoke a new and difficult language, knew nothing of history, and did not completely believe in ghosts.

Shocked and enraged, with María Bonita's trails completely tangled, overflowing with dead or lost friends, standing at the beginning of fear without money, Snatcher rented a room near the port, allowing himself twenty days of life.

He ate little and got up at nightfall so he could spend the night searching all the bars in the dock area for the face or familiar gesture that would lead him to María Bonita. On the corner from his boardinghouse, he found a foul, ruinous café, and took over a table next to the window, which was opaque with grease and always closed against this city of fogs and ghosts. For the price of a drink he would nurse for hours, he bought the right to examine his failures of the previous evening as well as his hopes and intuitions for the next. The theme of this return to the capital was changing in a dangerous way, becoming less and less María Bonita and the house and more and more himself, Snatcher, his youth and the past.

Grown old, aware of his dirty shirt, the hairs sprouting on his ears, the twisted heels of his shoes, his own solitude and rejection, he touched his shot of grappa with the tip of his tongue and imagined the cruel, young Snatcher, raging to live, the Snatcher of heroic and greedy nights.

At the beginning, he'd been that coarse thing, that twenty-year-old office worker who tried to satisfy an equally coarse, instinctive pride by getting everything he could from women—free. Later, no one knows when, the vocation appeared, as obvious as puberty, as an illness or a vice, but fixed in him. Almost nothing at the beginning, nothing more than capricious decisions taken on street corners in the outskirts of town, gratuitous cruelties in the family rooms of bars, a frenetic disdain for the confessions of his friends. Nothing more than that and the weakness, the anguish of knowing himself to be different from the others, the strange shame of lying, of imitating opinions and slogans in order to be tolerated but without the conviction necessary to accept solitude. Kept alert by the intuition that his destiny, that form of being he longed for, and in which he only vaguely believed, could not be carried out in solitude.

It was also the time of offices, of a hundred- or a hundred-and-twenty-peso salaries, of eight-hour days, of his own round, clear, even handwriting, stretching out, blue, docile, spontaneously tricky, on Daily and Other Expenditures, constructing the perceptible awareness of the columns in the account book. It was the time of the short, rapid smile twisted before bosses, accountants, and office heads: a desire, not a cowardly one, to be a nice guy, to impose on others an appropriate respect, to be accepted. And, at the same time, a will not to surrender, not to accept the extravagant world the others populated and defended.

But it was already, if precariously, the time for the brief and costly happiness of the barbershop, of the masculine, almost pointless self-abandonment in the violently perfumed warmth of those shops prolonged by mirrors that also seemed to reproduce arguments about sports, the hustle and bustle of the customers and the street; abandoning himself to razors, to an absence surrounded by moist, steaming towels. In the meantime, reality, still disconcerting and rebellious, communicated with his daydream without images beneath the asphyxiating, mentholated towels, all without interrupting him but strengthening him, by means of the fingers worked on by the manicurist and the shoe brushed by the shoeshine boy.

The woman appeared, the first real woman, the one who offered a contract with the necessary ease, and who was serious and sincere, who happily proved she was capable of doing what she promised. Room, board, and ten-peso notes deposited on his knee, under café and restaurant tables, bills transformed into a rigid slip of paper, stripped of any significance of value by sixteen or thirty-two folds, lent with the hope that he would never try to pay them back.

But Snatcher could only realize that the first woman had really appeared when he was already with the fifth or sixth. Nevertheless, the reiterated and delivered offers of room and board and uncounted bank notes for unforeseen and daily expenses lacked security and grandeur; they could only be thought of as transitory events, rehearsals, an apprenticeship.

It was necessary to go on running to catch trams, subways, or buses at seven in the morning—despite his exasperated and secret pride in the bank notes he hadn't earned, that he crushed in his pocket, despite his unwavering faith in an indubitable predestination. It was necessary to accept himself as brother or relative of the sleepy, overwhelmed men devoid of rebelliousness who pushed each other and smelled each other on these vehicles, maneuvering to read the headlines on the back pages of the newspapers, wearing hats that dripped soapy, shameful, turbid drops of water onto the backs of their necks.

It was necessary to punch the time clock, move along saying hello with a twisted mouth, the body slightly bent so that humility would eliminate curiosity and attention, between a double row of men bent over, men who hung jackets on hangers, women buttoning smocks, looking at themselves for the last time before noon in the little mirrors of their compacts.

It was necessary to listen to whatever the three men who worked next to him had brought with them from home or from the previous night. It was necessary to nod, to take the large books bound in gray burlap out of the safe, open them, slip on the alpaca sleeves that protected one's elbows and the whiteness of one's cuffs, and write out words and numbers, move and consult soft-colored papers, mask one's impotence, and sometimes grow distracted without revealing it, examining the pinkish glow of one's nails in the daily, essential light of the fluorescent bulbs.

At times he hated his cowardice and thought it inexcusable; other times he thought that this double life, the punctual yielding of eight hours to an absurd world, to an interpretation of existence he knew to be wrong, constituted a desirable stage, as, in the last analysis, the hours of boredom in high school are desirable and useful for the boy who wants to go to college and devote himself, finally, to his vocation.

He was working for a company that published magazines. He lived in a downtown boardinghouse with a woman older than he, a woman who was getting fat. Her name, to give her a name, was Blanca, and she tried to use him. She arranged him the way women arrange their makeup or modify their bodies with girdles to go out on the street. Humiliated but not hating her, the young Snatcher would receive on the first days of the month the three hundred pesos she earned as a schoolteacher. That's what they lived on, because it was necessary that the salary from the publishing company be spent on dinners and drinks with friends, that it not be useful for her.

But not even that or the planned-out violence, or the days of silence, or the surprising absences and unexplained returns managed to wash his original guilt out of the wrinkled bank notes that always fell on the table in the boardinghouse room. They added up to three hundred pesos, discounting pension contribution and maternity fund; they meant thirty days of room and board. The dirty, wrinkled money, mostly greenish, earned through work.

Like everyone else, she had a name, Blanca; but it was a name that didn't represent her, a name that could be applied to any other woman without modifying her. Her fattened body didn't represent her; neither did her fatigue and renunciation. They were all ferociously anticipated, with inexplicable urgency, almost with the pride of transmitting primary knowledge, through her eyes and her mouth in repose. For that reason, without a face, without a distinguishable voice, she attempted to exist, to place her own singularities in the world, separate from her, almost like objects to be contemplated with curiosity.

Desperate and timid, she'd taken the name Blanca and made it into Blanche, Bianca, Quita, Blan. She knew the name wasn't worth much. And Snatcher walked with her down the grand avenue almost every night, with a cigarette burning in the twist of his mouth, ashamed of the woman and ready to fight for her, distractedly proud of his new, freshly pressed uniform. The gray suit, the white silk shirt, a black slouch hat, the knot in his tie, also black, patent leather shoes with wide, heavy laces and long, thin soles. He walked clinging to every step, to every *ciao* from friends in cafés, to every finger clenched by Blanca (or Quita, Bianca, Blan, Blanche, Blancette, depending on which night it was), to the vulgar and irremediable quality of the money he was living on.

Sometimes, after dinner in the restaurant, ashamed of the prefabricated and complete sentences, sullied besides by the foreseeable moral and aesthetic intentions Blanca tossed out in front of the friends who sat down to have coffee, Snatcher suspected that the woman wanted to occupy a place in his world despite being fat and old, fighting against fatness and age as if they were alien things, obstacles in space, independent of her and her body.

But he had nothing to do with her or her desire; a face, blank, like her name, vague, bygone possibilities, and especially, under everything and making it all useless, that organic honesty which could not be renounced; the five hours of work at the school, the acts and the words with which Blanca daily saved—for herself, for the immortal particle of herself that had remained in her—traditions and points of view, inexplicable beliefs there was no need to explain.

Later the crisis came, the foreseeable moment in which every strong soul seeks solitude and destiny. Snatcher quit his job and separated from Blanca or the woman who'd taken Blanca's place. He rented a room in a neighborhood of cheap little houses, and every noon, freshly awakened, aware of the detour in his mouth into the smile just as he could have been aware of the particulars and the capacity of a tool, he took the tram to meet with his friends, be fed by them, and search the cabarets in the dock area for the woman adequate to his vocation, the absolutely essential woman he needed to begin living seriously, in accordance with his convictions.

Then he met María Bonita and became convinced that the realization of ideals depends on our capacity for renunciation. This certainty quickly became a dogma he wouldn't abandon for the rest of his life. María Bonita was prudent and immoral; prudent and immoral, he thought angrily, without understanding, as if he had accomplished the senseless task of pushing aside things that could not be mixed and which, nevertheless, were present in her, all combined, giving life to the woman, all transformed into her. Prudence and immorality survived all the tests he was able to imagine, escaped all the traps he set for them, went on existing, inexhaustible, vigorous, the same and in agreement, through punches, injustices, generous acts, challenges, cunning or sincere expectations.

He was by now in the time of friends, colleagues, some with nothing else to give him but camaraderie and lessons in style, examples of techniques that could be discussed or assimilated avidly. Others, almost always failed or approaching a poor, conjugal old age, his brothers in the intensity of the impulse that had brought them to a definable life or at least one that could be remembered by means of the smell of money, women, silk shirts, screens, abortions, grills where the country began, well-tended cheeks, nostalgia, and professed indifference. One intensity transcended them, went beyond bank accounts and the unconscious satisfaction of pride, beyond the possibilities of understanding what they had been given. They were his brothers; condemned like him, they supported tradition, they exaggerated their hatred for Italians and sought reasons to be confident in successive idolatries.

Some of them—silent, tense, defiant—showed themselves worthy of seeing him cry at the bar in a café that had two hard, perpendicular stripes of black crepe hanging from the empty guitarists's stand when the Marseilles gang knocked off little Julio at the door of a whorehouse.

Some wanted to help him get revenge, at least in its interminable preparatory stages. Also it would be in disobedience to the order to wait and mark time ordered by the native chiefs, the Negroid Pérezes and Giovaninis. In reality, and they suspected it, their conspiracies to take revenge, dragged out in restaurants, bars, and gardens, were nothing more than an extension of little Julio's wake, which no one could celebrate. Stories were told and unlikely-to-be-fulfilled prophecies made, courage was sought in pauses surrounded by shots of cheap brandy, and the hands that patted the butts of revolvers worn above the buttocks also measured out with stupefied impotence how really disconcerting, how really irremediable death is.

The later Snatcher of EL LIBERAL and the little house on the coast, who only had at his disposal for helping himself evoke the past the astonished attention and admiration of Vázquez or some young truck driver he'd stumbled on during Santa María's short dawns, would stand up and exhibit the memory whole before telling the story, before the initial negations which he would then erase:

"I don't know what his name was, his last name I mean. His first name was Julio. I didn't see him die, but I'd been with him a few hours earlier or the day before. He was twenty-four, younger than I was, a bit younger, but it was all the same: we were seasoned guys, men who'd done a lot before the Polacks came to knock off women in the basement of the Aiglon. We were real men, the kind they just don't make anymore. Well he was their boss, and they followed his orders. At that time, I'm talking about during the dictatorship, it was every man for himself, each one trying to screw his buddies for peanuts.

Not the Marseilles crowd; because it's always that way, they only worried about business and knew how to work together to protect it. The Marseilles guys and the Jews and later the Polacks, who decided it was better to be friends with whoever was on top, not counting that there were already wops, so you can see how it was. And he was a hope for all of us, older than he was, I'll say it again, tired of run-ins, men who'd grown up surrounded by whores and informers. At first, every one of the big guys turned his back on him, told him sure, looking down on him, checking him out, then kicking him out like some jerk who's just come on the scene and all of a sudden thinks he's a big deal, that he's carrying the ball and just looking for an opening. But he didn't ask them for anything, and if they offered, he'd just say no without making a fuss. Julio, see, worked this way: he'd patiently make the rounds, mixing in with everyone until he found someone having troubles with the sharks. Then he'd have himself introduced to him and bring up the subject of the Marseilles guys. Why is it we're always fighting each other while they're united to fuck us up; so why don't we organize and bury the hatchet and maybe together we can kick these guys out—after all, whose country is it? They tried to brush him off, like a pesky fly, when he bored them or if they got mad that a kid still wet behind the ears was coming around to tell them what to do. But he, with that young lady's air of his, next to guys who were wanted for murder, who had chains of whorehouses and who knew each other from head to toe—he went back to it again and again, always the same thing, the same advice, the same legal loopholes, laughing at himself when there was a reason, but always showing them with his eyes that he could run his own game. And nobody got tough with him; he told them his ideas without raising his voice, calm, looking them right in the eye. And he started growing little by little but without wasting any time. He asked nothing for himself; he had two women and wasn't looking for more. All he wanted was for us to unite, to forget the kid stuff, and to protect ourselves from the wops and sell-outs. It was a hope, you can just imagine; even before, all of us had thought the things he was repeating, and only he, a new guy, who had no problems with anyone, could go from one to another, discuss and convince them. How many times I saw him one-on-one with a heavy, always wearing gray, no gold, his hat tipped back; and I can tell you that the guys who wanted to start out slapping him across the face always ended up respecting him. I saw him just a few hours before, downtown. It was a Saturday and he called to me from the bar in that café that's gone now, the Dorrego, and invited me, laughing, to have a drink. He gave me a little hug: He had a newspaper under his arm and—this was the first time I ever saw him like this—wore a tie that wasn't black and a stickpin shaped like a horseshoe with tiny little jewels in it. I was in a hurry, so I couldn't stick around. The next day, Sunday, in the afternoon, as soon as the sun went down, he was standing in the doorway of a house with a grill-room and the Marseilles mob nailed him from a taxi, half a dozen shots in the gut. He couldn't even talk. It had to be that way. And then the whole country went down the drain, that was that.

CHAPTER XV

That was the beginning of the war, and to confirm it the anonymous letters instantly leapt into the pouches of the mailmen. They were blue, written in even, languid letters; almost all were sent to women to denounce the appearance at the bordello of sons, brothers, boyfriends, and a few husbands. They neither insulted nor lied; at that time, right after Father Bergner made his attack from the pulpit, they limited themselves to mentioning names, dates, and times, barely insinuating the reprisals that would soon divide the city.

Some of the scribes were almost thirty years old, but the majority were girls who'd met at meetings of the Cooperative Action Group. None conformed to the desperate spinster theory dreamed up by the recipients of those long envelopes covered with blue letters. Perhaps they all imagined the same woman, all concurring in the

arrangement of bones, eyes, height, complexion, length
of phalanges, shape of fingernails, configuration of her
knuckles as she wrote.

All of the recipients, without communicating with
each other, without knowing it, ascribed to the woman—
they wouldn't have thought the author a man, even
though it was impossible to tell from the writing, even if
the letters had been typewritten—a neat, tight-fitting lace
blouse, round at the start of the neck, with a thin velvet
ribbon, a cameo, or a gold coin made into a broach covering the collar button. They ascribed an immobile smile
to her, a sunken mouth, a sweet expression, and a severe
profile. They made her odious, but not repulsive, taciturn,
sighing, fond of plants and cats, devoted to the dawn and
the end of afternoon; they ascribed a wig to her or
bleached yellow hair, the habit of raising a tiny, initialed
handkerchief from her sleeve to her nose, to have the
pleasure of feeling alone and smelling perfume.

The first anonymous letters, those that sought vague-
ness and a prophetic tone, the ones that insisted on referring to the boys who'd drowned in the Rinconada
picnic, may well have emanated, as people said at the
time, from the sacristy. Some weeks went by without
punishments or visible catastrophes. The priest Bergner
showed us from the pulpit that this hiatus, this apparent
scorn or lapse of memory on the part of Divine Providence, was, because it was disconcerting and ominous,
infinitely more terrible than a concrete series of tragedies.
He recalled the lack of concern in Babylon and Nineveh,
he foresaw weeping and the gnashing of teeth in the
immediate but unforeseeable future, and he studied the
calm before the storm.

Then the girls from Cooperative Action, without anyone's being able to prove they were following orders or
suggestions, the clean, well-dressed girls from Santa
María, spontaneously, in the face of history, and without
obeying anything but their convictions and the sensation
of misery and danger that was altering the life of the city,
began to meet and conspire. They swore themselves to
silence and went on writing the blue letters of threats and
denunciations on fine, soft-colored paper in their tall,
traditional, and proud writing.

True, they didn't speak about the Middle Eastern cities which were eaten away by vice and demolished as
punishment; they simply mentioned the house on the
coast or María Bonita, sons, boyfriends, brothers and
places familiar to all of us; they confirmed coincidences
whose meaning was indubitable and transcendent.

Take, for example, the case of María Mann, the
daughter of the owners of the place that sold tents, mat-
tresses, and beach chairs on Urquiza Avenue, next to the
music store, almost on the corner opposite Barthé's pharmacy. She received, almost certainly in the first batch
mailed out, a letter that said:

> Your boyfriend Juan Carlos Pintos was in the
> house on the coast on Saturday night. Impure
> and very possibly sick, he visited you on Sun-
> day, ate dinner in your house, and took your
> mother and you to the movies. Is it possible
> he's kissed you, touched your mother's hand,
> the food on your table? Your children will be
> rachitic, blind, and covered with sores, and you
> yourself will not be able to escape from those

horrible sicknesses. But long before that, other disasters will afflict your loved ones who are innocent of sin. Think about this and seek the inspiration that saves in prayer.

Along with the others María Mann could contribute to bringing to life the image of the thin, rancorous woman with a biblical name and a lace blouse. They could all see her, alone, chewing her lip, writing at night while patting herself under the nose with the perfume of her initialed handkerchief. But the girls from Action who actually did write the letters were very different from the dried-out old maid.

Above all, they were sincere and acted cleanly. They did not seek to provoke any more suffering, fights and separations than those they thought essential for closing the brothel, for cleansing Santa María of that trash, the disgrace born on the coast and, full of insolence, incessantly working its way to the city so that it could scratch its antennae on their houses. They were not dried out by time or rage; they did not seek vengeance but merely to defend themselves from an enemy threatening their principles and projects, the personal future they all shared.

They did not want promiscuity and could not stand the idea that promiscuity was possible, easy, that it could beckon from the coast. They did not want to be compared in that violent manner, they did not want to tolerate the ability of the men to seek those women out, even if they were making a mistake.

At first they met in a room the High School lent them for the weekly meetings of Cooperative Action; later in the rooms of Julita, Malabia's widow, in the big old house on the road to Tablada. Fresh and healthy, exchanging giggles and squeals, each one defending the essence of their secret from the malevolence of the others, they made plans, they gossiped, and then, between sips of tea, lightly blushing, with their tongues between their teeth, getting ink on the tips of their avid fingers that slipped toward the nibs of their pens, they wrote out the anonymous letters. They were not surprised to discover that the feminine alliance to which they were giving form was centuries old.

It was stronger than love, capable of surviving any surrender to a man, any individual renunciation. Drinking tea and chewing cakes, smelling their inevitable perfumes, pushing back from the heat and humidity with smooth precise flicks the hairs that had fallen onto their foreheads, showing the whitest of teeth that announced and protected their guffaws, the girls wrote the anonymous letters to defend municipal purity and to keep the men from intuiting the key to their personality, from deciphering their only enigma, zealously covered by absurdities, cunning, by secular, constantly renewed misunderstandings.

Julita, Malabia's widow, had agreed to receive them twice a week. From almost a dozen photos, many of them pale enlargements of snapshots, Federico Malabia smiled or stared sadly at the lady writers of anonymous letters; the girls noted that the photos were aging rapidly: Every time they looked them over they seemed to have been taken two or three years earlier than what they'd estimated on their last visit, and the man seemed more dead, less credible. But they never spoke about that; gathered in the garden after saying good-by to Julita, they only commented on the eyes in the pictures, the dead man's shoulders, and the sweet line of his upper lip, the only softness in his face.

Sometimes they would find trousers and shirts that belonged to Federico scattered over the furniture, tossed onto the floor, and they would smell a trace of cologne and cigar smoke; it was as if a man had been there a few minutes before they'd arrived to take a bath, change his clothes, and then, indolent in the heat, to chat with Julita while he smoked a few of those thick cigars whose ash whitened in the only ashtray in the room. But they knew the clothes belonged to Federico, as did the smell of the tobacco and the cologne, even though it was impossible. They awaited Julita's face, her tired mouth, her hair that had grown out and was uncombed, her brilliant, dedicated eyes which she filled indefatigably with a look of furious ecstasy, a look that alluded to a secret, untransmissible triumph.

The girls would look at the woman's gestures. They would measure the slowness of the movement with which she brought her elbows to her waist—after putting the tray with the tea set and the cake down on the table and then smiling at them—the movement of withdrawing into herself and concentrating with which she gave solidity to her silence, defiantly invited a comparison of their happiness with hers, and proclaimed her isolation. The girls took note of all that, and one by one they foreswore the facility of malice, they became beautiful by forcing themselves to believe in the miracle or the madness, by deducing that the dead man who watched them from the walls, from the frame on the table, from the blackened fireplace, had been there that afternoon, fifteen minutes before the first of them knocked at the squeaky garden gate. Perhaps they might have passed him on the stairs, perhaps it wasn't absurd to imagine the simultaneously thin and corpulent man, standing still, bowing slightly, and patient at the turn of the stairs, allowing them to pass by.

On the afternoons when the girls would find Federico's clothes scattered around, Julita would receive them happily, her hair in a tangle; she would run, muttering excuses, to remove the trousers, the wrinkled shirt, and the snaking tie from the furniture. Before putting things away in the closet, she would bang the belt buckle against some piece of furniture or her own body; then she would open the window to clear the air of the masculine odors of smoke and cologne. With her arms outstretched, the light from the garden at her back, she would smile another excuse to them, blushing, sorry the girls had seen and smelled her intimacy.

She said only what she absolutely had to; with her hands plunged in the pocket of her robe, her eyes mad, smiling, she faced them as if from a nearby but unreachable height. She nodded assent, well disposed, when the girls would speak of vague, general things, the only ones they dared mention there; she would bring them tea, pens, and inkwells, boxes of fine, soft-colored paper. She never showed she knew why they came to her house; she let them talk and write.

Framed by hair that hung down rigidly and uncombed, her face devoid of makeup, shiny with sweat, fixed in a disinterested youth, not hiding, but actually showing the wrinkles at her temples and over her mouth, pleasantly denouncing the events with the angry shine of her eyes that refused to accept them, Julita's face stared at the girls with neither disdain nor enthusiasm. At times she twisted that face to look at her stomach. At other times she raised it to look over the girls, over their limited interests, over the acceptance of the definitive fact on which friends and relatives agreed every day, in order to participate again in unattainable events, in happy, accompanied moments, in scenes that were at least months old.

The chatter, the profiles bent over the sheets of stationery, the bare shoulders of summer, the very age of the girls, were nothing more than a cloud of steam between her and her palpable, present memory.

While they diligently wrote denunciations and suggested punishments in blue ink, Julita again touched Federico's arms and back, returned to the bed, to silent dialogues next to the fireplace, to winter dawns in the country, to solitary unions among frightened horses, shrieking birds, the smell of manure and toothpaste.

CHAPTER XVI

Lanza touches his moustache and again lifts his beer; along with the sticky cardboard coaster, he also brings up the theme I pushed aside a while ago by moving my fingers.

"The worst thing I can say about your poems," and then he says it, "is that they're good. I wish they were horrible, deformed, ill-born creatures, like little animals with too many or too few feet, eyes, horns. I mean . . ."

"Don't say anything more, I don't care. I don't care about those little verses I was ashamed to show. But I don't want to be sorry I wrote them. They were born and now they're dead."

"I mean," he persists sadly and resolutely, with a disproportionate gravity, "that they're bad because they're good. From a person your age and in this year and in this town, I would have preferred a shout, an incomprehensible grimace, some form of madness."

"Sure." I smile and drink. "My age, the times, Santa María, and, you forgot, personal circumstances."

He's left disarmed and sadder. He pretends to look for the waiter in the mix of smoke and words in the air of a Saturday night in the Berna.

"No," he whispers, looking at me. "I didn't forget, and you know it. Let this poor old man say his piece. I try not to annoy much. You understand me; because out of all the things I've read, all that's stayed with me are a few lines that touch on what I ask for, what you, unfortunately for you, are condemned to write. Forget mistakes, never waste time correcting proofs. Listen to what I did with this one:

> *"And I lose her, lose him, give my life*
> *in exchange for old age and the ambitions of*
> *   others*
> *each day more filthy, desiring, and cold.*
> *I should go and won't, should allow myself not*
> *   to believe."*

We order more beer, and I take a long time to empty and fill my pipe, commenting on the people coming and going. Lanza's face is good-natured and calm, with an attenuated victory in his moist, red eyes.

"Okay," I say. "I like it. But it hasn't got much to do with, isn't the monster with its feet on backwards that I gave you to read. It's much better, far away from the horror and the shouting."

"Don't believe it," he mumbles, decisively, through the foam. "I may be suffering lapses of memory, the confusion of an old man. But those four, mistaken lines . . . I find in them something disconcerting, the truth I asked of you or foretold. But it's useless. You already said it. In this kind of thing, opinions aren't worth anything. Anyone who takes someone else's opinions seriously is lost. And now, take a discreet look over toward the bar. Your relative Marcos has invaded, along with his usual parasites and a few women. All of it, the melancholy ruin of the Phalanstery."

I look over, and there they are, drinking and buying bottles. I turn back to the old man.

"One night he told me about the Phalanstery. I'd heard some bits of gossip, of course. But, really, I don't know, I don't understand."

Lanza laughs and smokes slowly.

"Got time?"

"All the time in the world."

"Lucky you. Light your pipe and brace yourself. Another tricky horror, in reality. A shame, if you think seriously about it. Marcos Bergner deserves neither the paternity nor the blame in this matter. What's the age difference between you two?"

I smoke, figuring it out. I can't guess what old Lanza intends with this prologue. Exordium, he'd call it. Anyway, the night is promising and threatens to be long. I know the tricks played by oldsters and young idiots alike to make a splash even if they're telling a trivial story. I remember how boring my father was.

"About ten years, I guess," I finally answer.

"And from when do you remember him? I mean a real memory."

"A real memory . . . Let's see. About two or three years

ago I started to see him. See him in the way you mean."

Lanza smiles happily and hesitates before rolling a cigarette.

"It doesn't matter. I'm interested in the Phalanstery."

"In that case," he goes on, relieved, "we're talking about different people. There was another Marcos. Look at him over there, drunk, fat, disgusting, puffy. The great disaster and the changes it brought forced me out of Spain, and here I am. Having enough time to do so, I studied my personal problem from all angles—logic, insomnia, despair. There was no lack of bad things. I had no option. They pushed me to settle down in Santa María along with Dr. Díaz Grey, our buddy Larsen—the philatelist of poor whores—and many others who are irrelevant, especially tonight. Here until I die," he says, shrugging his shoulders, behind the fingers he raises to cover a cough.

"There is sadness, and there remains the incomprehension. But neither drama nor melodrama. Phalanstery. I was talking to you about a Marcos Bergner you never met. Then he was probably the same age you are now. Maybe a year older, perhaps. But he had something, excuse me for saying so, you don't. He had that kind of health we call sanguine. You, writing poems, may or may not live the most important human experiences. That Marcos lived them body and soul—if he's got one—without having to write a single line. And Insurralde's girl, almost a compatriot of mine, lived those years with him. I really think that their real name must be Inssaurralde. But it's unimportant. Everything transplanted in Santa María dries up and degenerates. Let's not worry too much about a loss."

"Right," I say softly, so the old man knows I'm still

with him and not interrupting. "She was Marcos's girl friend."

"She and all the acres of open country her father bought. The Swiss had just begun to organize Colonia. Every six months families with tin trunks wearing strange, starched clothes would arrive—Bibles and pure will. But there was no Colonia yet. It's around that time, more or less, that the picture appears. Orloff, the prince who must have been running around these parts since the Russian revolution of 1905, or when Catherine the Great got fed up with Potemkin. Orloff could tell you anything and know how to persuade you. He'd say it with passion, without suffering. He lies better than I do. We both, I agree, tend toward anachronisms, exaggerations, impossibilities. But we're different: He looks for beauty, the literary vignette, what people call escapism nowadays, invention. It's an artist's position. I'm a poor old man looking for the truth."

Behind me, Marcos shouts in a threatening voice and immediately starts laughing. His friends cheer him and order more drinks.

"What are the women up to?" asks Lanza. I take a look and report unenthusiastically.

"One, the one with the sick face, as if she were going to puke, is smoking. Another is singing to herself and putting on makeup, as calm as if she were sewing a dress or straightening up the house, the room, whatever she lives in."

Two more beers appear, and Lanza touches the foam with his lips.

"Okay," he accepts. "Now Orloff and photography. I have a copy at home, for years now I've kept a notebook with everything I've wanted to keep. It would be a surprise. Someday I'll invite you to look through all those papers, so you can learn, it's your sacred patriotic obligation, the true history of Santa María. Meanwhile, my version of the photo. First you see a thin Marcos with satyr ears, long eyebrows, inquisitive, his nose hard, his mouth infantile. There is a black cape, maybe it's a poncho, over his shoulders. Emerging from the cape-poncho are two incredibly long hands, fingers he never had. I don't know how they got that effect. The cut of his jacket is old-fashioned, the vest high, and the funerary tie excessively thick. This Bergner, with a furrow in his brow, poses looking down. It may well be that in those days he too wrote poems. Relax and look at him, imagine. It's possible, now that I think about it, that in some year you might come to look the way Marcos does tonight. In the Lanza Museum and Archive, miraculously, we find yet another indispensable photo. It's the little Basque girl, Insurralde, Moncha.

"It's a poor shot, yellow, and faded, barely a newspaper clipping. But even then you could see her defiant eyes, her sensual, disdainful mouth, the strength in her chin. Let's not forget that she was older than Marcos and of age. If we study the second face carefully, we understand why there was nothing anyone could do about it, why old man Insurralde—the mother was already dead— had no choice but to play dumb and accept things. He did accept the Phalanstery, which was quite a lot to accept when we remember dates and geographic locations.

"There were six at the beginning, all rich, all young. Two married couples, Marcos and Moncha. In the period of grandeur, the number reached ten, not counting the children. No one knows—I at least haven't been able to find out—who proposed the idea and advocated it. Outwardly it was simple; very simple if we summarize it on a sheet of paper or discuss it after dinner. That remote Marcos Bergner offered part of his land and a ranch house that maybe you'll inherit someday. Property acquired through marriage, jointly held property, whatever repugnant definition you'd care to give it.

"In those days and nights, the three founding couples met to eat in the Progress Club or took turns inviting each other home to dinner. Also, some Saturdays, they gathered in Insurralde's house. The idea, let me say it again, was as simple as it was infallible: leave Santa María, settle down on the farm, harvest crops, rejoice in the growth and multiplication of the animals. First stage. The second included the purchase of more land, the import of thoroughbred animals, the inexorable accumulation of millions of pesos. It was a good and blessed project. All the pioneers had an economic cushion to fall back on in case (though no one allowed for these possibilities) of drought, disease, hailstorms, lean years. There would be workers, of course, so the men could concentrate on the intellectual labor of directing and planning. There were humble country girls so the kids wouldn't get in the way and so that day after day meals would be ready on time, and also, of course, it was a cooperative enterprise, at least with respect to the profits. In sum, a primitive Christian community based on altruism, tolerance, and mutual understanding.

"And they did it, started up. I can just imagine the little Basque girl, the only single woman on the Phalanstery, facing up to old man Insurralde, who could only beg or curse. Because Moncha was of age and because two-thirds of the Insurralde fortune belonged to her. I imagine her impassive and resolute, with that newspaper-photo face I tried to describe, giving her answer once and for all: 'I want to get to know Marcos. I have to know who he is before I marry him.'

"And naturally she went with the others. A few months later, as I said, two other married couples joined. And it's only proper to say that they did everything they'd projected for the first stage. The farm, the Phalanstery, was a success, a real success, for a year or eighteen months. We historians haven't come to any agreement on how long this fortunate period lasted. But when we combined our respective solitudes, themselves of diverse origin, to play cards, we agreed that history imposes itself with dates on a thing that is intrinsically confused and dumb. We agreed on historical objectivity, that is, on the nothingness of it, on its being the shell of an empty egg.

"We accepted the fact that after six months and twenty-three days, Moncha Insurralde fled the Phalanstery on a stolen horse, stopped off in Santa María to rest, and went right on to the capital, looking for a ship to take her to Europe. A few months later, her father sold out at a good price, and we never heard anything more about them. The truth was unknown, and we all tried to fill that empty eggshell honorably and decorously. The only problem was: who was going to tell us the truth? Because little by little the Phalanstery began to lose people, projects were interrupted, the plantings and harvests were left to rot, and almost all the animals were slaughtered.

"It was useless to think that any of the nine remaining Phalanstery members would explain the failure. However, if we remember that one couple of the four decided very quickly to leave the primitive Christian, communal experiment, this historian feels authorized, in the face of his professional conscience and standing before the bar of future generations, to take into account the quite similar versions of events extracted from the hardworking rural laborers who were with Marcos and company in the exodus and the campaign. Above all, we can believe the little that we learned from Barrientos, the man who was the overseer of that failed enterprise and who now, I think, has a store or something like that over near Enduro.

"With regard to Marcos, he was able to face the painful circumstances and knew how to deal with grief and adversity. Back in Santa María, he dedicated himself for a while to drowning his sorrow in public. Later on, he loaded his yacht with crates of liquor, acquired the fraternal presence of a few women and buddies and disappeared up river or down for a few months.

"The statements made by the sodbusters and cowboys may be, of course, the result of mere malice. A severe researcher might believe them. But he shouldn't use resentful gossip, so typical of the lower classes, to write and bequeath an INTRODUCTION TO THE TRUE HISTORY OF THE FIRST PHALANSTERY IN SANTA MARÍA. I did.

"I tell that six months or so after the undertaking of this colossal enterprise, a certain confusion was noted. It wasn't possible in the first instance to determine precisely who made up the sacred nuclear families. I must point out that, of course, the field hands did not often approach the phalansterial fortress. But, inevitably, the girls in charge of the kitchen and the kids did make their way into the citadel.

"Slowly, according to the calumnies spread around, the kingdom of the new couples, neither legalized nor blessed, was ruled, in substitution, by the criterion operative in the most highly perfected industrial societies of our century: Avoid at all costs any loss of resources or time. Around then, the Marcos Bergner of the photograph I described a while ago, had gathered numerous acolytes for his bacchic cult.

"According to evil and filthy gossip, the new and solemn rite was celebrated twice a week. They used dice or cards, innocent religious stamps stirred up in two hats. The Phalansterians rejected blind impulses, treacherous attractions. They honored the omniscience of the gods of chance and destiny to arrange their nocturnal partners twice a week. And the five women were young and agreeable. About the men I say nothing; I can only tell you they too were young.

"People also said that to vary their methods they used bedroom keys. An idea that has its charm and its fantasy. But I, as an irreproachable and honorable historian, have not accepted it. Because it isn't very likely that the bedrooms in Marcos Bergner's farm house would have locks and keys. Besides, they didn't need them, unless, and it's an idea we can only accept with reservations, they were used as symbols, as a poetic variation on ceremony.

"We must add more documentary dross, the kind that frequently will not separate from the shining gold of truth—as a mere curiosity. The powerful novelistic imagination of the illiterates adds that the chance couples yoked by the gods discovered in time that there is no solitude sadder than the solitude of two people alone. Ergo, they opted for the charms of social activities, for the pleasures of collective works, which are so superior to those individualist, petit bourgeois egoism can offer.

"Now, in my relentless pursuit of the truth, I must bring up two points in my story that are not completely convincing. Even taking into account human nature, a very important factor we all pretend to understand, no amount of reflection has allowed me to clear up the reasons why the Phalansterians took so long to initiate their fatal promiscuity. I use as a starting date the angry, shocked flight of Moncha Insurralde. I also don't understand how, once they'd accepted the wholeness of communal existence, the characters in the drama could live together so long without turning to guns or fists. And I add that it's curious to see and hear your relative Marcos organizing a Holy Crusade against the humble bordello citizen Larsen, alias Body Snatcher, out on the coast. Considering the matter from the psychological point of view, it may be the common vocational rivalry which has always characterized artists. Now, if we apply a Marxist criterion, it may be that the origin of the grudge is the fact that the three women in the sky-blue house don't work for nothing, are not moved, in bed, by the noble love of the profession. So different from the women Marcos had and knew in the brief, idyllic time of the unforgettable Phalanstery."

CHAPTER XVII

I t's a Sunday night," said Snatcher. He was sitting at one of the little tables in the patio, swirling the liquid in his glass before drinking it, tossing half-smoked cigarettes onto the tiles, certain that she couldn't understand what he was thinking. "A Sunday night or a Monday morning. Do you realize that?"

"Realize what?" asked María Bonita from the window. She leaned her head against two window bars and held a glass in her skirt, in the space between her legs.

"You don't realize anything. Were you listening? If you'd realized, you wouldn't be asking. You know I don't like to talk, but when I do talk I like someone to hear me."

María Bonita laughed so that Snatcher could hear her. She settled her buttocks onto the window ledge and lifted her head, sliding it on the two bars.

"You weren't talking about the fact that it was a Sunday night. You were talking about something else." She lowered her eyelids and looked at the shadow of the solitary man in the patio surrounded by empty tables and the sad, furious, midsummer heat. There was no other light but the candle in the niche in front of the gilt print of the Virgin bent over the Child.

"I'm not going to ask you questions as if we were in grade school," said Snatcher, sticking a finger into the glass to remove a hard green bug. "I'm always thinking about buying some of that cloth they use to keep the flies off the meat in butcher shops and putting it in the windows. But the bugs come in anyway whenever you open the window. The other night the place was full of those big ones with hard shells, and I don't like it when people smash them."

She lifted her head from the bars and softly banged it against them. Outside, the night was like a black limit that contained the heat and the unknown world of Santa María. She knew that the girls carried jasmine, that they were blonde, and that they strolled around the plaza and the docks. The stories Nelly and Irene told on Monday afternoons slightly modified the image she had of the city: Some store would have a new display window, an anecdote would reveal an incomprehensible tradition, a man on horseback began an eternal ride around the plaza she remembered.

Snatcher filled his glass and lit another cigarette. Inside, in the darkness, asleep, nowhere, dead, one of the women snored. Obliged to rise and fall with the rhythm of the breathing, wounded by those whistled s's, sinking into the round, absorbent holes the mouth of the sleeping woman opened in the air, Snatcher confirmed that she would never know what he was thinking. He told himself that someone else was using him to try things out.

"It's a Sunday night," he said. "Whether you realize it or not."

"Of course I realize it. For me Sunday is Saturday. So I have to realize when it's Saturday, right?"

Snatcher shook his head and took another drink. Later he aimed a smile at the white form in the window, knowing that she could not see him, smiling with the intensity of a cynical confession, of an act of love.

"This is coming to an end," he said. "I'd like to be with a man so I could talk."

"What's coming to an end?" asked María Bonita without lifting her head from the bars. "You can talk to me. You always said you wanted to know, but were in no hurry. You never believed in all this, you'd always breathed the presence of failure here, like a smell, like the aromas we've got to accept along with old houses and furniture."

"I'd like to be with a man. I'd like to be with Dr. Díaz Grey. I don't know if he's really a man, I don't know if he'd understand, but I'd like to have him here now, at this table. This is coming to an end. There's the priest, the guys outside in the car taking notes. People are afraid of saying hello to me, of being seen with me. Even the wops are afraid of selling me stuff. I'm not afraid, we've got legal permission, they can't throw us out. But I realize what's happening."

"Only now? I figured it out the first day, when we drove through the town in the car, and everything was closed, and nobody stuck his head out to gawk or even to insult us. But you always said . . ."

"I said what I said to keep your spirits up. And because

I thought it would blow over. It did. But now it's coming back worse, now it's for real, and they won't let up until it's finished."

"Okay, so we go somewhere else. We've got something. We can go to Rosario or the capital, or even better, we can try in another place like this, a small city. It's a big sacrifice if you have to live locked up the way I do, but the money comes in regularly and without problems. You don't have to worry, sweetie. If there's anyone to be sorry for, it's the girls, because they'd concocted so many illusions."

"Yes," said Snatcher. He lit a cigarette with the one he was smoking and began to play with the candlelight shimmering through his glass.

María Bonita suddenly bent over and emptied her glass. The taste was indefinable, a burning in her chest, the short, fleeting memory of each one of the drinks she'd made up out of the glasses left on the tables after closing time. She lay her head against the bars again.

I must be getting old. Reaching the end of the Santa María adventure with much less money than she thought they'd have didn't matter to her. The cordiality or unfriendliness of the heavyset man rocking back and forth in his chair in the patio, linking his movement with the rhythm of the snores coming from the bedrooms also did not matter to her. Now she thought she understood the meaning of "It's a Sunday night," but its meaning didn't interest her. She felt at peace, unprotected by the diminutive hatreds and the familiar greed that engendered her strength, her desire to live. *I must be getting old, old,* she repeated without emotion, moving her tongue inside her half-open mouth to form the words.

Maybe the failure was real, maybe she was condemned to close up the little house and cross the town in the opposite direction in Carlos's Ford, this time going up the steep, dry, clay streets lined with honeysuckle, eucalyptus, and shade trees whose names she didn't know. Back in the train station as if only a few days had passed since their arrival, as if this were the end of a visit, a holiday, and she would have revisited the places she'd only glimpsed. Their memory she'd perfected uncertainly through the tales of the girls, Nelly and Irene, and quotations from the conversations of the liberated, recovering men who stayed on, drinking in the patio. She would go through the city for the last time, with no hope of overcoming that angry rejection of intimacy shown her by doors and windows and by the few backs, the few impassive, blind faces she'd seen through the useless skeleton roof of the ancient touring car, with no springs, shaken almost regularly by the broken surface of the streets. So, she thought, she would have lost Santa María forever.

"I wish he were here so I could talk to him," said Snatcher, immobilized, staring at the light of the last cigarette on the ground. "He wouldn't understand, you don't seem to understand much either tonight. Sunday night, Monday morning, it's all the same. But that's the way it is: He'd think something else about all this. About me, about you, about the business."

The snores were no longer audible. After bubbling and fading, the light from the candle extended a poor yellow over the print of the Virgin.

"What would he understand?" murmured María Bonita, scornful, adulating.

A man almost as old as she, heavyset, wide, dressed in black, splayed out on his chair in the center of the empty patio. She could remember his name and his habits, recognize him, enumerate the things that linked him to her and even stuff it all with a precise meaning, the convenient and friendly meaning. She raised her empty glass and began to breathe inside it. Her breath erased the light of the candle down below. *I'm getting old, I'm lying, I should have stayed in the capital, he gets mad if they call him Snatcher, maybe Nelly will stay on with the wop, I've got a few thousand pesos and whatever I get from what we sell off, tomorrow I'm going to sleep until I can't sleep anymore, better to try again in a small city, I spent the summer stuck in here, if we go I have to cancel the liquor order, I'm getting old and I'm blowing into this glass as if I were a little kid.*

"Once and for all," said Snatcher. Again he rocked in his chair and smiled looking straight forward. "But I put up with a lot, I don't know if you understand. I put up with too much, and now I want to shake myself and show them who I am and who they are." He had a hard shock of hair hanging down to one eye; his smile and the movements of his hand with the cigarette made him look younger, his face, in profile, became thinner as it entered and left the light from the candle.

María Bonita felt the night behind the nape of her neck as she leaned against the bars, as if it were a different night, easily separated from the rest, a night that could be saved and taken away. *A whole summer, locked away, who'd believe me, not once on the beach.* She set the glass down on the window ledge and tried to sleep. But she rebounded into lucidity, into the nervousness of fatigue, into all the possible motives for fear and remorse.

None of it mattered to her: failure, the disdain that had pierced the place and that awaited her, alert, patient, confident, on the other side of the window bars and the sky-blue paint of the little house. But she was ready to weep for the definitive loss of the Santa María she'd imagined and had never dared to compare to the real one.

She was sure that if she worked up the courage to go out, tomorrow morning, Monday, for example, and, arm-in-arm with Irene and Nelly, scramble up the dirt road that led to the corner of the plaza, she was sure that if she took a walk, leaning on the girls, past the doors and windows of the shops, and went down later, taking lazy steps, toward the promenade, she would not be able to recognize the city she'd been constructing, with no intention, daily, out of the sentences and laughter of the clients, out of the smells the wind carried or the summer gave off, out of the news gathered weekly by the girls, with her worn-out memories of another small city, surrounded by farmland.

CHAPTER XVIII

The snoring of one of the girls—either Nelly, the skinny one who slept alone, or Irene who was accompanied— jumped out of the rooms: Regular, whitish, it established itself intermittently in the patio like a small frog that had fallen, moistened and boned.

Snatcher drank and tried to assign the snoring to the proper mouth, Nelly's or Irene's. He didn't imagine the girls asleep; he simply considered them his, the way an ordinary distracted and melancholy father considers his daughters his. They were a family, and the unforgettably transitory nature of the quartet only increased the voices of alarm and hardened prejudices, impeding any con- fusion of evil with good.

Through the failures, the bad moments, the years of testing and egoism, of unforeseen lessons, Snatcher had come to discover that what makes sin sinful is its uselessness, that pernicious mania for being self-sufficient, for not deriving from anything, for the lack of any need to transcend or leave palpable things, numbers, satisfactions that can be shared in the world visible to others.

They were a family, he, María Bonita, and the two girls, all united in their intention to make money in a provincial town next to a river, between a river and a colony of blond men who were stronger than he because they did not need to discover and adopt their prejudices by means of suffering and defense. And so, like other families, this one had been created and supported by an accident that might be absurd, that might be felt to be deliberately injurious.

Their purpose was identical to the one determined by the attitudes and thoughts of the men in Colonia and Santa María—Snatcher was capable of imagining the others—to earn money. But not only that way, by establishing a direct, fantastic relation between a desire for money and money, but going to it, working at it, from the natural coarseness of desire, through techniques, experience, perfection, legitimate cleverness, newfangled tricks that become practice. The means were there, as were the people he'd agreed to call the means; they were there, besides, to defeat him, to try to bring about his degradation, tear to pieces what was vulnerable in his vocation, to tear to shreds disloyalties, denunciations, and the simple abusive caprices that were born from that agreement.

Finally María Bonita lifted her head from the window bars and straightened her body. Smiling, barefoot, she made her way to Snatcher's table and let down her hair. She filled his glass and bent over to kiss a corner of the man's mouth, softly, pausing to smell the alcohol and tobacco.

Snatcher shook his shoulders and a hand, and she went back to the window. She settled down in profile to the night, her wrists clasped around her knees. "Why wouldn't it be any good to talk to me?" she insisted. "Talk to me as if I weren't here. If we have to close up, so what? We'll go somewhere else. I know you don't love me, that way, I mean, completely, the way you used to. Are you listening? But you do love me and you're going to love me as long as this time of ours lasts. Talk to me as if I weren't here."

"It's no use," said Snatcher. The wheezing of the sleeping woman was now much more rapid, almost jolly, as if she were calling to someone, guiding him through the darkness. "It's no use."

"Talk to me about how it all was before, about you and me," whispered María Bonita, without any hope.

Snatcher was immersed in all of that, he couldn't remember any moment beyond the frontiers of the Santa María adventure, this perfect opportunity he'd desired for so many years, and which they were threatening to kill right in his hands. His courage, his hate, or his inexpressible love would not be of any use to prolong or defend it.

But it was useless to talk and especially with her. And if he'd imagined having Díaz Grey there, if he'd imagined a violent need to feel sorry for and contradict the weak little doctor, it was, had to be, for the pleasure, the irritation, the conscious despair that abandoning himself to the uselessness of talking promised. Everything was lost, and not because a new failure had hit him there in Santa

María as he was turning fifty. It wasn't because of being rejected by the city, not because of the anonymous letters, the hysteria of the young ladies, the insane energy of the priest Bergner, not even because of the poor devils keeping an eye on the bordello, yawning inside their car.

Everything was lost because the unique, irreplaceable story of that man who had various names, Snatcher for one, a man that he could brag of knowing better than anyone, was coming to an end. He could transport Snatcher, just as a woman carries a dead fetus; using his memory, he could play at being alive. But there were no more facts—the small renascences, the modifications, the upsets, the progresses, the pleasant rectifications that each true fact means—except a series of reflex actions, visible from this death until the next, and imposed by the past which was just over.

No one. Not even this woman who was whispering and cuddling herself next to the bars in the window with her long legs that raised her knees to the same height as her face. Her knees held up a full glass, just tipped so that she could twist her neck and drink, in an infantile way, keeping her hands useless, under her buttocks. Not even Dr. Díaz Grey, cordial but separate, tepid, alien, not equipped from birth to understand the only thing that mattered about the deceased Snatcher, about the legend that would begin to grow vigorously and to become corrupt. Not María Bonita, not Díaz Grey, not Barthé, not Vázquez.

No one. Dead, stupefied by the conviction that the always sudden end had come despite bravura and intuition. He could only talk about Snatcher with himself. He foresaw the measured gestures, the immobile, red eyes of the soliloquies, the desperate effort, the will to abstain, the pure curiosity and justice with which, from now on, he would have to evoke the passages of his terminated life in order to be able to reconstruct the history of Snatcher and calm down, before his definitive death, with the security of having obtained a manageable interpretation. Only in that way, believing he knew what it was that was dying, could he die in peace.

"If you're not going to talk, let's go to sleep," said María Bonita. "But you're going to stay right here, right? Anyway, if the thing is coming to an end, what can it matter to you if you sleep here or not?" She was standing in the center of the patio, finishing her drink with her eyes open, looking forward, with the same pensive, absent, and confident stare of a child. Even barefoot, her head was even with the reluctant little flame that crackled in the niche. *Not even forty*, joked Snatcher. *She must be just a little over thirty. But her body has already begun to weigh on her, as if she were hanging, just the opposite of the María Bonita I met when she was a girl and had another name. Even though she was tall, everything in her moved up, wanting to grow. Taller than I am, than almost all the men; but she looked up and stood straight and raised her arms. Now she's coming back, everything on her hangs, wanting to go down; her stomach, her bosom, her face, her swollen hands.*

"I'm not leaving. Go to bed."

"Got cigarettes? There's the bottle, but don't drink too much."

"It's Saturday night. I haven't gotten drunk since this thing began."

María Bonita crossed herself before the niche and moistened a finger with saliva to straighten the candlewick. She dragged her feet over the coolness of the tiles

going toward the shadow of the house, toward the fluctuating grotto of concord, exile, and autonomy the watery,
disconnected snoring of the sleeping woman, Nelly or
Irene, excavated in the darkness. She stopped and turned
her head.

"I feel like cleaning up. See how the filth piles up? It
doesn't take long."

Snatcher waited for the noise of the door opening and
closing. Then, glass in hand, even with his chest, he went
to the window and put his nose between the gratings.
There was the car: black, immobile, sterile. A cigarette
glowed, fixed, hanging out of someone's mouth. The silence of the night—the roosters and dogs, so far away,
didn't count; nor did the shaking of the worn-out tracks
on which the last tram descended toward the sleeping
streets near the dock—seemed more intense around the
car, fortified by what the three sleepy, cramped men were
thinking without saying it.

"Assholes," said Snatcher, turning to look at the small,
tiled patio, the little tables with light-colored table cloths
which had lost their symmetrical distribution. He sat
down again and lit a cigarette. The night was definitive,
interminable, seemingly nurtured by the rhythmical tune
swallowed and exhaled by the woman. Happily, he was
not with Díaz Grey, and María Bonita had gone to bed.
She would go to sleep without waiting for him. He was
now with Snatcher, susceptible to comprehension and
dead. He lifted his glass, said, "Cheers," and drank; smiling, confused, excited by good intentions, he put the glass
on the table and softly tapped it with his fingernails.

CHAPTER XIX

Marcos woke up on the floor and instantly had to shut his eyes. He saw the height of the eight o'clock sun in the sky, stained, interrupted by the branches of a euca-lyptus barely stirred by a wind devoid of coolness; between his feet, he could see a fringe of sandy soil, dry grass, the reflection of the light in the river. The moist nape of his neck hurt; the memory of the night and the dawn whirled around under his back, rising up to cover him completely and take possession of his entire body where zones of heat alternated with prolonged chills.

From the gallery on the second story of the house, a woman's voice descended:

"Don't you think we should wake him up? It's got to be bad for him to be sleeping out in the sun with all his clothes on."

"I hope he blows up," said Ana María, and the other

woman snickered mockingly. She seemed to appropriate a piece of the morning's joy, peck at it like a bird, then swallow it up quickly. She prolonged her laughter, with disdain, mock courtesy, and an impersonal form of rancor. Marcos felt the sweat on his head and stomach; he acknowledged the drops rolling down his ribs, under his shirt. A cup or pitcher hit something up above; in the gallery, one of the women made a noise with her mouth, and the other laughed.

"The others are still asleep," said Nena. "When I went to wake Mario up, he told me to get the hell out. He'll stay drunk until noon."

"The milk still hasn't come," said Ana María. "This is yesterday's. I thought it would be sour."

"I don't know why we have the cow when the German only milks her when he feels like it. Maybe he sells the milk. No one checks on him."

"The sun won't hurt him," said Ana María. "It's not the first time he's slept that way."

"Don't bother him. What they say is dangerous is the moon. It makes you crazy. But he's already nuts."

Nena laughed again, but now she seemed to let the laugh die with her mouth still open. They were having breakfast in the gallery; they hadn't taken a bath yet and still had makeup and greasy streaks on their faces. Nena might have been polishing her nails.

"They're all half-crazy," said Ana María some time later. Stupidity stood out in her voice like a foreign accent.

"Were you ever in Rosario?"

"No, I already told you. I don't like it."

"You can't know if you've never been there."

"I just don't like it."

In the silence, pretending to sleep, Marcos, angry and

compassionate, thought about his immobile face turned toward the sky, defenseless under the eyes and thoughts of both women. He imagined he needed an expression of admiration or love from Ana María; he imagined himself on his knees, bent over his own enormous, closed, red, bodiless face in the grass. But it wasn't he who was looking at it but the women. Ana María and Nena were looking at him from the gallery, squinting and scratching the indolence and ill-humor on their heads, trading stupid remarks, drinking their breakfast, staring at their nails, abandoning themselves unenthusiastically to the pursuit of the nebulous meaning of their idiotic sentences.

They were looking at him, looking at his naked, defenseless face. Perhaps they squinted because the morning sun shone on the gallery; on each of Ana María's temples, a small fan of wrinkles would be opening, two triangles capable of provoking rage. Our faces have a secret, not always the one we try to hide. The women were up there in bathrobes, sitting on the canvas chairs with their legs spread, above his face reddened by the heat, by the wine he'd drunk at dawn, by the hate that made his carotid arteries tremble, above his face corrupted and aged by remorse. *Damned pair of whores*, he thought, retaining the laziness of a tranquil sleep on his eyelids. But they didn't count. They were everyone, everyone else, those who examined him by means of the pair of immobile women up in the gallery, who now fell into a nasty silence.

Without haste, they stared at his sweaty, red face, the cowardly corners of his mouth, the double chin that raised the collar of his shirt made of hard cloth. They could discover his lies, smell his stench, feel sorry about insecurities and tears; they could see him, judge him, know what he would never know.

The wind died down, and the sun climbed high over the topmost branches of the eucalyptus. Two helpless horses neighed without urgency near the barn; above the trees on the coast the birds made a wheel of shrieks, a noise like rags being beaten.

"I don't like it," said Nena. "Give me a beer."

"Like him," said Ana María. "Just because he drank it."

"Okay," said Nena. "Stop screwing around. I don't like it and that's that. Tell me the rest."

One began to laugh, and the other helped her finish.

"Nothing much to tell," said Ana María. "I was in the Trocadero, on a whim. The kid came over and invited me to a private room. He always gave me vodka, and that's how I learned. It's like a brandy, like any whiskey. But you get drunk without feeling that your stomach's too full."

She always says the same thing when she talks about vodka. A little black guy who looked like he had TB, who bought her vodka in a cabaret up north with the few pesos he'd earned by the sweat of his brow. A couple of worn-out whores, the others sleeping off the liquor I bought them, and me turned into a disgusting mess stretched out in the morning. Sunday morning getting later, and my sister crazy because that jerk died and left her with no one to sleep with, and the Jews getting rich off the whorehouse.

"That's the way it is, and there's nothing you can do about it. You just have to understand," said Nena.

"You might be right, sweetie," answered Ana María.

It was that time of day when they called each other sweetie, when they pretended to respect each other and take each other seriously, each one building up her ideal image of herself with phrases and smiles directed toward the other.

In the meadow, the cows were mooing, coming over to the fence. Marcos raised his knees and arms, stretched out by rolling in the grass; the pain in the nape of his neck was fixed and deep, his despondency was as concrete as the filthy taste in his mouth. He stood up and walked toward the wooden stairway to the gallery, heavily, feeling waves of nausea. He turned around to look at the day, the river. Ana María spoke behind him. Yawning, he went behind the canvas chairs and shouted an insult to answer the women's ironic greetings. Only when he was in the kitchen did he realize he was barefoot; he drank a glass of water, washed his mouth out with the second and spit it through the screen on the window.

He went into the bedroom to look for his bathing suit; a fly buzzed around his back as he looked through the dresser drawer. Standing there, he examined the shadow of the mat on the bedroom window. Guided by Ana María's perfume, he made his way to the bed and sank into it. His hands folded on his chest, he tried to sink into his memory of the night, descend to it, and smash it. The prologue to sleep always promised reconciliations, agreements in which nothing needed to be explained, a definitive and tacit understanding. The fly went on buzzing, looking for the opening in his shirt. Marcos got up and seemed to drag the smell of the sheets and Ana María along with him, on his shoulders, something like threads that instantly fell off.

He left the bedroom, banging his heels on the gallery floorboards, again insulting the backs of the canvas chairs occupied by the women, and then jumping down to the lawn. Standing straight, smiling, wishing he could fight, rejoicing when the stones and thorns hurt his feet, he walked down the path to the river, taking off his shirt and loosening his belt.

The water was cool but not cool enough. He swam, first underwater with his eyes closed. The silent, indifferent, and blind coolness, the form of the water touched his mouth, his nipples, his stomach, and his testicles. All those parts of him became lost in the past, behind the soles of his feet; but the same feelings came back, persistent, punctual, disinterested, to caress his lips, his chest, and his stomach.

He raised his head into the air to breathe and swam toward the imagined, invisible shore while he tried to remember his thoughts to the rhythm of his shoulders as he blew out water and tried to know what it was necessary to think. He turned over on his stomach and unhurriedly returned, his eyes half-closed against the sun, his mouth round and open to spit. He smiled, began to wake up, exaggerating the sensation of cold in his armpits and groin. It was as if the water washed away, along with immediate, recognizable smells, abandoned years and anecdotes in which he'd willfully persisted. Vertical now, happy, his arms spread to tread water and not drift downstream, he began to see the familiar landscape through the drops of water in his eyes. He'd prayed, cunningly, indirectly, for this to happen. He let himself sink and rocked back and forth until he had to breathe; then he surfaced and shook his soaking head under the sun.

He looked at the fields and the beach and had to rack his memory to convince himself he'd seen them on a thousand similar mornings at one time or another beginning when he was a child. However, despite his memories, he was seeing them now for the first time, seeing them as if his eyes were creating them, as if his head or his refusal to see signified the annihilation of the river bank overgrown with weeds, of the summer sun, of the gallery held up by oblique beams and the smallness and colors of the clothes worn by the two lazy women chatting and drinking beer.

Limping, Jorge came out from behind a tree and bent over to pull out a weed. He was wearing blue trousers that were wrinkled and filthy, and his shirt was folded over one shoulder. He was thin, blond, and his ribs pushed against the skin and the sides of his stomach. Now Jorge was down on his haunches, smiling as he chewed a stem, friendly and tolerant. Marcos sat up on the shore and looked at Jorge's white, silent shape, his visible teeth, the bitten stem trembling in the light breeze.

"Sorry about last night," said Marcos, sincere but without conviction.

Jorge shrugged and went on smiling. Now he looked into the distance at the shining water, wrinkling his face into the sun.

"I forgot my sunglasses," said Jorge, slowly and placidly. "I was sure I'd left them next to the radio. But this morning . . ."

The women laughed again; a cup smashed on the gallery floor. Standing up, shouting, Ana María slapped her skirt with both hands.

"The bitches," said Marcos, quickly smiling. "Did you bring any cigarettes? Me either." He hesitated, then sat down next to Jorge, leaning on one arm which in turn was in the sand. "Listen: I'm asking you to forgive me, really, for last night. But I'm partly happy it happened."

"Why? It's not important. A few too many and we

threw some punches." He touched his right cheekbone with a broken fingernail. "It still hurts a little, but it's nothing." With no effort, his protruding teeth formed a smile.

"I didn't want to hit you," said Marcos. "I'm not trying to justify myself, but I didn't want to hit you."

"Nobody's to blame. The thing is you're just too big. It's true. It's also true that I visit Julita almost every night without anything's happening to justify jealousy with or without too much to drink, and that sometimes I think she's crazy and others I don't."

"I know," answered Marcos, turning his head so Jorge could see he was smiling. "Just too much body."

"It isn't that," said Jorge. "Besides, I don't have any. Too much body, too much time in the gym, too strong. You were always like that. And strength is like money: When you've got it, you feel you have to spend it. But it's not important."

Two sculls from the rowing club passed by at a distance heading toward the port; three bare-chested men and one wearing a white shirt rhythmically bent back and forth.

"Right," said Marcos. "Know why I was happy about last night? Because now it's all over."

"It's all over?" Jorge laughed. "What's all over? Oh sure, you swore a few times that you were going to work as a field hand on the ranch. Just like Federico. And you were going to stop drinking and send Ana María to the capital. But you were always drunk when you repented. Now it's morning, and you've just had a swim. Doesn't the ranch belong to your sister? The whole ranch I mean. Because maybe I have a part too."

"Don't talk about my sister," said Marcos rapidly.

Then he added, more softly, "I think Julita's crazy, seriously. This mourning's getting out of hand."

"She'd just gotten married. And she loved Federico. At least that much is true."

The last sentence, as twangy as an insect, hovered over Marcos's closed eyes. Just one hour earlier, he'd been trying to fall asleep on top of Ana María's perfume, underneath the fly's intermittent noise. He remembered tepidly hitting Jorge's face, trying to believe he hated him, that he had faith in the argument and in the punch. Now too he wanted to commit himself, to speak with the hope that the words could transform the feelings he had while swimming into facts.

"Now I want to smoke and get drunk again. But it doesn't matter because it's all over. You have to understand me."

"All right, but what's all over?"

"Everything. That's why I'm happy about last night. Because while I was fighting I began to realize things. You finished yourself off in order to begin, because you're closer to everything. You, you visit my sister, you're Federico for the second and final time. It didn't matter to me then, and whatever happens now doesn't matter either. Don't take offense. And Ana María and the Phalanstery are also finished, like this way of living."

"Okay," said Jorge, while Marcos imagined Jorge's teeth taking a sunbath. "What are you going to do? For example, with the bordello."

"I don't know. Not more than I was doing. Just for starters. And from now on. It's something."

"Well, it might be nothing or too much."

"Now you'll see," said Marcos, "that I'm not as big an idiot as people think. Once, we were drunk, it was when the guy called Blackie came back to Santa María. We were playing a game, telling what we each thought of everyone else. You must remember because I told you in my sister's room."

"Sure, I remember," said Jorge. "And the night ended with a fight, as usual."

"That night," Marcos pronounced slowly; he got up, then sat down with his back to the house and to Jorge. His body was dry and hot again; the surface of the river was empty and foamy, with tiny white cones that floated up and went out like lights.

"That night, not my night with Blackie, but your night and mine with Julita, you tried to tell me what you thought of me. You said you'd only tell me when we separated once and for all, never to see each other again."

"I remember," said Jorge; even his voice sounded different, less bland.

"So you have to tell me now. After lunch, I'm leaving. Will you tell me?"

"Sure, I'll tell you. But I don't want you to feel you don't have to see me anymore just because I told you. Maybe I bother you; but I'm good for you, I'm sure, even if you don't realize it."

"No, I've made up my mind to end all this. When I started swimming, I realized. I didn't think about you at all."

Jorge laughed again, his old laugh, almost all of it.

"When you're drunk, it seems easy. But it's long and very complicated."

"We've got time," said Marcos. He went on smiling because he didn't want to get angry. He was nervous and anxious, acquiescent, with a slight sensation of disgust.

"If you like, we can go to the house and get drunk. If you feel you need to get drunk."

"No, I don't. I never do. I mean that it's more comfortable. I'm always a little afraid I'm going to use the wrong words."

"No matter, let's get on with it," murmured Marcos patiently. Perhaps silence would force the other to talk, perhaps silence would annoy him, like an imposition.

"I'm not going to talk about Julita; not even about Federico. As far as they're concerned, we're closer in opinion than you might think. Are you going to leave Santa María?"

"Yes, I'm going to leave. But anyway, I don't ever want to see you again. And I don't think you'll come looking for me."

"Just as you say," said Jorge. "This isn't something between us, that you must know. All that matters are the years when we were friends, despite the difference in our ages. Now when I think about you, I don't really see you. I don't think about you but about these years. I mean that I think about myself. Almost everything I thought I did I did with you."

"I get you. A little while ago I told you the same thing talking about Ana María, what she was for me. But outside of that, you know or think you know what I'm like."

"Well," said Jorge, laughing again. "I'm not worked up, really It's like getting married. Friendship is over right away, and we go on for no good reason, out of laziness, because the other guy did things with us and is now part of us. I did things, imagining them, with Federico and with you. Federico is dead. I never could talk about it, but you understand. I'm not going to tell you everything I think about you because I couldn't remember it all just like that. The most important things are your body and that you've got money. You've got that body, strength, energy, but it's all useless. Well for women, sure, and for fistfights in Santa María. You're strong and you don't do anything that matters to you with it. That poisons you. As soon as someone new comes to the Phalanstery, you take off your clothes and practice gymnastics so they'll see you. Sometimes you slap Ana María around. But these things don't give you any satisfaction. So you spend your life asking for more. And in Santa María there is no more. That's the way you live, wasting yourself on cheap cruelty. Just to find some meaning to your strength, you impose it on others. But there is no one. You can break a cow or horse's back with a stick. But what can we make out of that? You can go to bed with Ana María and leave the door open; you can threaten everyone in Santa María and all the foreigners in Colonia; you can, like last night, smash every bug that comes close to the lamp. And since you have money, you don't have to waste your energy on anything. You're generous; but I think that's just another way to show how strong you are. You could also say you're a contradictory guy. Contradictory because you want all that on the side, because you're aware that your strength doesn't do you any good. So you're inferior to your strength, inferior to what at first sight you could be. That's why you turn out to be weak. And you want to keep people baffled so they don't figure you out. Now you've come up with this thing about the bordello, now you made up this jealousy thing about your sister, jealousy from before and from last night."

"I don't get that part, I don't believe it," said Marcos with equanimity. "But it doesn't matter. In general, I agree with you. Even though the other guy can't know everything. Isn't there anything good in me? You're right, it doesn't matter. During my whole life I've never done anything but make plans and fool around. The difference between us is that you think, still think, that something's going to happen someday, something you've talked about, projects, desires. I haven't thought that for years. And despite our age difference, we're the same. Until today, as far as I know, you've never done anybody any good. You're like me. You always gave tips, every night you give a tip to my sister. When I write to the ranch, it's a tip. When I kiss Ana María, it's a tip. If we really think about it, we're really screwed. But we don't really have to. Anything else?"

"No, nothing that matters now. I hope it's true that all this is over for you now. I'm young, but you live a poisoned life."

Marcos stood up and smiled again; he stretched his arms and flexed them until he touched his shoulders with his fists.

"Projects and parties; let's see. Anyway, everything you said, I said myself already."

The women had left the gallery, and the smoke from the kitchen floated weakly over the house. Crouching again, with his thin arms wrapped around the knees of his blue trousers, Jorge squinted as he looked at the river. Like a sudden change in the direction and temperature of the wind, solitude, heartbreak, and a rapid maturity entered his narrow, bent body.

"Anyway," said Jorge, showing his teeth, "I can still be your friend."

CHAPTER XX

Twice in one week, the girls from Cooperative Action parked their bicycles in Julita Malabia's garden and marched resolutely up the creaking stairs to finish writing the anonymous letters of the third era. These put us on guard against the pleasures offered by the little house with sky-blue shutters and urged us to reflect on the treacherous nature of those pleasures and the disproportionate price we risked having to pay for them.

During these two meetings, the girls were made more uncomfortable and were more disconcerted by the new, rejuvenated Julita, now gay and neatly dressed, than they had been in the company of the earlier version, who was badly dressed, unkempt, whose face was distracted and greasy.

In two afternoons, working with scarcely a pause, refusing to take part in the frivolous chitchat the widow proposed with exaggerated cordiality, they almost completed their task.

They learned how to defend themselves from the atmosphere of resurrection that surrounded Julita. That air seemed atrocious to the girls because they knew in their heart of hearts that she wasn't behaving that way merely for them. But there she was, doggedly maintaining and propagating it. They heard her give shouts of joy standing at windows open onto the dry, hot landscape; they saw her sudden flights to the mirror, the cigarettes she smoked in silence with a mocking, little-girl look on the mouth that held them; they put up with her questions and answers, which followed hard on each other's heels, with no interruption: questions about the bordello, municipal indignation, and about the letters they were writing.

In those two meetings, the girls almost finished their job, closing in on the last name on the list on the previous series of anonymous notes, those of the second era. Unfortunately, no visible catastrophe, no impressive, collective disaster had come along to match the capsizing of the boat on the Rinconada.

The League of Decency, or League of Knights as it was called then, was not founded or suggested by the priest Bergner, although many people in Santa María still think it was. It came into existence a few years before the establishment of the brothel for the specific purpose of keeping the only movie house in Santa María from showing a German film on childbirth that included details of a Caesarean section. The League of Decency, founded by the priest Peña—a little old man from Andalusia who died of an angina attack and who was replaced by Father Bergner—consisted of four farmers from Colonia, and a businessman from town, Ramallo, the hardware man, father of the current Ramallo.

They had no trouble whatsoever in keeping the good people of Santa María from seeing the film. The owner of the theater was a Swiss who instantly understood the advantages in losing the business he thought he'd get by showing the scientific film.

The result was that the members of the League of Decency, after hearing the Swiss's explanations and accepting his promise not to show the film, after deciding to pay—out of their own pockets—his expenses for renting the film and for the advertising he'd taken out, probably innocently and with no bad intentions, immediately found themselves with nothing to do.

Separately and in a friendly way, they visited the shops beginning to open around the lot covered with weeds and delineated by useless chains that was set aside to be the plaza. With no difficulty, they obtained promises from all the owners that none of the future display windows would contain feminine underwear. Later they had a warning published in EL LIBERAL concerning the dangers of magazines sent in from the capital. Father Peña repeated this warning from the pulpit on three successive Sundays, at much greater length, much more comprehensibly, and much more severely.

The League maintained its secret, theoretical existence until Father Peña's death; his successor, Father Bergner, could find no practical, immediate purpose for the League when he took charge of the parish. But because he was intelligent, providential, and liked organizing things, he took the League in hand, changed its name to the League of Catholic Knights of Santa María, and set about replacing the farmers who made it up with elements of the "intelligentsia" starting to appear in the city. From then until the opening of the bordello, the League of Knights limited itself to acting as an advisory body for Father Bergner, to raising funds for the construction of the church, and to supplying scholarships to seminary students. The League of Knights also published admonitions and judgments about books, magazines, films, fashions, and mores in Santa María's newspapers—besides EL LIBERAL we also had EL ORDEN.

After his first bellicose sermon, Father Bergner behaved as if he had forgotten the problem, as if he knew nothing of the presence of the women in the house on the coast and the visits the men paid them. He celebrated Christmas and then, on New Year's Day, when the feast of Saint Silvester was celebrated—January first fell on a Sunday that year—he wished the faithful filling the church, those who could not come as well as those who would not come, a year of happiness, repentance, and moral improvement. He asked God this grace and made no references to the bordello.

But when Mass was over, he asked all five members of the League of Knights to come to the church lecture room on Monday at seven o'clock. I don't know what they discussed and resolved at that meeting, which was declared secret even before it began. From the secrets that leaked out much later despite all the vows, it seems that Father Bergner made the League of Knights see the gravity of the threat as well as the scandal now introduced into the city. It's almost certain that he revealed to them the source of the anonymous letters in blue ink that kept all the rest of us apprehensive and on the alert, that he encouraged the five men listening to him to be inspired by the action of the girls in Action, to imitate them, and to give them the audacious, unhesitating support they needed and deserved.

The Knights, it was easy to see, agreed and proceeded rapidly. Beginning the next afternoon, at six in the afternoon on Tuesday, January third, a car—there were three and they rotated daily—appeared, parked just a few yards from the house with the blue siding and on the other side of the dirt road.

At first, the car was there around the clock; then the Knights realized it was useless to expect guilty parties to appear during the morning hours: the women slept until noon, and even if they didn't always sleep alone, their companions, who entered the white light of summer bedazzled and hesitated for a long time at the sky-blue entrance, as if they had just been born or were returning from a distant land and were finding it painful to acclimate themselves to the city, were, in any case, already on the list compiled by the preceding patrol, which ended its tour of duty at dawn.

Inside the cars, smoking, almost always silent, nudging each other with their elbows, hissing to each other, with huge revolvers under their arms, were the three men that made up each patrol—sons and nephews of the Knights of the League, young friends of the sons and nephews. They stood their watch and tried to use an exaggerated indignation about the men who had knocked and entered to compensate for the boredom they felt when there was no one.

Any idea they might have had that they were ridiculous or that they were carrying out acts of espionage was destroyed, dissolved by the idea that they were doing their social duty, by their sense of passive heroism. This they created virtually out of monosyllables, nurturing it all afternoon and night. The solitude, the hardness of the revolvers in their armpits, and the monotonous distance that twisted its way down toward the invisible river and the shacks in Enduro also reinforced their feelings. They thought they were witnesses and judges, that the short, irregular lines they were writing out by the light of the dashboard could modify a destiny or change someone's idiosyncrasies.

Thanks to them, the new era of anonymous letters could begin. They were vastly superior to the first ones in terms of accuracy: They mentioned names, times, and dates. Very soon, we were all convinced that the anonymous letters were true, that those denounced in them had visited the little house and on exactly the day mentioned in the letter. From this exactness, from the absence of any intention to get revenge or simply to calumniate anyone, was born the strength of the letters sent by the girls in Action. As we read them, we did not think about anonymous letters, we did not imagine the people who had written them, or who had done the spying. It was in reality as if a superior power were pointing out to the guilty parties and others that it was impossible to defend oneself hypocritically against the wages of sin.

It's been years since all that happened. Evoking it now makes us think we're seeing Santa María and its inhabitants just as they were and not as we saw them then. Nothing essential links us with what we remember; but, fundamentally, this distance is not the result of time but of disinterest.

Santa María and the land around it contain no significant elevations. The city, Colonia, all the landscape visible, let's say, from a plane, slopes gently until it reaches the river. It forms a semicircle. Going up from the river, the land is flat and even, with no notable high point except the mountains. But now, as I tell the story of the city and Colonia during the months of the invasion, even though I'm telling it for myself and making no commitment to precision or to literature, writing it to amuse myself now in this moment, I imagine there is a ridge next to the city, and that from there I can see houses and people, laugh or feel anguish. I can do anything, feel anything, but I cannot intervene or change anything.

I also imagine Santa María from my humble height like a toy city, a naive system of white cubes and green cones through which slow, indefatigable insects are walking. Then I see the diminutive town and understand its geometry, its heights, its balance; I understand, because of its almost invariable reiteration, the reasons why the insects are nervous. But I cannot discover an indubitable reason why all this exists, so I'm shocked, bored, and discouraged. When discouragement weakens my desire to write—and I do think there is in this labor something of obligation, something of salvation—I prefer to play the game that consists in supposing that Santa María, Colonia, even the river never existed.

That way, when I imagine I invent everything I write, things acquire a meaning, an inexplicable meaning, true enough, but one I could only doubt if I simultaneously doubted my own existence. There was never anything before, or at least, nothing more than a stretch of beach and some fields along the river. I invented the plaza and its statue, I made the church, I laid out the streets that lead to the coast, I put the promenade next to the docks and determined where Colonia would be.

It's easy to draw a map of the whole area and a plan for Santa María in addition to giving it a name. But you've also got to put a special light in each store, each doorway, each corner. You've got to give a form to the low clouds that drift over the church steeple and the flat roofs with their cream and pink balustrades; you've got to dole out disgusting furniture, accept things you hate, bring in people from who knows where so that they can take up residence, dirty things, move us to tears, be happy, and waste themselves. And, during the game, I have to give them bodies, the need for love and money, different and identical ambitions, a never-examined faith in immortality and in the idea that they deserve immortality; I have to give them the ability to forget things, along with guts and unmistakable faces.

There is no doubt that the League of Knights was revived by Father Bergner and that he organized it, set it in motion, and transformed it—we have to remember the general mediocrity of the Knights he had at his disposal—into an efficient, disciplined weapon, almost always up to the operations it had to carry out.

If we stick to the facts, we can accept, following certain historians, that Father Bergner committed one error: He put himself on the defensive and never attacked until the enemy had breached the walls of his fortress. In the salacious, direct account of these events that Lanza, the proofreader at EL LIBERAL, seems to have written, he reveals the passivity of the priest right from the start. It's true that Lanza has only allowed a few pages of his work to be seen and even then not always to people who could recount them accurately. Some fragments, nevertheless, whether he knows it or not, were copied and may be consulted. And on more than one occasion, Lanza commented to Malabia's son and to others in the Berna, when talking about the attitude of the priest during our unforgettable emergency:

"I just can't understand why the hell this guy stood back and let things happen without saying a word until we were up to our ears in sluts."

The most believable explanation is that Father Bergner wouldn't admit that such a thing could actually happen. We all accept that death exists and that it will visit each one of the beings we know, but it's impossible to believe that we too are going to die. Well, the priest felt (we assume) that bordellos, undeniable realities, although they exist merely as theories, could establish themselves and function in the capital, in Rosario, in Salto, or even in some dirt-floored hovel in a nameless hamlet, almost anywhere in the country or the world except Santa María. And he believed these things without vanity, with no other defect but innocence, because it was in Santa María that he officiated at Mass, baptized babies, used, wisely and with inspiration, the pressure of his big hands to facilitate the passing of the moribund.

The most laborious and perhaps the most truthful explanation, the one most widely accepted by revisionist historians, tells us that Father Bergner knew that this time, this year, the ideal of Barthé the pharmacist was being nurtured by the votes of the conservative members of the town council. With resolution, with irrefutable evidence, it may be proven still today that the small, faded, blinking Dr. Díaz Grey, willingly transformed into destiny's agent, into messenger boy for Arcelo, Barthé, and

Body Snatcher, brought his objectivity, his desire for nul-
lification, to the point of informing the priest that the
representatives of the people had reached an agreement
about the so-often-defeated bordello project. So the priest
knew the devil was coming to Santa María and chose to
allow him to enter.

If we persist in this explanation and want to go about
it properly, we'll have to accept that at this point it bi-
furcates. One branch contains a Father Bergner who foresaw the coming of the moment promised to all, although
the offer is only rarely carried through, in which he would
have the opportunity to realize himself totally as an individual and servant of the Lord. He would be, without
any mutilations, Anton Bergner. He would face up to and
fight a manifestation of evil that had a stature and a
strength worthy of his hitherto unused possibilities. He
would be up against someone who had all the elusive,
personal, uncertain characteristics, all the wretchedness
of sin, of imperfection, that the priest had to withstand
every day, like fleeting plagues, like someone who can't
decide between an origin of frequent repentance or rachitic vanity during the tongue-tied routine of confession.

The other branch of the confused explanation leads
us to a Father Bergner who wanted, accepted, and per-
mitted the arrival and the settling in of evil so that the
inhabitants of Santa María and Colonia, the sheep left
to his care, would have their collective, obvious opportunity for temptation, combat, and triumph. So that they
would show—not to him; he didn't count, he could only
pray, whatever the results might be—their will to achieve
salvation while still on earth.

But independent of the veracity of the theories that

explain Father Bergner's slowness in opposing the realization of Barthé's ancient project, the one indisputable
fact, the one Lanza himself, with increased perplexity,
recognizes, is that from the moment the priest decided,
for one reason or another, to take up the fight, he kept
at it until the end in exemplary fashion.

CHAPTER XXI

Moving at the same speed I've moved at on so many other nights, knowing that without wanting to I'm copying gestures I've made on so many other nights, feeling pride, melancholy, and postponements revive in me, I stop writing.

I button my shirt, I put on my beret and then pull it down over one eye. After putting out the light, I go to the window to look for the moon, see it smashed in the garden, smell the flowers, and look at Julita's door. My face is hardened, resolved, composed by me alone: I don't know what it expresses.

As I walk downstairs, I think about an unknown plant, I think about the best—which is almost never visible—in every person, I think about the situation I'm in with Julita, my dead brother, and the baby she doesn't have inside her stomach.

I stop halfway through the garden; I'm opposite Rita's darkened window. I remember stopping on this same spot on other nights with the same tricky smile on my face. "Like a good husband," I mutter, just to annoy myself as I put the key in the lock. Holding the door motionless in the shadow of the vestibule, I wait in vain for the church bell to ring eleven times; the wind must have changed direction. I discover huge clouds that stretch out while they climb toward the moon.

Humiliated and protective, I announce my arrival using the smooth explosion of the steps; I open the door and walk in. There are no wrinkled pieces of male clothing on the chairs, the bed has a new, light-colored spread, she's wearing a sky-blue nightdress that reaches her shiny shoes. She's sitting next to the fireplace on a very low chair. She doesn't look up at me but merely slides a wide bracelet up and down her left forearm. The nape of her neck is hidden by a hairdo she could not have arranged by herself.

My decision to stop putting up with this climbs through my body again and leans me, holds me against the wooden door. On the little table are a bottle and two almost-full glasses. She won't show me her face until she comes over and speaks to me. I'm discovering that my undefined resolution not to go on putting up with this is the same as my desire, an old one I've postponed a hundred times, to slap her, just once, with all my strength.

I want to call her, but I hold back. Hatred dries out my tongue. I'm as sorry for myself as I would be for an irreplaceable, lost friend. She won't turn around. She takes another drink. Her short laugh, so short that no jokes, no happiness, and no expectations could fit inside it, mixes with the noise of the glass on the table. All I want to find out about is her narrow, round, sky-blue shoulder. When I try to distract myself by figuring what kind of madness Julita has invented for this evening, she abruptly turns her head to show me her face, which is serious and alert, as if she'd just taken off a mask. The falsity may be seen in the imperious, long movement of her arm, which she uses to offer me a drink.

"Hello, Jorge," she says, as if she'd been practicing the greeting.

I'm Jorge, nothing more than Jorge, alive and lucid, sorry I felt that impulse to abandon myself. But I've stepped down from my mature attitude and take up my position next to the fireplace.

We drink, cautiously scrutinizing each other, pretending to take anxious swallows. I sit down and curl up in front of her. She smiles and again plays with her bracelet, sliding it in a spiral from her wrist to her elbow. Her arm is tan; I can't imagine the moments when she's been out of the house and in the sun. I think all this must be absurd, impossible to understand, incapable of being formed into past times and compromises.

"Jorge," she repeats, so I won't be confused about who I am. "I've been waiting for you since this afternoon. I mean that since this afternoon I've been waiting for eleven o'clock to come so I could see you and talk to you. I think starting tomorrow I'm going to eat in the dining room. It doesn't matter to me anymore, I haven't any reason to stay locked up. If you only knew . . . Days, over a week ago, I discovered the truth. But I didn't really know I'd discovered it. I didn't know until today. Do you understand? And so, since I had it inside me for so long, I couldn't wait until you came and I could tell you."

There's something strange in the bedroom. I look at

the new bedspread, the clean, orderly furniture, the figures in the carpet at the foot of the bed. I take a drink
and light my pipe as I listen to her and look at her with
the most infantile expression I can muster tonight.

"Doesn't it matter to you? Don't you realize that everything's different?"

"Yes, I feel that everything is different, but I don't
understand."

"Tomorrow I'm going out. I'm going to eat with all
of you and live in the house."

She looks at me, searching for my astonishment, as if
she hadn't said it before. Then her face calms down,
becomes sad, with a sadness that comes from outside and
settles on her skin without penetrating it, without putting
any pressure on it.

"How can I explain this to you? In what way should
I tell it to you?" she asks herself, showing the fireplace
her immobile, well-displayed smile.

I confirm that I no longer believe in her or her setting.
I admit to having doubted her madness for some weeks
now. So, I think, something's going to happen, something's coming to an end tonight.

Since I don't answer, she has to hide her teeth and
pull her head back. Her sky-blue body retreats, standing
erect. Suddenly, she's left in isolation on her chair, her
knees even with her navel, her hairdo intensely yellow,
the expression on her lips no longer congruent with the
outline she made on them with her lipstick. Alone on the
low chair in the center of the room, she's separated from
me and my memory of Federico.

"I think you're a bit stupid tonight," she says sweetly,
the smile she no longer has on her face illuminating her

voice, making it persuasive and tolerant, emphasizing gifts, patience, secrets.

"I always was. Sometimes I think I was an idiot from the beginning. I never wanted to tell you, because it doesn't matter to me and because you wouldn't have understood. Just as I don't understand you."

She looks at me and narrows her eyes. Now her smile does not suggest ecstasy: It's white, happy, narrow, and totally her own. It's the smile that she used to ask me tender, common questions before my brother became ill.

"Jorge, please . . ."

I raise my hand, but she thinks I'm trying to protect myself with my five fingers, with the moisture on the palm I turn toward her.

"We've always understood each other. . . . That's the reason I'm alive, really, that's the only reason, because we've always understood each other. I wasn't reproaching you, it was just a joke, I'm the stupid one because I had the silly idea, the lazy thought that you could guess everything without my having to talk."

I get up, go to the fireplace, and knock the ash out of my pipe. I don't listen to the things she goes on saying in the same tone my mother uses to explain how serious the future is, to enumerate my privileges, and to convince me that my father gave up something for my well-being. I empty my pipe and suck at the stem. I go over to the window, but I don't have the nerve to open it. Her sweetened voice goes on explaining my long comprehension of the past, transforming these eleven o'clock interviews into high-school classes.

"You could understand each one of my mistakes, you were never afraid, never thought I was insane. You were

Federico, you knew you were Federico. And it was a lie; it passed. You knew I was going to have Federico's child, you knew Federico was dead. And all that turned out to be a lie as well. But before it was a lie, you knew just as well as I knew. Don't tell me you didn't, don't tell me you didn't believe it."

"No. That's right. It doesn't matter to me that it's a lie today. It wasn't a lie for me."

I said it with my slow, serious man's voice, which didn't fade, didn't crack. I can open the window, smell the air, reconstruct the landscapes in the darkened distance, feel I'm alone and stronger. But I am afraid of bouncing off the blackness and going back toward her, toward all that, humiliated and even younger.

"Well, Jorge? How can you say we don't understand each other, that you've been stupid from the beginning?"

I don't want to look at her. She's talking as if she'd been crying and now, consoled, she's trying to laugh to please me. Something important happened, something's finished forever, and I'm not happy about it. The photos of Federico have disappeared from the walls, the mantel, and the little table. I'm alone for the first time in my life, and for the first time in my life, the idea of solitude doesn't anguish me. So much the worse for her, I think, because I look at her again and don't desire her, and it's as if I had always despised her and wanted to knock her down, the way it must be with whores.

"Don't stay so far away," she says. "Today we've got to talk. Today I have to explain the truth to you. Tomorrow you'll see how from now on everything will be marvelous. Beginning tomorrow, right now. You know, when you discover the truth, you think everybody knows it and there's no need to say it."

She's lying again, but now she doesn't believe her lies. She's sitting on the low chair, not using the backrest, desperate, twisted. The shine on her old, sagging, beggarwoman's face is turned toward me like a hand or a claw, like a spotlight. She's losing her footing and only her defects are holding her up. Before, on other nights, pity protected her and separated me from her. Now it separates me from myself. I want to push her aside, to be and to know myself.

She asks a question. I avoid the hand that comes to touch my head.

"All of this," I say. "What was I doing here? Why did I come every night? Who was I? Because I wasn't here, I didn't count. It didn't occur to you to think that I was someone else, that I wasn't Federico, that I wasn't you, or God, or a piece of furniture. I'm alive, I'm not Federico, not Federico's son. I'm someone else, I told you. I was always someone else."

She empties her glass and gets up. The sky-blue dress swings back and forth, close to the floor, spreads and closes. Julita bends over to smooth the bedspread, rearranges the sweet peas in the vase on the night table; I see her standing straight, still smiling, flicking a flower with the index finger of one hand, resting her other hand on her backside.

"Absurd," she says, waiting for me to ask.

Still looking at her, I refuse to light my pipe, I stop paying any attention to her madness, I see her, blonde, almost thirty, thin, wide, infantile.

"Isn't it absurd?" she insists. I hear her say "My God" several times. Then she throws herself onto the bed.

I say something because I have to, not at all concerned that she listen to me:

"It is absurd, it's all absurd. So what? I was here all those nights and during the days as well. I would come and listen to you, the two of us playing your game, the Federico game. But I have other games to play, other misfortunes. I don't know how important they are, but they are my misfortunes. And they were my misfortunes, I had them inside me, while I came to sit here and listen to the lies with which you tried to defend yourself. Maybe not, maybe you really are mad. If you are, you won't suffer because I say so, if you aren't mad, then you deserve to hear it."

"Jorge," she says, "Jorge . . ."

Looking at the unlit pipe, I know, as if I had seen her, that she narrowed her eyes, that she's smiling at the ceiling, and that she's doing everything possible to heighten the pity she feels for herself.

"Don't go on talking that way. I don't want you to be sorry for having told me. . . ."

"I know I'm not going to be sorry. But every night I would be sorry because I didn't tell you, and also all the next day. I was sorry as I walked downstairs to the garden every night. Shall I go on or leave? I'll listen to whatever it is you want to tell me, then I'll go."

"No, no," she says, and I understand that she feels herself strongly again, that she's sure she hasn't lost me. "It's better you say everything. You should have told me before."

"Before I couldn't, and I don't know why. I don't know why I can today."

"I'm happy you can, I want to listen to you. It's better, necessary that you say it all. I want to tell you everything too. It's going to be like beginning over, but now with the truth. Give me some cognac."

I bring her my glass and leave it on the little table so she doesn't have to move to drink it. She's staring at the ceiling with her arms crossed. Her face is rounder, younger. I start to leave, but she calls me. I stop with my back to her.

"Jorge."

"Yes?"

If my brother can remember, he'll probably remember with some frequency that horizontal face, plump at the chin, under the ears, and in the cheeks. Again, with a different, more profound and less hopeful, curiosity, he will bend over the brilliance of those teeth and eyes, over the ambush in those lips and half-shut eyes.

She puts the empty glass down on the little table and coughs. Now she makes herself comfortable with her arms at her sides, with the same smile of willful placidity. Pregnant or not—every one of her lies may step forward tonight and occupy a space in the world—her sky-blue dress forms a curve over her belly, clings between her legs. Partially moved, I recognize her madness in her velvet slippers with their enormous heels, unused, still shiny where the sole curves.

CHAPTER XXII

On Sunday nights, bored and old, Larsen would think about María Bonita, about when her name was Nora, about the series of phony names of forgotten origin that stretched between the first and the last. He evoked the capital, bent curiously over a time and an impulse that now seemed to him alien, dead, and, nevertheless, as surprising as unexpected news. His hand unnecessarily held up his face, his sleepy eyes on the disconnected parade of memories and doubts, the unpremeditated escapes toward parts of the city without familiar names, incredible places, toward intersections overheard in a conversation or discovered in advertisements for sales.

For hours, between lunch and nightfall, he would sit there over a coffee cup filled with cigarette ashes, and examine, through smeared windows where white letters often slithered to announce the imminent visit of billiard and guitar players, the landscape of the slums, wires covered by creepers, repair shops filled with automobile skeletons, awnings bent back by the wind clinging to the brick façades of shops with feminine names.

He would walk along the worn-out or recently opened streets, trampling the tenacity of the weeds poking up between the paving stones, memorizing streets, imperfect corners, shops with memorable merchandise. And all for nothing, as he found out later.

It came without his having looked for it determinedly, like a simple consequence of tenacity and faith: the time of the car, the apartment, the shirts made of Japanese silk, freedom from all undesired promiscuity. And when, dangerously, he'd begun to believe that all of it was the truth, when he felt himself sharing his friends' pride and ambition, the providential catastrophe came: six months in jail, exile to the interior.

In jail, he could verify that María Bonita's prudence and immorality were somehow in agreement with what they essentially were, the ideals they'd been defining during their hours of boredom and renunciation. She would arrive punctually, stocked with jokes, encouragement, cigarettes, cynical advice, clean clothes.

She was there the moment visiting time began, her mouth swollen as if she were afraid to laugh out loud, casting her short, inescapable glances of defiance and pity over the faces of the guards. She would comment on how thin Larsen was, show off each gift, and enumerate, until it was time to leave, the events of the lost world, the monotonous vicissitudes of women and friends. And not as if it mattered to her or that she thought it mattered to

Snatcher, but patiently, encouragingly, honestly, as if she'd found out somewhere that it was proper to talk about such things, appropriate to the circumstances.

When the six months were up, he concluded he'd been born to achieve two perfections: a perfect woman and a perfect bordello. For the first, he would need the complicity of Providence, in finding the hypothetical girl born for such a destiny; for the second, it was absolutely necessary to have money and a free hand.

Shortly after getting out of jail, fed up with being followed or having young men in white raincoats walk into the café to ask to see his papers or fat, mocking detectives make him wait for hours before listening to him construct explanations about how he earned his living, he decided to go to the interior in search of both things, the woman and the money to set up the house.

María Bonita refused to go with him, and he understood that she was right, that it was better for both of them: the future perfect woman had to come to him without experience or deformations. But the girl never appeared; nor did the opportunity to create the dream house, which became more expensive and more impossible with each day that passed as he improved it in his solitude in cheap cafés and boardinghouse beds. He had to live somehow while the years slipped by; and since he'd have to live for the moment when he'd stumble over the girl or could inaugurate the perfect whorehouse, he committed himself not to look at himself, not to make judgments, not to know anything about the grotesque man he was becoming.

He had to live somehow, which is why he invented the business of the poor, old, worn-out, and disdained whores.

Impassive at the center of ironic stares in restaurants that served stew at dawn, smiling at the fiftyish fat ones, the bony old ones in party dresses, paternal and tolerant, always there to listen and give advice, he showed that for him anyone who could manage to earn money and who had the necessary and desperate confidence to give it to him was still a woman. That's how he won the name Body Snatcher, won sufficient beatitude to answer to that nickname with no other protest than a small smile of cunning and commiseration.

If he'd had the slightest suicidal impulse, the courage necessary to stop in front of a mirror, interrupt his siesta and examine his conscience, he'd have found he was exactly like the image of a long-haired, threadbare violinist playing medleys and waltzes from operettas without the permission of the owner in second-class cafés located in third-class cities. There he'd be, his head held high, variously scornful, his large mouth fixed in a smile that could withstand any interpretation, confident that something essential was safe as long as he didn't pawn the greasy, darkened violin, as long as he didn't play tangos, as long as he protected his music from the accompaniment of drunks and disgusting women, as long as, every three numbers, he could make the rounds of the tables and hold out a tiny metal tray onto which fell the coins he could empty into the pockets of his black jacket without having the skin on his hands participate in the joy and humiliation. Sometimes showing a yellowed concert program, worn out in the folds, hard to unfold, with his still-recognizable photo on it, with the word *Wien* underlined in red by himself so that it could be found rapidly among the others, which were incomprehensible, and pursued by diaereses and curves devoid of sweetness.

Still, for years Snatcher patrolled dance halls, slowly, swaggering, skillfully constructing the simulacrum of security and calm appropriate to the man he imagined himself to be, distributing false greetings with a slow, cold hand and sitting down at a table to offer his love and consolation to the piece of debris whose turn it happened to be. As if he'd dragged a valise filled with junk over to the rough, badly lighted corner, opened it onto the table, and skillfully but unenthusiastically put his merchandise on display, certain that no vendor could ever convince a customer, certain that in the act of buying, of paying a price for something, the only thing that matters is an obscure combination of vanity and sacrifice. He was offering an acceptable substitute for hope, for overwhelming masculine desire, for the lukewarm experience that can console, understand, and tolerate, almost without limits.

He would set up his tent, his cheek touched by four manicured nails, the cigarette holder between his teeth, his other hand grasping the tiny glass, at a table set faraway from the dance floor, near the spring door and the enameled sign: LADIES. Every woman in the place would pass by there more than once over the course of the night, not hurrying, not slowly, raising an indifferent expression. He didn't waste time looking at them or insinuating the good qualities of the merchandise he was offering. Everyone knew who he was and what he could give to them or ask of them. The women he liked, those who were still young, still pretty, who blinked over his patience at the table next to the bathrooms, who revived old projects and attitudes in an ephemeral way, who were impossible, had no good reason to be with him. The others, those already corralled by old age and the absence of a man, would come on their own, one night or another, sit down at his table, and ask permission to get drunk. Their stories almost always began that way, and if he had had humor and memory enough to compare them, he would have noted that all their stories were in fact one single story, one single inevitable event in the lives of all women, like puberty, menopause, and death. He knew how to listen with the appropriate gravity and smiles; he knew how to pat a scarred hand with bulging veins, the kind of hand that can no longer be hidden; he knew how to make fun of their apprehensions and repeat expressions of affirmation and optimism with measured spontaneity. He never offered vague consolations, never mentioned the well-deserved rewards they would surely receive some day: He offered himself, lying in state, from that night forward.

Without asking, he knew how to get the bedazzled woman to pay the bill for her own drinking; that way their future days were free of erroneous or confused interpretations. And every time, in the epilogue of those wedding nights, when the fat or skeletal cadaver he'd just added to his collection or herd decided, always provisionally, to stop her tears, her puking, or the worn-out tender phrases she whispered between his shoulder and ear, Snatcher would raise the cigarette stuffed into the holder toward the ceiling and meditate for a few moments on that failure, on that sensation of failure, linked to all women over forty, and seeming to be waiting for them from the beginning, from birth or adolescence, like a robber along a road. Or it was a failure the women carried within themselves and fed with their own blood to which, some inevitable day, they would give birth in order to see themselves strangled by it, by failure, so they could then blame their existence on the others, on the world, on the God they imagined after turning forty.

This sense of shipwreck—which he saw take place independently of any imaginable circumstance—this biological condemnation to disillusion, linked all women to him. But, at the same time, since female failure was irremediable, and he, to the contrary, had not yet spoken his last word, he could behave like an older brother with them, understand them before the fact, without having to hear them lie; he could direct them and use their money to buy them cheap, daily, and concrete stimuli.

CHAPTER XXIII

As if he knows I'm thinking about the time, my father interrupts himself to take out of his vest pocket the gold, triple-covered Omega that bears an inscription speaking about goodness and probity, the watch the employees of EL LIBERAL gave my grandfather twenty-five years ago. Blue-shirted workers, failures in bow ties from the editorial office, slumped-over characters from the business office wearing glasses and cloth protectors over their shirt-sleeves. All rotten by now, I hope; all of them at that time gathering together, like coins collected for a collective party, their repugnant, soft individualities, their similar odors of tobacco, laundered shirts, sweat, bachelorhood or matrimonial bliss, conceit and servitude.

My mother knits with her head tilted forward; she's either counting stitches or praying. I don't know why she's got a yellow flower hanging from the brooch on her bosom. For a long, long time, she's known she's a wife and mother; I've always known her with either one face or the other: the sweet, impersonal eyes, the kindly and embittered mouth, varying the proportions according to the day. I think I remember that at one time I tried to imagine how her face would be if she weren't a blessed mother and a faithful spouse, if she weren't anything but a woman. However, after Federico died, I found out that the mask was definitive, that it would go on destroying her over the years with no more real changes. She's looking at me attentively, begging me to be a good boy; she looks at my father tenderly, a bit admiringly; I don't know what she's thinking about—maybe she's not thinking about anything. When my father goes back to strolling between the window and the table, I see that it's ten to eleven by the wall clock. Julita's probably beginning to wait for me.

"You will inherit some money," my father repeats; I distractedly suspect he interrupted himself and took out his watch because he didn't know how to go on. "I don't know how much, perhaps only a little, perhaps enough. In any case, much less than I would have wanted to leave you, less, I'm sure, than you deserve." He rests his hand on the table and smiles at me sadly. Modest, he instantly averts his eyes.

I'm sixteen; I understand that tenderness between men has to be a veiled thing. My mother looks at us, looks over the table, up to the vase, over the black pile made up of the photo album, EL LIBERAL's first account book, annotated by my grandfather, and the Bible imported by her grandmother. She's at the center of the wave of tenderness and understanding flowing back and forth between father and son, uniting them in this after-dinner gathering. She sighs to show she's participating and then goes back to moving her needles.

I shake my head and smile. I want to say that money doesn't interest me, that I don't deserve anything, and that my father is immortal. He might be expecting just that because he exerts considerable pressure on the table with his fingers before he gets up and continues talking.

"But I think—who knows if you can understand it today—I'm going to leave you an example. I don't mean an example for you to follow. I understand that we're all different, and the fact that you're my son . . ."

I come from him, from that body, from that walk, from the things he believes in, from the motions he makes as he puts his hands in his pockets and then caresses and weighs his belly. I can't find another expression of touched, reflexive idiocy for my face. I change the position of my legs and start to tangle my fingers in the fringe on the table cloth.

"I shall leave you . . . the image, the memory of a father you won't have to be ashamed of. I hope to leave you a business, EL LIBERAL, a newspaper, which, I must say, is something of which Santa María and the nation can be proud. Not that I created it; I found it in place, all I did was interpret someone else's will, someone else's wisdom. Perhaps you, having a different education, the child of a different age . . ."

He doesn't finish saying what it is I might do with the newspaper. I try to tie the fringes into a sailor knot, and I remember the dramatic days, the expressive silences, the mutually planned avoidances that took place three or four years ago when Federico left the newspaper and said he wanted to get married and work in the country. They thought it was a good idea for him to marry Julita because she was rich and a good rather than a strange person. But Federico was their firstborn and was supposed to take his place in the newspaper tradition of the Malabias, write editorials about the price of sunflower seeds, about Santa María, bulwark of the purest traditions, Santa María, bold standard-bearer of progress. He was supposed to believe that our grandfather—small, round beard, short nose, positive eyes—would have accomplished, written great things if he had been able to renounce the civilizing, apostolic mission of making a small fortune out of two linotype machines and a rusty Marinoni press.

The result was that my father decreed a week of mourning, nostalgia, and making amends, all as a tribute to grandfather and to himself, the sustainer. A silent reproach, after the shouts, the exhortations, and the dusty anecdotes uselessly tried to stir Federico out of his tedium, ingratitude, and lack of understanding.

It's eleven ten; if I make Julita wait too long, the lies and inventions she stockpiles for these nights ferment, become deformed, impatient, get all mixed up in her mouth and eyes, try to jump out on me, confused, hating each other, destroying their individual meanings.

"Money was never important to me," says my father, serious, his legs spread, his head nodding resolutely. He's not sorry about this aspect of his character and is always ready to suffer the consequences.

"I know," I say in a tone of high emotion. Either the fringes or my fingers are no good for making sailor knots. An expression of sensible disdain for money in conversations not directly related to money is another family tradition. My mother drops her knitting onto her lap, and picks up what's left of the cold herb tea in her cup. She looks over at my father, accentuating the habitual sweetness in her face, almost smiling, republishing tolerance, old forgiveness for loans she could never collect, debts never called in. He turns toward me and raises his hand; he's got a face like the one I'm vainly trying to compose: good-natured, distracted, slightly dumb.

"Because I—I want you to pay close attention—could be happy even if I lost everything, everything except you two and a typewriter. It might even be a favor."

I'm struggling to show him the most appropriate smile, an undefined enthusiasm in my eyes. He looks ridiculous, fat, solemn, and false. But, in this very instant, I know that I love him, that I feel love and pity for him, that I will always respect the undefinable virtue I imagine him to have underneath all his defects. If I could believe he mentioned the typewriter because he read my poems or knows I write them . . . But I heard him say the same thing years ago, give the same bravura performance during an argument with Federico. It's a quarter past eleven; fortunately my mother gets up and goes over to kiss him.

Hanging onto his shoulder, she looks at me and smiles. I think: She isn't a person, a woman; she's my mother. She has no face: Her nose, forehead, mouth, height are only the steps she's taken to be my mother. She smiles at me to tell me my father's right, that I shouldn't associate with friends who go to or who even go near the little house on the coast, and that, nevertheless, whatever happens, she has faith in me and is on my side.

"Someday you'll understand all this," says my father, extricating himself from her embrace without violence.

"You'll understand our motives, you'll understand us. And what seems intolerance to you today . . . Someday you'll have your own children."

My mother laughs without joy, as if she were alone and remembered.

"The opinions of this grumbling old man . . ."

My father smiles, puts an expression of security and nostalgia on his face, looks, without any visible impatience, without humiliating himself, for some kind of emotion on my face that will allow him to end the interview. It's almost eleven twenty. I get up and let them see the tears in my eyes.

"My boy," he says, satisfied, patting me on the back. My mother kisses me and says, for his benefit: "Don't stay up writing now. Don't smoke too much. And don't go to bed late."

"I'm going to take a little walk," I say, ashamed. My profile turned toward them, as they embrace again, I put on my beret, drape my raincoat over my shoulder, and, for the first time, show my pipe. Three infantile manias that make my mother laugh; she does laugh.

"I didn't know it was raining," says my father, looking at my raincoat. I say good night, and with consoled heart, bent over in a laborious child's gait, cross the room, leaving them as I walk out into the garden.

It's hot, and the sky, filled with stars, is dark red. I open and close the door, as if I had gone up to the bedroom. I wait for a few minutes and fill my pipe, trying to hear something in the maid's, Rita's, room. *It's possible that everything will come to an end tonight. It's possible that Julita will wake up and that everything will be the way it was at the beginning, that it will start over again, and we will find each other, she and I, together on the day after Federico's death, talking about him. It's possible she won't want to take me again or let herself be taken.*

I cross the garden biting my cold pipe, making no noise, carefully trailing the empty sleeves of my raincoat over the night, discovering that our thoughts are not born in us, that they are simply there, in any place outside our heads, free and hard, and that they enter us in order to be thought and then, capricious and unchanged, abandon us when they've had enough.

When I push the upstairs door, I hear Julita run and trip over a chair. I stop to give her time, and when I open the door I find her sitting on the floor next to the empty fireplace wearing a dark fur coat, her knees drawn up, smiling at me. With no conviction, as if she'd been preparing the phrase for hours and were incapable of holding it back, she protests:

"I've been waiting for you since eleven. And you knew that today it was important, that you had to come early. Don't tell me you didn't find the note."

"No. I found it. It's that I couldn't come, they were talking to me."

But I remember that it was only my father who talked.

"About me?"

"No, no, no. About everything else: my future, morality, the bordello, the sacrifices they've made, Santa María, our good name, conscience, experience, EL LIBERAL, and my grandfather. The usual sermon, except that this time . . ."

As I enumerate, standing next to her, not sure she's looking at me, I accompany each word with a shake of my head, with a sarcastic, mature grimace. I catch a glimpse of her heavily made up face, fallen now, directing her old smile of secrets, passivity, and madness toward her knees. I drop my raincoat on the floor, sit down, cross my legs, and light my pipe. I try to hate Julita, I try to convince myself that she needs me and that her need authorizes me to disdain and protect her.

"Talking about everything else!" she whispers, shocked, as if the very idea were unimaginable. Now she caresses the part of the coat covering her legs, one hand for each leg, up and down her torso, from her thighs to her ankles. She holds her feet, in slippers, motionless against the floor. Her smile, fixed, slightly surprised, referring, I'm sure, to things not even she could name, fills me with disquiet, causing a cold, foreign hatred to be born in me different from the hatred I want to have for her.

"What did you do today?"

She stops, and very slowly raises her shoulders, letting them fall suddenly. She starts to move around again, accompanying the back-and-forth movement of her hands over her coat, over her legs. I think the scene tonight in the living room means that my parents have accepted Federico's death, that he's no longer here, that suffering and memory cannot be touched, that it's not possible to associate with or fight against the dead because they are excessively malleable and servile. So now, for them as well, I am Federico, the sustainer of the sustainer of an undying Malabia who founded Santa María's EL LIBERAL.

"They were back again today," says Julita, still moving. "As always, pitying me, just as I pity them. But besides pity, they display a filthy curiosity. Did I ever have that same curiosity, as filthy and mean as theirs? When I was a girl like them."

But not completely, not yet. My brother's death is still

not definitive, and they, my parents, haven't imagined a
future devoid of Federico. Like Julita; and like Julita they
think I'm too young to fit into the attitudes and circumstances they've imagined over the years for Federico.

"I don't understand," I say angrily. She stops and
looks at me, almost serious, without finishing the with-
drawal of her smile. But she doesn't understand that I
love her, doesn't know she's mine, and that the time of
games and stories has just ended.

"Who? What girls, what pity, what curiosity?" I ask
without getting excited, as if I were talking with my pipe.

Disillusioned, Julita starts her back-and-forth motion
again and recovers her drowsy smile. But I don't want to
give up; I'm afraid of silence because she's a woman,
older, with many more things to keep silent; I rummage
through my pockets and inform her without looking at
her:

> I have to see you because it happened. We shall
> pray together. Not one minute after eleven; you
> have to help me make atonement for all my
> shameful moments of doubt. At eleven, earlier
> if possible.

"Well, here I am. What happened?"

She raises her face and stops moving her body. With
her mouth half open, hardening her eyes, she looks at
me as if she could see, surrounding my face, the tone of
voice in which I spoke, the short straight forms, the dry
colors of challenge, of calculated indifference. For the
first time, it occurs to me that she's got the ability to be
proud, that she looked at her parents in the same way

when she was a child and then later on at Federico. She may prefer catastrophes to explanations.

"Nothing. I wanted to see you, so I sent you the note. Aren't you happy?"

I shrug my shoulders, puff on my pipe, and watch the smoke dissolve in front of her face. Still openmouthed, she waits, pretending to believe I can offend her.

"No I'm not. All that stuff, the sermons, the tenderness they heap on you, that lack of discretion, of fair play . . ."

Now she's beginning to smile with the ends of her lips, recovering the affection, spreading her lips as if they were two hands she could use to measure my height. She doesn't want to help me.

"All that stuff. Why do I have to have parents? I know everything about them, but they know nothing about me. But I love them, and I can't stop pretending, I can't show them that they should see the justice in relationships like that, so I do nothing more than put up with them."

"Is that why?" She's lying; she doesn't believe me, has to accept my lie, and goes back to stroking her body. Once again, she's got the smile of ecstasy on her face. She hopes to wear me down and console me in order to impose her story, the roles she's imagined for tonight.

"That's true, or it should be true, because I don't . . . But it must be worse not having parents; I mean it would be worse never to have had parents."

I get up and walk toward the wall where my brother's photo used to hang. I sit down on the bed and open the box on the night table. There are hairpins, folded papers, an aroma of wood and medicine, the tube of sleeping pills slides toward the light; another, unused, trembles on top of an identification photo. I watch her fur-covered shoulders go back and forth, her hairdo falling over the nape of her neck without touching it. I look for memories that will help me despise Julita's body. She calms down to talk to me in the hoarse voice she uses for deceptive secrets. I recoil, and before I understand what she's saying to me, I bend over her and ask:

"Why shouldn't I go to the bordello? Why can't I do whatever I like?"

Whatever she was saying, the words and their lost suggestions, return and cover her over; they stretch something thin, without consistency, over her head and shoulders. Just sufficient to separate her from me.

"Why can't I go to the whorehouse?" I repeat coldly, in a calm, loud voice.

She leans forward, rests her head on her knees, and breathes noisily, as if she were making a hasty effort to recognize the significance of an odor. Later, with her cheek and temple, she tries to find the meaning of touching things; she fails and comes to rest. Below me, closed, immobile, I have her face in profile, feigning thought, dreams, and abandon. She has gold trinkets in her hair; elsewhere there are also rapid, still infantile curves, lines and hollows made by despair and time. Tears begin to glitter, and all the features of her face, which is alert but pretending renunciation, seem to turn their back on weeping, not wanting the inevitable blinking, not wanting to calculate my reaction here above.

I think I can save myself from her, from my cowardice, from my dead brother, from my parents, from memories and premonitions, by exaggerating—until I can touch it, until the point of terror and vomiting—the diminutive disgust I get from knowing she's older than I am, from knowing that she's already been where I have yet to tread, from knowing she wasted what I have yet to touch, from knowing she's already squandered the opportunities still waiting for me. I sit down again and smoke; she can accept the idea that I didn't see her tears.

"It was an impersonal question," I whisper coldly. "Why can't I go to the bordello? Why can't someone seventeen years old go? Not that I want to go. But, if you can listen to me calmly, if you feel it's necessary to be as stupid as the rest . . ." She shakes her head, separates it from her knees, and goes on shaking it while she looks at the ceiling. They're all stupid. I'm more intelligent than they are, I'm different. Why do I have to say yes to everything they believe to be good for them, everything they were preparing because they got here before I did?

I believe what I'm saying, but not now: It doesn't matter to me right now. She's going to explode, to reveal her game for tonight down to the last detail if I mention Federico.

"My father's been to a whorehouse. Besides, he rents the house to Snatcher and the women so they can carry on their business. Maybe it's one of your houses, a piece of the property that belongs to you, one of the pieces of fixed property brought to conjugal society."

I don't look at her; my pipe goes on burning. The bedroom seems astonishingly small compared to my memory of it. For example, it seems to me that all I'd have to do would be to stretch out my hand to touch the wall where Federico's photo used to hang, use my fingernails to caress the flowers carved into the headboard. I want to hurt her, not with words but by giving her a sudden, strong sensation of her own stupidity. I want her to hate me, even if it's nothing more than a distilled hatred, and I want to stimulate myself with that hatred in order to separate what's mine and protect myself.

"The little house may well be part of my inheritance. Yours or, more likely, mine because my parents will die first. And he, my father—who forbids me to go to the whorehouse, who doesn't even bother to forbid me but instead makes the necessary effort to reason things out with a poor little boy, without wounding any sensibilities—has gone to whorehouses. And I think it's a good idea. He laughed with the women, touched them, paid for their anisette, went to bed with them, and added a tip to the price. He was a Malabia. And Federico, I'm very sure, didn't lie to you."

"Federico," Julita interrupts me, as if she hadn't named anyone, as if she'd mechanically repeated a password. I feel liberated and rest, with a sigh. I uselessly puff on the pipe and wait. She makes an incomprehensible noise, like a deep, thick groan devoid of sadness. She lets the silence grow until it's as high as her chin and then repeats the noise. I catch sight of the shine of the moon in the windowpanes, in a triangle of peace and cold, a remnant of last winter revealed by the curtain. I am empty, as if I had nothing against her, Julita, as if I'd discovered that feelings can be freely chosen and adopted, and that we have go through a certain number of sleepless nights in order to see them grow. I am empty, and I turn around to look at her.

"Federico," she repeats, looking for the accessible part of the word, its weak point. She smiles at me, calm, solid, on the way back from danger, and the glint of her tears extends her smile to her cheekbones, finding sanctuary for it in her chin. "Federico went, was with, knew lots of women. But there is no Federico, there never was; that's why I called you here tonight, to explain it to you. And I don't want to explain anything to you, things have to happen without words. He was dead, I looked at you and chose you. But not even that's true, it wasn't I who chose you, I had no will to choose. I was forced to choose, without voices, without explanations. What does it matter? It's still not the right moment, and that's why I don't want to tell you about it. You thought I was crazy, you've thought so all this time, from the first day. Marcos comes and thinks the same thing, the doctor comes, my uncles come and push their chairs back, they don't want to drink anything as if my madness were contagious, and your mother, when she thinks I'm not looking at her, weeps quietly and prays. And I'm going to explain it all to you because I don't need anyone. All I need is this room and to be alone to live what they can't live even if they live to be a hundred. Not even Federico; there was no Federico, you're afraid because you always thought there was one. My fault, I know, I don't need you to say so."

She clasps her hands over her knees again and starts her back-and-forth motion again. A corner of her fur coat hangs down and touches the bricks in the fireplace floor. I see her leg, I see she's naked under the fur.

"I know the room and your solitude are enough," I say. "I'd like to know if they were always enough. Do I also think you're crazy?"

Without answering me, serious and concentrated, she pushes her face forward, pierces the air with it, immobilizes it for a second, stabs it into the air, holds it there for a second, and then pulls it back, as if she were leaving the form and the expression of her profile definitively, as an answer to me.

"There never was a Federico, the world is gone, there is no Santa María. Everything you see outside of here is a lie, everything you touch. Even what you think outside of here and what you think while you're here and not thinking of me. With all this. With you and with me. With this room."

A little message for every sentence, like a parasitic fish. I'm beginning not to understand her, not to know who she is.

"Who else could it be?" she asks. "The girls were here last night to write anonymous letters. I don't love them, they must be virgins. It must be for that reason that I find them filthy. It's this way: All they have, the clothes on their backs, everything clean, cared-for, chosen, everything gives me the sensation of scum, of something unclean, of old fat which is stuck on, black. That grease of the years in the kitchen corners where no one can see. The newly made dresses, short sleeves, and décolleté, their arms, necks, so clean and so annoying. I know what the underwear they have on is like, I know they washed after the siesta, that they put on perfume before coming over here. They drink tea and write, they do not want to look at each other with their brilliant eyes, they try to act as if they were working in an office."

She gets up, patting the coat in place to keep herself covered and smiles at me. She shows me her teeth, stretches her lips and joins them again. "What do they matter to me?" She comes over to me, bends over, and kisses me. "Does any of this matter to you? All that . . . sometimes Marcos comes and tells me. But it doesn't matter to us."

She caresses me, lifts up my head, and kisses me again. Her eyes are opposite mine, but she isn't looking at me; she squeezes my shoulders, raises me up, moves me along, puts me in the bed, bends over to pick up my legs. I want to loosen my tie, but she slaps my hands.

"Don't get undressed," she says without lowering her voice. "Don't put out the light." She takes off the coat and there she is, naked, touching my hand with her knee. She doesn't desire me or expect my desire, she's simply showing me her body, expecting me to say something I can't imagine. Then she sits down on the bed and puts her hand on my chest.

I wait for what's going to happen as if I didn't have to do it myself, as if I were a visitor, someone, another person who crosses the garden, goes up the stairs in the shadow, step by step. I close my eyes and see myself, as if I were looking down from the ceiling or even higher, immobile in bed, sweating, with a perfume set against my cheek, covered by her and her madness, covered by my age, by my faults, by the walls and the air of the room, by the distance that separates me from death.

I lean on my shoulders and one arm, make her roll over on her back, and I slap her face, just once, not violently. I hold her and kiss her, I make her bend one knee and, almost laughing, thankful, free of her, happy now for having patiently passed through the extremely long prologue, the game, and the wait which she knew how to impose, I enter into the tremor of her body, I love cruelty and joy.

CHAPTER XXIV

Marcos dreamed about a fight, about a voice repeating domestic admonitions concerning the slow, elastic back-and-forth movement of the furniture, the weapons, and the arms that tediously and perpetually constituted the static character of the quarrel. It was a voice whose mere sound resolved all doubts and provided a consolation for every failure to understand.

But now he couldn't get back to sleep to go on listening to it. It was also useless to try to induce sleep by the infantile method of rubbing his half-opened, saliva-filled mouth against Rita's ribs. He opened his eyes toward the clarity of the night fenced in by the garden, toward the crickets, the wind, the insignificant and distant noises; he heard the church clock and deduced that the wind was blowing from the west. A good night for fishing. Now he was totally awake, on the defensive, hating himself for being alive and lucid, swollen by hatred as if by pain. Nervous and nauseated, he turned over to get away from the girl's smell and from the plant twisted around the bars over the window. Hunkered down, he took a drink out of the flask he'd left next to the bed and lit a cigarette; with the same match, he lit the twisted candle stub on the table next to the wall. Its light was superfluous in any case because the moon, wide and triangular, covered the bed and almost the entire visible floor of the small room.

"But no, but no . . . ," Rita insisted in her sleep without moving.

The yellow light rose, rubbing over photographs and cheap prints, a big nail with a key ring hung on it, a mirror, a horse's tail. It shone on the table, the edge of the washbasin and the handle of the pitcher, a disorder of hairpins, packs of cigarettes, soap dish, comb, bracelets, a magazine, a stack of coins, a compact.

Marcos picked up a towel to dry the sweat on his face and chest; he'd gone to sleep with his watch on; it was barely, almost eleven. He took another drink and put his cigarette in his mouth. He wouldn't be hearing the voice from his dream again; he'd lost his total relief forever. He slowly lowered his head to look himself over: tall, tan, and white, legs spread, giving off the smell of summer, of sleep, and of a woman. His big feet, caked with mud, were surrounded by the design in the rug. As sinuous as the path it would have to take through the hills covered with orange trees and property boundaries, beyond Enduro, a freight train blew its horn twice, exaggerating the silence of the night, the distance, the unbearable solitude. Marcos took a step and kicked the bed, making the girl's naked body thud against the window wall.

"Yes," she said, hoarse, without expression. She instantly sat up and stayed erect, dazzled by the uncertain candlelight, sluggish, trying to guess what she'd have to do to free herself from fear. "Yes. What's happening?" She recognized Marcos, smiled, and pulled up a corner of the sheet to cover herself, relaxed her fingers, and smiled again. "Yes," she repeated, knowing she could say yes to anything.

"Nothing," said Marcos. "I woke up. It's early."

She looked at the cold, enraged whiteness of his smile; she saw the nickel and leather flask as if it were melting in the moonlight. Because she believed that at heart he liked to hear her, she repeated her habitual remark: "Don't drink so much." She insisted, with the careless question, "Why do you drink so much?"

"Listen," said Marcos, coming over to her. "Cover yourself up, don't be naked." He sat down on the circular rug, covering himself with his folded legs, his hands on his knees. "Cover your breasts too. I was dreaming about a fight, and I woke up. You have to listen to me. Did it ever occur to you to kill someone? Don't bother answering, you're going to say something stupid, the way you always do."

"Yes," said Rita. She began to laugh, doubled up, decapitated by the sheet, laughing at all the darling, stupid things she could remember and foresee, happy because of the irresponsibility of stupidity, feeling that stupidity would protect her until the day she died.

"But you've got to listen to me. When Caudillo died, I didn't want to have any more dogs. I always talked to him, and it was better than talking with people. He was a dog, a friend. I woke up knowing that I had to kill someone. I'm with you, and I get crazy. Then I'm disgusted with myself, I already told you that. But it shouldn't matter to you because it always disgusted me. After all, women are all the same thing, any woman. And that's all right, it occurs to me, because we aren't one flesh, and only matrimony can make two people the same flesh. My uncle, the priest, could make us into one flesh, and then I wouldn't feel disgusted. That's a fact. You think it's funny; but if we went to church and my uncle married us, we would be one flesh. Understand?"

Marcos looked at her as if she really were asking. He kept his mouth half-open, his eyes toward her, sighing as he took a drink from the flask.

"It'd be more respectable," Rita answered. "I wouldn't be ashamed with you, but sometimes the lady looks at me and I think she knows everything. But you'd have to be crazy to marry me."

"Don't talk," said Marcos, setting the flask aside.

She saw his head in the moonlight, as if he'd deliberately put it in the perverse, soft light, as if it weren't simply there, at the same height as the bed, blond and handsome, accidental, seeking with his tiny eyes things that were not and could not be in Rita, looking through her at things that she, because she was tactless, condemned to be tactless, disfigured with fog and apprehension. She saw the shiny moisture that slipped from his lips separated by his painful, prophetic smile.

"Don't talk. One flesh. It has to be that way, it must be that way because if it weren't, everybody would have committed suicide. Nobody could stand it. We're all unclean, and the filth we carry from birth, men and women, is multiplied in the filth of the other person, and the disgust is unbearable. As my uncle the priest says, we need to support our love on God, God has to be in bed with us. Then it would be different, I'm sure. You can do anything with purity."

"Don't shout," whispered Rita.

Marcos interrupted himself to look at her wide, soft mouth, her open eyes, her temples, her face with its Indian features, patient, with her hard, tousled hair, sullenly profiled against the nocturnal clarity and docility.

"I believe in prayer," said Marcos. He could barely speak, he stuck out his tongue to touch the sweat above his lip. "I have to kill someone. Our race is the fatherland. I'm no wop, no German, and no Swiss."

"Someone's down in the garden. Shut up."

Marcos got up with the flask in his hand, walked on his knees over the bed until he could lean his forehead against the bars on the window. He recognized the night with its promises, its postponement, a special night, his night, repeated forever with variants that were of no importance. A shadow zigzagged through the plots, passed by limping under the hanging branches, stopped to cough and mutter something like an owl outside Julita's door. Marcos identified the beret, the way the body was bent forward, the infantile, excessive posture of the silhouette that turned around to study the sky and the solitude of the garden.

"It's the kid." He got off the bed and looked for a cigarette. "Today he decided not to look through the window," he whispered, crouching down as he lit the cigarette with the candle. "What's he doing with my sister at this time of night?"

"He goes up there every night," said Rita softly, stretching out in the bed as if she'd just carried out an imprecise act of revenge with disinterest. "At about eleven, every night, or almost every night. I hear him because of the stairs or the door latch. The young madam comes down and lets him in. They must be talking about the one who passed away."

Marcos began to get dressed. When he'd arranged his trousers, he put out the candle with a saliva-moistened finger. He came over and sat down on the edge of the bed to tie his tie.

"He's just a kid," said Rita, fearful now. "You're not mad, are you?" She had her eyes closed, protecting them from the moonlight with one hand, with the border of the sheet. And in the silence, in the blackness, she tried to dissimulate for the room and for Marcos, she tried to blend into the absurdities of the welcoming dream that was soon to come.

"My sister is crazy," said Marcos when he'd put his jacket on. "As if all men had died for her. But she's right, that was true because they were one flesh. That kid is an idiot, a spoiled brat. You never felt a desire to kill some-one, and if you did it was only for a moment, you forgot about it and asked forgiveness. There are three whores in the little blue house, and I'm sick and tired of them and the guys who see them, I'm sick and tired of all the talk and argument about them, sick and tired of what my uncle the priest says every Sunday. But my uncle is a great guy. Ciao."

He walked out and saw the empty garden. He was looking at the small, curled-up clouds that drifted east-ward, their borders disintegrating while he measured his drunkenness and the limitations it implied, while he twirled his key ring around his finger. He went back to Rita's window:

"And I'm sick and tired of myself. You can't understand."

The red car was still twisted among the orange trees, facing the road. Marcos advanced in a swagger, breaking up clods of dirt, twisting his head around so he could look at the square, sad light in Julita's window.

CHAPTER XXV

Father Bergner did not kneel. Leaning lightly against the pulpit, he humbly murmured his request supplicating through the fingers on his hand, begging that the triumph of the devil in Santa María be impeded. A few feminine sobs trembled, short and controlled, like bubbles forming and bursting on the surface of the silence. Wide, bent forward, offering their backs and napes to fear, both men and women sank under the threat they detected in the conclusion of the sermon.

"And let it not be said that the shepherd abandoned his flock. The flock had already turned away from the shepherd, become stiff-necked. Preferring to be hospitable to sin, they banished the Sacred Heart from their lives and replaced it with vice, the filthiest of vices, the vice that is like a blight which gnaws at the soul and eats it away. Let it not be said that the shepherd abandoned his flock."

Each one peered into the personal sufferings and fears he excited and forced to grow. He used those sufferings and fears to widen the great, general fear, the fear of a punishment that would include all of them, them and their children, the fear of the enormous black cloud that would detach itself from the sky and cover both the city and Colonia.

Almost all of them were blond; their hands were big, red, and rough. Their faces gave the same sensation of use as their hands: They seemed to have dealt with joys, memories, fears, and convictions by touching them, holding them, rubbing them against themselves. Doing that made these people lose some of their original form here and there—in their temples, their eyes, their foreheads, around their mouths.

Almost all of them had arrived in broken-down automobiles, in two-wheeled carriages, sulkies, and trucks, making their way up the road between Colonia and Santa María under the white, seemingly immobile, Sunday-morning sun. The men, now down on their knees, dressed somberly in tight-fitting suits, wearing high vests that came out of the closet on Sunday only to go right back in, into the soothing smell of mothballs and enclosed space, right after lunch was on the table, a table extended with boards and sawhorses. The men snapped the reins and urged the horses forward with blows and casual insults; their women on the rear seats smelled of the cowshed, sweat, and cologne. The girls took the risk of introducing into the open air the perfumes they'd secretly bought in town or from the Lebanese traveling salesmen who visited the farms. Chatting about work and illnesses, marriages, pregnancies, and birthdays, they were sticking their fingers between their collars and their necks to get some relief from the heat, flexing their feet inside their shoes, draping shawls over their shoulders, shawls they would later use to cover themselves in church.

And all of them, in their heart of hearts, beneath the surface of their conversations and self-absorptions, beneath their immediate concerns, were trying to figure out exactly what had happened since the preceding Sunday, what advances and retreats had occurred in that filth ensconced in a sky-blue house somewhere on the coast. They were thinking of the injustice—well deserved of course—in the fact that the scorn, threats, and punishment that were the mainstay of Father Bergner's sermons included them, the inhabitants of Colonia. That they should have to suffer and pay for the sins of Santa María, for the shameful habits and affairs of dark-skinned city men.

And now they were on their knees, humiliated, offering their silence and faith as weapons that God might perhaps accept to defeat evil. A moment before, they had seen Moses climb the mountain, summoned by Jehovah; they confused Father Bergner with Moses and admired his ascent to Sinai, where, for six days, the glory of God rested. They had seen God raise His hand to order Father Bergner: "Go, descend, for your people are corrupted. In but a short time they have strayed from the path I marked out for them. Now, let my wrath blaze against them and consume them." They listened to the sadness and anger of God, the shame and anger of Father Bergner.

The shining, peasant images so familiar to them in the sermon vanished; they no longer witnessed the dialogue between Father Bergner and God, but they hadn't committed the sins of the tribe camped on the flank of the mountain. They did not anguish foreseeing the destiny of the earrings Aaron gathered from their ears, nor did they grieve impotently at the jubilation of the revels that surrounded, beginning at dawn, the gross majesty of the Golden Calf. They were on their knees in silence, troubled. Their mute, mobile lips seemed to labor to taste all the bitterness obtainable from the threat of being abandoned by the priest, something he'd insinuated this Sunday more directly than ever before.

For an entire hour, Father Bergner had maintained a hermetic, separated, antisocial expression that befitted a sick man. He had not bent his huge peasant's shoulders. His movements, if anything, were slower, hindered by a careless slowness, distracted by an obsession.

His head had been raised to a wider angle than was usual in him—although it wouldn't have been necessary to knock it down with a brusque blow, loosening the muscles so it would fall, as if separated from him, like an object that could separate from his shoulders, fall to the ground, and roll away. It was separated from the height of the other humiliated heads, from the same surface of clods and sprouts, from the riverbanks, streets, and gardens Santa María presented to the clear sky of Sunday.

The priest's voice had resounded during the sermon and Mass with a dry, severe tone, with the perceptible resolution to be no more than the instrument of the sentences spoken, incapable of expressing emotions that would alter, invigorate, or calm the feelings that charged his words.

A body whose gestures, voice, and direct gaze would not stop and recognize anyone, did not want to be distracted: The priest wanted to be an essential, anonymous means by which repudiation, condemnation, and vague threats could be spoken and expressed. More effective and frightening because he had dispensed with himself, the priest Bergner had emulated invariable faith and the birth of an earthly despair. But it was only visibly dramatic at the end, in the murmur where he caused the last sentence to die in the sermon in the prolonged, indecisive, reticent, prophetic silence which preceded the three words of command and dismissal, in the speed with which he stepped down from the pulpit and avoided the eyes of the parishioners, who stood up dizzy and awkward, all sighing at the same time.

They walked toward the summer light, went their ways amid gestures of greeting made above the noise of feet dragged to the sulkies and the dusty cars with which they'd surrounded the plaza. As they moved along, taciturn, stretching their legs, feeling elements of rage and sparks of resolution as if they were small, weak animals, they walked toward the return journey, which would be ill-humored and silent, only interrupted by trivial remarks and nods. They walked toward an interminable lunch, the relief of siesta, the boredom of the idle, burning afternoon, with the insincere bustle of visits, with the perplexed sunset, the buzz of streetlights in whose white light they would watch each other grow old, parsimonious, equable, not drawing any conclusions.

CHAPTER XXVI

At the garden door, mysteriously unlocked tonight, I hear her idiot laughter and realize once again that everything comes to an end.

Upstairs there is no one, nothing, nothing but Julita stretched out in bed sprinkling perfume on her bosom and the nape of her neck.

She looks at me, and I know that I don't count even though I'm irreplaceable. Neither do my problems, my soul, or my desires. Not even my beret, my pipe, the confused anguish of the verses I was writing. I remember the yellow, round moon in the garden's diminished sky.

Now Julita laughs again, but more slowly, prolonging the pauses, using all her hysteria and happiness.

"Idiotidiotidiot," she greets me tenderly.

She's smoking in bed, wearing a black party dress, with gold around her neck and on her arm. She contemplates the ceiling beams with a perfect, cold smile. I am the owner, the indifferent man, the cuckold. I sit down next to the dying fire and slowly, awkwardly fill my pipe.

"There's a bottle with the underwear and other things in the dresser. That's where the bottle is. I drink and hide it; we don't need glasses."

We drink in silence, taking turns drinking out of the round cognac bottle. I put it back and cover it over with clothing.

Slowly, leaning on her elbows, shifting her huge hips, squeezing her cheekbones in her hands, she manages to sit up in the bed and laugh again. Her legs were never prettier.

"Am I drunk?"

"A little, I think," I murmur, trying to guess at what else awaits me, guessing wrong.

"Federico," she says. I don't believe her.

"Certainly."

"Federico or whatever I choose . . ."

"Sure."

"Get it."

While I go back to the dresser and push weightless, odorless panties out of the way, I listen to her:

"A thrush, a rosebush, a morning, a crippled dog. I was transforming myself. It was inevitable. And the distance between the bed and the bathroom never changed."

I lay the bottle in her lap and sit down again. The noise of her swallowing disgusts me; she calls me, and I don't answer. She gets up to see whatever she can of the night through the window. She pronounces my name; she repeats it like a cat meowing, not expecting any answer. She laughs again, and now I feel she's laughing at me just so I'll hear her. She calls my name and begins to strip, tossing her clothes against the walls and windows. Narrow shoulders, small breasts, each one a perfect handful; below her waist everything widens, exaggeratedly, almost bestially. Naked, she makes herself comfortable in the bed, drinks, curls up to die, drinks, and calls me. I remember the switchblade in my pocket; I hide it under the pillow and get undressed. Julita mutters stupidities, smiling, her eyes closed.

She spreads her huge thighs to let me enter. It's always different, always the first time.

"Like that," she says. "Don't move."

There is a silence in the night, and I'm sure that she made it. After a while, I hear her weep, almost without adding any noise. I barely feel the tears sliding down her cheeks, the agitation of her chest. I think about an old, worn-out title that may be dead; I imagine that the trip and the rest of winter have finished forever.

After a while, after making love, after the forbidden words and the sigh, she speaks. Her voice dominates the room, erases the distant dogs. She's not talking to me, not telling me anything. She's describing the things that she's seeing, that she sees or remembers. More than myself, it's my lucid hand resting on the coolness of the knife that listens to her.

Suddenly she moves her hips, pushes me away, and asks me to light her a cigarette. Now she's sitting on the edge of the bed; again she speaks for the air polished by the smoke or for no one. I'm afraid she's talking for herself. Her free hand rests on her thighs; she's heavy and strong, very white. She says something, and her hand goes up, caresses, and separates.

Julita smokes and tells things; she smiles so happily that I suffer envy and tenderness. Her muscular body is almost adolescent. I observe the puerile, rhythmic caress of her fingers, hope she doesn't open her eyes, that she knows, that she's coming to know that there's no reason to open them.

She tosses the cigarette aside, collapses onto the bed, curls up like a fetus, and clenches her fists. Now she has no breasts, her pubis is bald; she whispers as her nose seems to get smaller, turned up. Finally she falls asleep. I lean over to kiss her feet, her knees.

Without violence, caressingly, the morning enters through the half-open curtain and wakes me up.

I blink before Julita's half-open, rosy penumbra and begin to understand. Half asleep, I think about the night and the dawn, the excess of cognac, the woman's vertiginous madness, her gallop back to the past until, dangerously, she touches the border of infancy.

I kiss her again, barely touching her so I won't disturb her sleep, her absence, the immodest and abandoned posture of her thick legs. Noiselessly, I light a cigarette and stretch out on my back, protecting myself from looking at her, recovering the mild terror the memory brings close to me.

Now there is no difference between night, dawn, and morning. It's all the same, an eternal present time that was imposed on me by Julita's madness. Ashamed as I look for an ashtray, I think, I compose the lie that I will recite to my parents before midday, right now. The prettiest, the least credible I can think of is my obedience to my impulse to search, walking at dawn on the farms or along the river. They know I sleep until noon, but they might also remember Federico's walks, believe me, and be happy.

It's night, dawn, and day. I have Julita naked, wise, a bit curious, and sympathetic, teaching me, with a desperate tenacity, all the forms of lust, perversity, inventing absurdities, laughing as madly as if she'd lucidly created new ways. Nevertheless, I feel, there's nothing new in the intimacy, the shown, happy physiology. I never did it before, that's true. But I did imagine it, want it, and thought it many years ago, from the time I have a memory of myself.

Irrepressible, with an indirect smile that repeats itself with no change, Julita fills the pauses and rest periods by talking to the ceiling and the dark red beams, to the nothingness:

"Why did Federico have to die? I say 'have to,' without asking why he died. I know what he did. It was an obligation he had to carry out. The things we mentioned had nothing to do with it. Not falling off the horse, not what they called pneumonia. Maybe he postponed it once or ten times; nobody can know that but now, I'm sure we knew it, he and I, that we knew it from the beginning, stronger and stronger every day, as our happiness sank its roots deeper and deeper. Because real happiness can't grow, get bigger. It's there. And we laughed at each other, stared at each other, touched each other with love. But we both knew, embraced knowing and crazy with fear and each one hiding the terror from the other. At night we went to bed on top of the danger, we saw each other wake up wondering whether it would be that morning, that day. He and I, of course. Fearful that it was the other's turn to carry out his obligation, horrified by cowardice, the selfishness of being left alone, of carrying out the other horrifying obligation of suffering and remembering.

"He looked so much like what I had imagined that almost instantly he became exactly that. I would imagine him with the boys from Colonia and how he would be when we came to Santa María with our parents and girl friends to Sunday Mass, to pay visits, to stroll around the plaza wearing those long dresses with the color and hardness of uniforms. I see their dresses, clothes that only a mother embittered and disenchanted because she was transplanted here could cut and sew for a daughter whose breasts had begun to swell.

"Later comes boarding school, the nuns' school. Skinny, sad, as lonely as I could possibly be; still flat-chested, sensing the secrets and vacillating about them. I can't talk about stupidity if I remember my school friends. I'll only say that they were different, almost all of them pretty, full of jealousy, malice, and lies. And each one playing her game, me too of course, trying that sinuous and patient style that only we women know and dominate.

"I see, later, the visits of the priest, fights with my brother, my father's surly, prematurely aged face giving thanks before dinner and preaching obedience to us in a loud, slow voice, as if he were in no hurry, as if we weren't hungry. Enormous, wearing mourning, never thanking God for the liters of wine he drank, alone or with friends, invariable, stripped of happiness.

"I'm looking at the big bronze pot hanging in the fireplace. I'm little; sitting in the big chair grandma left us, I swing my legs back and forth looking from a distance at the burning splinters and the Christmas Eve lights that mix with the sparks, I swing my legs and wait for sleep, the order to go to bed with my doll, because I'm a very little girl and they don't want me to go too near the fire."

CHAPTER XXVII

I carefully put on my clothes and had just finished combing my hair when I heard the light but prolonged complaint of Marcos's horn. I hurried downstairs to keep the Alfa's noise from waking Julita. It was strange: The steps on the old staircase creaked more that morning than they had on all those remote nights that all resembled each other. It was still not possible to call the clarity in the garden morning, the mist rising from the grass that tangled in the leaves of the trees and then broke up.

I looked around and tried to imagine what had brought Marcos while I stopped to fill my pipe and light it. He was leaning on the little red car, protected from the elements by a leather jacket, his long cigarette with its lazy smoke horizontal in his mouth. I advanced in the cold, gray air, put on my beret and pulled it down over one ear.

"What's going on up there?" asked Marcos, indifferent, as if he'd simply said hello.

"Same as always. She talks about Federico, cries, talks about Federico, and then gets drunk. Now she's asleep, she must be happy. I'm more and more convinced that something's got to be done. Put her away, even if it's against her will."

Without moving, permanently encrusted on the car door, he looked at me lying, smiled, and dragged the cigarette to a corner of his mouth. He wasn't drunk.

"So lovingly in agreement . . . Whoever told you that you were born to know about women? Do something against her will? Julita would smash you with one slap of her hand. When you sleep with her, it's never against her will. It happens when my inconsolable sister feels like it. Spotless wife, exemplary widow. It's morning now. And since eleven last night you've been listening to chapter one thousand of the Federico novel. That's right: I came to find you, and here you are fully dressed, all prim and proper, like a gentleman. But your hair's wet, you've got shadows under your eyes, a sleepy face. I knew where you were. Sometimes you spy on Rita; sometimes she spies on you. What a shock for your mom and Julita."

He laughed, spit out the cigarette, and pulled himself away from the car.

"If that's what you think . . . ," I started to say.

"Don't say a word. No need for explanations, fairy tales, or excuses. I like the idea that she chose you. And don't kid yourself, she did choose you. And about her being crazy . . ."

He looked into the distance at the clouds gathering to block the rising sun. I judged him to be watching the freedom of the morning, the incomprehensible injustice of life.

"She's crazy. Always been crazy. I've seen it. She was strange even before becoming a widow, even before she met your brother."

"So why don't you put her away, take care of her, watch out for her?"

"Because I don't want to. I don't see her very often, but I need to know I've got her nearby. But I didn't come to talk. I came looking for you to do things, to do something. Not that I really need you. Get in."

I obeyed, and he settled in behind the wheel, yawning. He started the motor, and while it warmed up, he said:

"It's a good time of day. The time to take over police stations and army barracks."

I rubbed my face with my beret to clean off the sleep.

"I don't understand."

"No? That's odd." He lit another cigarette without offering me one. "It must be three or five in the morning. It's Sunday. And I haven't had a miserable drop of alcohol in my gut for hours."

The motor was warmed up and the car was shaking. Marcos stayed still, leaning back in the chair, letting the cigarette in his mouth burn on its own. When he spoke, his voice was slow and dangerous.

"A long time ago, some night or other, you promised to be with me when I decided to do this, to do things. Now, I don't know why, the time has come. I could get someone who'd be more useful, some ass from among my friends. But I remembered that I promised you the honor of accompanying me. After all, we are related.

After all, you do sleep with my sister. And if you forgot or deny your promise . . ."

Surrounded by the mist, it was indubitable that we were together and tired at the beginning of a Sunday morning, and in Santa María. I could just begin to smell the grass. Out of the corner of my eye, I looked at his solid body, gone to fat in the last few months, soft, indolent, sitting on the red leather seat. His smile was turning toward mockery and humiliation. I hid my pipe before I said anything.

"No," I said after a while. "I don't remember any promise, and threats don't matter to me. But I'll go with you to look for whatever you want."

"You never knew me, kid."

"No. Other people had to tell me. Too bad, when you think about it."

"Who'd they talk about?"

"I forget the name. A girl, a Basque. An old story."

In silence we both waited for and received the intimidated beginning of the wind, the cries of the birds. Then Marcos, looking old, put the car in gear and sped for the gates. He turned, and at sixty miles per hour we went looking for whatever was still left at that hour on Sunday. This time he did offer me a cigarette. I heard him laugh out loud, choke, and cough.

"Just a minute," he said. "First we have to go by the Plaza. After all, we're gentlemen, descendants of the founding fathers."

"At this hour?"

"Don't worry. For me, they're always open."

He left me on the corner, yawning out the remnants of my sleepiness into the cool air, in the grayish but already implacable morning light. I bit my pipe again, I listened to the tolling of the church bell; I made an effort to forget the previous night, that mutual and insane perversity trying to reach a beyond, a truly impossible ending. I could not think about Julita with Marcos nearby or next to me; the visible resemblances between him and his sister repelled me.

Finally he came back, emerging from the Plaza's small side door, carrying a squarish bottle, his pockets bulging with packs of cigarettes.

"Yes," he said, sitting down in the car. "Fine liquor and filtered cigarettes for ladies. Born in a golden cradle, painstakingly educated. But I forgot that your father could write it better than that. His specialty is obituary notes, isn't that right?"

I don't answer, and the car starts moving, instantly recovers its former speed and its excessive shaking. Marcos is whistling happily. He speaks only once, just before we arrive:

"I'd pay anything to know where Ana María is. One of these days we're going to find her in the little house on the coast. I remember that one night I asked her or advised her to go live there."

The clouds were slipping over the sky-blue house when we got there. Marcos noiselessly parked his car next to the ditch that separated the road from what was supposed to be the sidewalk. Then he imitated his earlier position, leaning his body on the door and lighting a cigarette. He had the bottle under his arm, while he slowly and confidently spun a black pistol around on his index finger.

"I've been waiting for months. Try to understand me, kid. If I don't dirty my hands, it's as if I were allowing them to dirty them for me. There are lots of 'them' in

Santa María." He roused himself, raising his head, and started walking toward the unchanging, blue sky of the curtains on that cloudy, indecisive Sunday morning. He pounded on the door with the butt of the pistol, and we waited for a while. The youngest of the women, the blonde with the round face, slid back the bolt, opened the door, and looked at us sleepily, calmly, as if she'd been expecting us.

"Hello," she muttered toward the pistol in Marcos's hand.

We walked in, blinded by the half-light. We figured out where the little tables were by the way they were arranged, then discerned the prints on the walls, the withered, forgotten flowers, the hostile doors of the bedrooms. A second later, we saw the man sitting at the big table in the middle, with his hat on, playing solitaire with a greasy deck of French cards. He put the cards down on the embroidered table cloth and greeted us calmly.

"Good morning." Putting his hands together, Larsen twiddled his thumbs.

Marcos advanced step by step, put the bottle on the table, and emptied his pockets.

"For the ladies," he said.

"They'll appreciate it."

Marcos brought his pistol right up to Body Snatcher's face. Snatcher looked at it distractedly.

"I've come to clean out all of this," Marcos explained without raising his voice. "Let's get this straight: I don't have anything against you personally. You don't exist. I just don't want a whorehouse in Santa María."

The plump blonde, Nelly, was next to me, smiling at me tenderly, patiently.

"Would you like to sit down?" she asked.

"No thanks. I see better standing up."

Nelly shrugged her shoulders and went over to the table. Brushing against Marcos, she reached for a pack of cigarettes.

"Excuse me. You did say they were for us, didn't you?"

Without answering her, Marcos went on playing with the gun. The woman lit a cigarette and smoked it as if she were hungry for tobacco. Then she lazily walked away to open the curtain. The morning light was inappropriate to the scene. The woman walked past me and entered one of the bedrooms without making a sound. The two men went on staring at each other. They were calm, one standing, the other sitting. Only Snatcher's thumbs and Marcos's pistol were moving. After a while, Body Snatcher, with a bored air, took a silver watch out of his vest. Marcos stopped twirling the pistol.

"It's six," said Body Snatcher in a melancholy tone. "Which is when I thought I'd go to bed. After all, looking at it from my side of the table, you have your desire and I have mine."

Marcos leaned one fist on the table, spit into Body Snatcher's face, and slowly straightened up.

"Jew bastard."

Motionless, looking out of the corner of his eye at the embroidered flowers on the table cloth, Body Snatcher began to smile, to rejuvenate. He seemed separated from us, from the moment, by a long distance of many years. Finally, slowly and clearly, he whispered:

"Neither the one and barely, from what I've heard, any of the other."

Marcos laughed mockingly and sat down opposite Body Snatcher. He put the pistol on the table and opened the bottle.

"There are glasses over there."

"Jorge," said Marcos.

I went over to the sideboard and hesitated a moment. Then, smiling, I brought three glasses to the table. Marcos looked at me suspiciously for a second, then filled his glass. Almost instantly, I poured whiskey into the glasses I'd brought for myself and Larsen.

"Know something? It's been a long time since I've used guns. I mean since I carried one."

We all took a drink, and in the pause afterward, we heard the voices of the hidden women.

"That's a Luger, isn't it?" Marcos refilled his glass. I saw no saliva on Larsen's face. One of the invisible women shouted orders. Snatcher set his empty glass aside and picked up the pistol. Marcos observed him without moving, smiling, disdainful.

"A Luger, of course," confirmed Body Snatcher with a happy expression on his face. "The best I've ever seen. I've got a thirty-eight in the back someplace. Later I'll ask the girls to bring it out. They're like twin sisters. And yet, if you ask me . . ."

Courteous and proper, he put the pistol back next to Marcos's elbow. I filled the glasses again, and we drank. Soon I felt happy and a little drunk—the cognac from the previous night, the same night, still alive, my not having slept. Then, tripping and dressed up, gay, the women came in to greet us.

Marcos stood up, bowed, and told them our names. He brought glasses over from the sideboard and offered them cigarettes. Later, smiling, excusing himself, he tried to find tangos on the little white radio, and danced with María Bonita.

That's how the six of us began to live. I don't even

want to know how long we lasted together. I'm determined to forget—and I will—the routine events and the absurd situations. I can think we were happy until the end, until the cop and Medina knocked at the door at a forgettable moment and spoke to Marcos, pretending not to see me, handing Larsen a copy of the governor's order.

CHAPTER XXVIII

Erect, taking huge strides, the priest Bergner walked into the sacristy, still wearing the expression of sickness, distance, and insomnia he had kept on his face during Mass, despite the smile he'd directed to three old women in mourning who stood up from a bench against the wall, sobbing, murmuring confused phrases of supplication. He heard them speak and blessed them; his smile softly illuminated the suffering adrift on his cheekbones and in his eyes: It revealed suffering without contradicting or magnifying it. The deputy priest stood waiting for him next to a corner of the table, his hand resting on a portfolio. His shoulders stooped, but there was admiration in his fixed and shining eyes.

"Only God knows," said the priest, and the three mourning crones repeated the three words at different speeds, consoling themselves. The priest looked at them, their watery, faded eyes, whose irises were streaked with bloody lines, with stains similar to those tobacco makes on the fingers of smokers. He allowed them to kiss his hand by way of farewell.

Seated at the table, while he opened the portfolio his deputy pushed toward him, Father Bergner looked up at the portrait of the pope on the wall and thought, vaguely, as if he'd just discovered its existence, about the heat. It was a bad portrait, in merciless black and white, with emphatic intentions that pulled the pope's eyes out of their sockets and transformed the austerity of his mouth into rancor; a geometric dove crucified itself in the background against a large window filled with indefinite images.

The only thing of any importance in the portfolio was a report from the League of Knights; after they detailed the names and numbers, the total number of visitors to the bordello during the last week, compared this with the number from the week before, the Knights asked permission to make some suggestions to the reverend father: They advised "proceeding to the publication of the names of all the bordello's clients, whenever possible, using whatever media deemed appropriate. Truth should not shame us."

"They say that the Jew . . . ," began the deputy; his clear, guttural Spanish accent made the priest's head rise. "Well, I mean the man who brought the women. They say he's leaving, that he's giving up the hotel to go to Rosario."

"Maybe so, but it doesn't matter," said the priest. "We aren't fighting him or Barthé, not even the women. We're not fighting anyone in particular; we are fighting evil."

"All I meant to say . . . ," complained the deputy. "If he's really leaving . . ."

"Thanks, thanks for the information. I always think it's necessary to point out that we don't want to persecute anyone. We want Santa María to wake up; the towns-people themselves must desire to save their own souls."

Smiling, with an old man's expression he would excuse without humiliating himself, Father Bergner dug in his pockets until he found and unfolded the handkerchief he used to dry his forehead and lip.

The portrait took up a third of the height of the wall; it was a present, it was bad and disagreeable to look at, a symbol, alternately, of the idea that good intentions are not always sufficient and that he who gives what he can gives everything. Now, in the heat, as if stunned, made sleepy by the sensation of the departing summer toasting the grass, the priest allowed himself to think about the subjects he'd explained so often on winter nights. He had known the man who painted the picture when he was a boy; he saw him, once or twice each autumn, ever since the portrait was hung on the sacristy wall, that thirty-year-old face which clung to adolescence for reasons the priest could not understand. Each autumn, accompanied by his aunt, the school principal, he would come by after the last Mass. And it was his aunt who brought the picture to the church and offered it to the priest with the moving certainty that through her gift she was conquering a reward no one could grant her on earth. It seemed necessary to believe that she had painted the portrait, to doubt the existence of that artistic nephew, and to suspect that the horrifying picture had an ungraspable meaning, a secret and fantastic value. But the nephew did exist; that little boy who at some time or other impossible to date had decided to run away with nothing more than the most absolutely necessary clothing, a train ticket, a few pesos, and the jars of paint he'd bought, God knows how, from some traveling salesman. Now the painter, back from mystery and silence, had set up a studio over in the Old Market.

The priest knew, without going beyond simply knowing, that the simulacrum of youth was determined in the nephew by things more serious than vanity; or by a different kind of vanity, more important and harder to forgive than the vanity that impelled the weak aunt to use rouge and hide her white hair with a hairdo and with the round, resolutely horizontal hat she still wore for Mass.

The deputy yawned with hunger, raising a hand that was too late to reach his mouth. Father Bergner glanced for a second at his bony, clean-shaven, dark face. Like a fat summer fly, ill humor buzzed between the two men, colliding with their foreheads.

"The young ladies from the League will be here just after lunch," said the deputy. "You have an appointment with them. The woman asked if there was anything she could do."

He yawned again behind his hairy, crooked hand while the priest got up from the table, again thinking about the heat, trying to discover an important, original meaning in the image of the city and the peaceful farms under the intense whiteness of siesta. He snatched up the handkerchief, certain he'd forgotten something, that something was being wasted forever.

"At exactly three, we'll receive the young ladies. Now, let's eat."

He touched the other man's shoulder lightly to head him to the door.

"You understand, don't you? I'm grateful that you gave me that information, and it may be important in a certain way. But I don't want, we shouldn't personalize things. This isn't a political struggle."

Walking along the corridor, which was cooler, over the slap of the deputy's shoes on the red, moist tiles, the priest thought that man's misery reached the point where it dimmed the grandeur of the disasters he had to withstand and turned tragic symbols into mere anecdotes.

"I was telling you because that was what people were saying," the deputy insisted sadly, pausing in the smell of the food outside the refectory door. "They say the same thing about you, that you're leaving."

Father Bergner touched the man's shoulder again and smiled mechanically, even before he knew what he wanted to express with his smile. The deputy's face seemed to grow blacker as his whiskers grew, and his eyes cautiously revealed curiosity, a bewildered, apprehensive love.

"Let them talk, son," answered the priest. "Let's eat."

Then the deputy took a step in the direction the pressure of the priest's hand on his shoulder indicated. But he stopped instantly, hirsute, pained, staring at the blotches of color on the three bottles resting on the set table.

"Father, they've also told me something they don't want you to know. But I can't keep silent. I was praying all morning, and now I know that I must tell you. Even so . . . They've told me that your nephew is in the bordello."

"My nephew?" The disconcerted priest wrinkled his face incredulously, grieving at the indisputable fact that he too was linked to others by blood. "What do you mean 'in the bordello'?"

"Just that, father," purred the deputy, recoiling under the priest's hand, repentant and guilty. "Marcos Bergner, your nephew. He went out to the house last night and stayed. They say his car is still there, parked right in front."

They walked forward separately, silently, shortening their steps and straightening up, as if they were sliding over the checkerboard tiles, as if they understood each other, as if they'd rehearsed the scene. At the head of the table, the priest's hand and face authorized the others to sit down. Father Bergner thought objectively, preparing himself. *Marcos Bergner. Marcos. I thought I saw him this morning in church, as I do every Sunday. Actually, this doesn't surprise me. I never liked hearing his confession. He's young; physically he resembles me.*

Immediately he felt ready to deal with the scandal, measure its consequences and use them. During the entire lunch, intervening regularly and distractedly in the conversation, losing arguments about dates, accurate memories, and the taste of wines, he could imagine Marcos's small red car abandoned in the gray clods on the steep street, shining like a bonfire under the whiteness of the sun, attractive and unmistakable in front of the closed wood of the house. Bent over the dishes the old woman carried in at extremely long intervals, scattering the buzz of the flies with his handkerchief, separating it from the noise of drinking and chewing, it occurred to him that perhaps it might not have been the devil who led Marcos to the bordello on the previous night.

He wanted to be alone and on his knees, to give thanks for that confused sensation about the heat and the landscapes around Santa María at siesta time, that premonitory image which could include, in a dissimulated way, a red car on an insignificant street parked in front of the sky-blue glare of a poor little house, out there on the unknown coast.

CHAPTER XXIX

Marcos Bergner received the little card at eight in the evening at the Plaza bar. Earlier he told María Bonita:

"I'm going on vacation for a few hours. Take care of the kid for me. And hide him."

In the Plaza, he thought vaguely that his uncle must already know about his personal bordello adventure. The card invited him to enter the church one hour later through a side door, to meet in the sacristy with the priest, a shoemaker, an auctioneer, a farmer, a student, a wheat buyer, and a Swiss-German grandfather.

Between drinks, as he tore up the card, he mockingly analyzed the name "League of Knights" and informed his friends at the bar.

"You can't do anything in this country. Everything's filthy and worn-out. But maybe it's just that we're wrong when we decide what really matters. Ana María disap-

peared more than a week ago. One of you must know
where she's hiding. And if one knows, all of you know,
except Marcos Bergner. Which proves that all of you, my
dear friends, are sons of bitches. An indispensable cat-
egory if we want to achieve equality among men. But
you're right. I don't want to go looking for her. She'll
have to come back on her own; we're going to have fun."

He asked for another drink as he slowly felt young
and happy again. Outside, the summer was coming to an
end and the flowers in the plaza were pouring out their
last perfume. The river was lapping quietly against the
dock, against Latorre Island and the opposite bank. All
possibilities—saying "no," saying "yes," inventing something different, without a past—were outside again, as
usual.

At a quarter after nine, he told the bartender he was
paying for everyone's drinks. He smiled as he thought
up a lie, wondering if anyone at the bar deserved it.

"I'm not self-centered. Some night or other, I'll take
all of you, when I get bored. But the early bird has some
rights too. Now I don't know whether I should go back
to the whorehouse or go over to the church."

For a few blocks he made the noise of the red car echo
as he left town and headed for the coast. Then he silently
turned around, returning by dark, bumpy streets until he
stopped in the shadows a hundred yards from the church.
Above the narrow door, a cautious yellow light dissolved.
He entered without knocking, moving through the smells
of wax, age, benzoin or incense. On some remote morning, his mother had burned similar perfumes, blowing
on an indolent smoke in order to expel the devil, illness,
and bad luck from the house. He stopped to listen to the
voices in the sacristy. "The best among us must gather

together in moments of danger," the priest Bergner had written on the card. Marcos knocked at the door with one finger, and advanced his insolent smile amid sentences about prophylaxis and the immortality of the soul. Around the oblong table, the same poor men he expected to find.

"We've been waiting for you, my boy." The priest greeted him in a barely exaggerated tone of rejoicing and enthusiasm.

"Please go on talking."

Marcos stepped back a few paces and then retreated until he could lean his shoulders against the wall. He took out a cigarette and listened to the silence, the bother, and the stupidity. The badly formed sentences, the commonplaces, the conflicting discourses resumed. Leaning his head in front of the tight vest of the shoe salesman, someone proposed:

"Gentlemen, since our friend Marcos Bergner has decided to honor us with a visit, I think it's only appropriate to inform him . . ."

Marcos separated the cigarette from his mouth and stretched out a negative arm:

"Thank you. But I'm not here to attend this meeting of the League. I have to speak with my uncle. Family matters. Urgent family matters."

He begged their pardon, nodding his head while the priest left his high-backed chair and walked slowly toward him, trampling the brusque silence.

"And again, please excuse me," said Marcos.

In the refectory's long solitude, sitting at opposite ends of the naked, interminable table, the priest and the nephew stared at each other.

"What is all this, Marcos?" Father Bergner finally asked. "Nothing like what you said, I'm sure."

"Nothing. Everything's fine, the same. Julita's crazy. As for me, we don't need the secrecy of confession. The whole town, all those idiots gathered in there, know that I moved into the whorehouse. But it's just a kind of tourism, a reconnaissance patrol into enemy territory."

Father Bergner turned his face toward the door of the sacristy where the angry, confused voices again grew loud. Amused, he smiled, calmly stroked his stubborn chin and sat down in another chair, closer to Marcos.

"Nearer so we don't have to shout."

Marcos agreed, felt for another chair and finally sat down on the table, directly opposite the priest's intelligent expression.

"Anyway," Marcos excused himself, "since the saints don't eat much . . ."

"They eat a lot. And it doesn't matter. Just as the stupid life you're leading doesn't matter for what's really important. Going to the bordello for you was nothing more than what you and your friends call being a real man. Even so, without knowing it, you're helping me, serving my cause."

Marcos smiled as he took out another cigarette. Then he affectionately reached out his hand to caress the priest's brow.

"That's what I like, uncle and father," he said. "The intelligence, the tricks, the game. And it's really true. I'm there as one of your allies. And it's possible that I didn't do all that unconsciously. That I didn't invade the bordello only to chalk up another 'real man's' deed, as you say. Now something's got to happen."

"Yes." The priest took out a handkerchief and began playing with it: He stretched it over his cheeks and nose. "Something. But, if you don't mind, I want to take advantage of this visit to ask about your sister. You aren't drunk, are you?"

"That can't happen. I'm always drunk; consequently I'm never drunk. That's what we call casuistry. Hard to explain."

"Quite comprehensible!" The priest calmed down. "And how are you doing in the little house on the coast?"

"As we Bergners always do, father. I went, I saw, I conquered. I keep on seeing, and there are no more victories. I get drunk with the incredible Body Snatcher, we play cards, we take turns telling each other finely wrought lies. I scared off two or three idiots, and I can't help but abuse my *droit du seigneur*. Slightly modified, of course. But, for better or worse, we have to respect traditions."

"Fine," said the priest. "That's good enough for me. What about Julita? I'm worried, and I don't understand. She never comes to Mass, doesn't want to visit me or receive me. Maybe it's the Malabias. Maybe they're estranging her from me, from God. But Julita knows I'm not the kind of man who goes in for sermons or arguing."

"Except . . ."

"Except when people demand it of me or just plain demand it. It isn't like that in this case, as you well know."

Marcos straightened his body and looked at some Madonna or other on the wall above Father Bergner's head.

"Maybe they're estranging her from God. . . ." He repeated the phrase tenderly, softly, savoring it, almost without moving the cigarette hanging from his lips. "No, the Malabias have nothing to do with it. As for me, I've never seen anyone live as close to God as she does."

The priest helped him in the pause. Again he played with his handkerchief while one of the invisible Knights raised his flutelike voice amid short, defiant laughs.

"And why don't they go screw themselves?" Marcos muttered under his breath.

"Not so fast. Soon they'll be going out to the house. And what about the Malabias' son?"

"That's easy. We were talking about Julita. And I tell him that I never saw a woman so full of love. So absolutely insane, so highly charged. By which I mean: so indifferent to all that we call the world, to the smell of the clothes covered with acrid scum scattered all over her bedroom. She believes in a living Federico. And she summons the Malabia boy so they can exaggerate the merits of the dearly departed in a duet. Or so she can have an ear who will listen to her, maybe a chorus. We've got to leave her alone and wait. In the meantime, pray."

"Wait," commented the priest, shaking his head. "Give me a puff, Marcos."

Marcos passed him the cigarette he was smoking; the priest inhaled deeply twice and returned it to him.

"Wait for what? Wait until Julita, alone and surrounded by all of you, finally turns the madness she chose as a refuge into something permanent? I want to see her."

"You will," promised Marcos. Then he began to laugh. "I can just imagine the interview. You, fully aware of what's going on. Fully aware of our homegrown version of Philip the Fair and Juana the Mad, Federico and Julita."

Father Bergner quieted him, raising a hand.

"They're not shouting any longer. That's dangerous. I have to go back to them. We'll speak again soon. I don't know, I can't know when. In any case, it will be without alcohol and after the eleven o'clock Mass, the hour of the whited sepulchres. But I asked about the Malabias' son. Where is he? His mother came to see me. She thinks he went with you."

"With me?" Marcos pretended to take offense. "He must have run away to the capital. I swear I don't know anything about that idiot. He must have run away from what's left of his disgusting family. I'm not my brother-in-law's keeper."

The priest stood up with an ironic, tolerant look in his eyes. They looked at each other awhile, studying their mutual resemblance. With one hand on the doorknob, Father Bergner said:

"For the greater glory of God, Marcos Bergner, I bless you. I want to ask you to do something very important. I want you to go back to the bordello. I want you to stay there at least until Sunday night."

Still sitting at the table, Marcos bowed. "That's a promise. It will be my penitence, father."

CHAPTER XXX

Díaz Grey was alone, drinking beer at a window table in the Plaza bar. It wasn't chilly, but the lowered curtains cut horizontally across the Sunday afternoon, imposing an unconvincing penumbra on it, a fragile shadow reminiscent of closed, moist patios or bedrooms protected from the heat since morning.

The four boys and one girl were drinking sodas and glasses of *caña* or cognac near the bar, at one of the wicker tables that would be put out on the sidewalk when the sun went down. They moved little and cautiously, holding back their vehemence without succeeding in suppressing it, each one challenging the others with a blond, tanned, prematurely aged face. They were probably between sixteen and eighteen years old, although the skinny girl looked younger. She was wearing brown, rolled-up velvet slacks and a plaid shirt. She smoked with her elbows on the table cloth, removing the cigarette from her mouth at regular intervals, first with her left hand—two short, strong, neglected fingers without rings and almost without nails—and then with her right. She was determined to keep her body from participating in the laughter and forced herself to remain calm, distant, not shaking her head while she allowed her dry, high-pitched guffaws to ring out, always interrupting them before they dropped in tone.

Díaz Grey knew she was the granddaughter of old Petrus, the owner of the cannery, the real estate around the spa, and the dry dock, but he did not recall who her father was or which of the daughters of old Petrus had placed her in the world. *And it may well be that I helped her be born, her or a cousin, in some brick house over in Colonia, scaring the calm, white women so they'd give me more boiling water in some kitchen with immortal stains and smells of smoke, frying, and moisture. But that can't be because it wasn't so many years ago that Brausen brought me to Santa María; but even if it can't be, it's true that we're separated by the same amount of time, and it's true then that I lifted her out from between the milky, bloody legs of one of old Petrus's daughters, held her in the air, amphibious, sticky, and red, that I gave her a couple of slaps on the ass until she cried her short, cold, impersonal cry, just like that laugh she forces out, expels, in the presence of these four pimple-faced aspirants to the first bloodletting, who treat her as a pal and ostentatiously take no regard of the small breasts with which she, humiliated, inflates her work shirt.*

The boy in gray set aside his glass to bend forward over the table and lispingly whisper the story of a scientific method to win at horse racing and the man who invented it, put it into practice in Mar del Plata and the capital, who was now enjoying the fruits of his labors in Paris or Cairo. *They say Marcos Bergner went at dawn to live in the bordello. They say he brought a Luger and the clothes on his back. But his uncle, the priest Bergner, never mentioned it in his sermon this morning, never talked about the prodigal son, or the lost sheep, and did not take any examples of apostasy from the Bible. But the story of the Golden Calf, already used up, was about the apostasy we've all committed, his people, and doesn't warn about or exemplify this personal, more shocking apostasy of a favorite nephew: anti-Semitic, anti-liberal, anti-Yankee, anti-Soviet.*

The blondest of the boys lit a cigarette and fixed his face in a sarcastic, reticent, tamed smile until the smoke left it naked and visible. "Systems," he said when the others looked at him. "Let her tell you about the Gaucho and Peeping Tom. You'll see what these systems for gambling really are. Gambling is gambling." He was wearing a very tight, blue, three-button suit he could only button by making an effort. It had very narrow lapels; on the left was a monstrous sprig of freshly cut jasmine. The collar of his tieless, yellowish, silk shirt spread over the cloth of the suit; like an improvised plaster pedestal, it held up his golden head, educated to be sensible and indifferent, covered by short, hard, incongruous curls. The girl began to laugh and waited.

Then, suddenly, taking advantage of a lull in the conversation, the afternoon revealed it was passing, that it had not promised to become eternal in the hotel salon or to eternalize the warm half-light, the lines of gold and dust on the windows, the quintet of adolescents sitting in wicker armchairs, the clear noises free of the ice, glass, and gambling chips that clattered on the bar, falsely distant, falsely involved in the corroboration of a symbol. *I helped all of them to be born, and it may be that I was imagining a kind of superiority above their howls, their livid, miserable bodies, perhaps I imagined that they accepted owing me some kind of thanks. And now they've reached fifteen and begun to take their places and displace others, begun to believe that the old, tedious, and exciting adventure, the interminable reiteration of commonplaces, actually starts with them and that they are discovering and creating it. And it's true, I have to accept it; enthusiastically, submissively, they are writing the chapters of the inveterate story and don't know that it existed before, that it re-creates itself with them, that it made them and makes them in order to consummate its maniacal obstinacy.*

"On Sunday, the Gaucho came to this very table," recited the Petrus girl in a monotonous voice whose high notes easily rose above her deliberate hoarseness, "he came and told me he was going to put twenty and ten on Southern Boy in the fifth race and did I want to bet anything. I didn't move a muscle, told him I did and laid down a hundred pesos next to his hand, between his hand and his glass. None of you was here, remember? That was the Sunday you stood me up because of Cota's birthday. But Gaucho came, and I was here alone from lunch until three with the other waiter, the Italian, cracking jokes. Because I was alone and calm. I went along with him and laughed. If no one came by three, I was going to get on my bike and place the bet. And all because of a dream, I dreamed about the woman from the Old Market's kid, he's three, dreamed that he followed me home and that I was going to sleep and he was looking at me with his head poked through the door. Really. He looked at me until I pushed him out and closed the door, and then I saw him looking in through the window. Then the other day, I looked at the paper and said Peeping Tom, I'm going to bet on Peeping Tom. And the Gaucho, when I gave him the money and he was laughing at me and at all of you because you'd stood me up and gone to the birthday party, made a face as if he were disgusted and told me I was crazy. He knew that Southern Boy was going to win, knew that Peeping Tom was a donkey. 'I don't want to help you throw your money away.' 'Gaucho,' I said to him, 'look, it doesn't matter to me; if you don't do it, I'll get on my bike and place the bet myself, which I'll do right now just because I feel like it.' Finally he took the money and went. He didn't pay up, I told my brother; Peeping Tom paid off twenty to one, and now I'm waiting for the Gaucho to turn up so I can wave the money in his face."

"So much for systems," said the boy without a tie as he got up to make a telephone call.

Díaz Grey ordered another beer and noted the weakness of the afternoon in the light falling on his hand.

In the south, Villa Petrus, right at the beach, had grown. It grew on its own, under the indifference of Petrus, who had planned it as a big spa business. When he didn't get the support he needed immediately from Councilman Veronentas, he lost interest. It was the young men from Colonia who years ago began to build little houses in Villa Petrus, mostly for weekends and amorous excursions, at first with maids, then with their social equals, the sisters of their friends, the kind of girl it's possible, though not necessary, to marry. So after years of this kind of growth and clandestine preparation, suddenly we found out that Villa Petrus was a real place, *the* fashionable place. It became necessary to own a bungalow near what people called the beach, although the sand there was no different from the dark sand mixed with muddy earth that extended along the entire coastal region. And, absurdly, Petrus's original and very large house, set on top of a hill, which stood as the foundation stone of the entire spa, was turned by its owner into a boardinghouse.

For a few weeks during the summer it was almost filled with tourists, the farthest of whom came from three or four miles away to breathe the same air and to admire a landscape approximately identical to the one they could see every day, if they'd wanted to, in the place where they lived and worked throughout the year.

But Villa Petrus, very quickly for those who knew how to observe, became something more than a jumbled, cheap copy of a seaside town. Something more or something essentially different from the ambition the names of the "hotels" announced: Ostende, Biarritz, Monte Carlo, Lido, Atlantic. Almost none of them offered more than bedrooms, given up during the summer by the owner's children or in-laws, who would gather for the duration of the "season" in the few rooms remaining or in sheds or garages. There were only two with more than twenty rooms, the old one and the new one, the first made of wood, the second of cement.

The little town was a not very convincing pile of small houses barely distinguishable from each other except in the details their owners managed to add, the painting of façades, for example, because the builder, Ferrari, constructed them according to a conventional model of Swiss chalet he was more or less incapable of altering. The chalets were at different heights, surrounded by wild weeds that no civilizing or aesthetic effort, no summer heat for that matter, managed to kill, separated from the river by boastful rows of tamarind trees that never grew and were never necessary. This landscape was at first a symbol and then a reality; it was a kind of bastion or island where, especially during the summer months, the social life of the new generation from Colonia took place, excluding Santa María and, especially, its inhabitants. So, year after year, and with greater and greater intensity, resolve, and a disdain that required no comment and perhaps wasn't completely conscious, the children and grandchildren of the citizens of Colonia were relegating Santa María, from December to February, to the well-delineated status of social center, to a place they could not avoid visiting if they wanted to shop, make bank deposits, or pick up letters at the post office.

But Santa María itself never became aware of that spontaneously organized excommunication. The scorn of the young foreigners, naturally and solidly seconded by their parents—who set about substituting the makeshift, adventurous little shacks with real houses with tile roofs and decorative stairs made of flagstones, houses fit only for large families, not furtive couples or little groups— was not something that could interest much less wound the city which with each harvest was growing by leaps and bounds both in population and wealth. It was only noticed by the boys, who on afternoons, summer evenings, or Saturday nights would go from Santa María to Villa Petrus to have some fun in what was at least a different place, a different bar.

At that time in Villa Petrus there were two spots where it was possible to drink and even to dance: The Breezes, a café, and a tiny operation open only at night called the Wilhelm, but referred to as the "boîte."

Juan Carlos Onetti

We are, or in any case, I am in Santa María at the end of a summer, telling the story of the bordello on the coast, the story of Barthé the pharmacist, the priest Bergner, María Bonita, Body Snatcher, and, when you get right down to it, the story of all of us, the rest, the city, and Colonia. Now, on this Sunday, we have reached the stage of the apocalyptic anonymous, linked letters, trying to find the meaning, the importance, the consequences of the fact, apparently so easy to tell, that Marcos Bergner, nephew of the priest, had entered the whorehouse at dawn with a Luger in his hand, and is still there, as can be scandalously confirmed by his red sports car, which is parked diagonally in the ruts along the dirt road.

CHAPTER XXXI

In those days, we felt our faith in the existence of a disillusioned, mature, woman doggedly writing the anonymous letters begin to decline. We no longer believed in the features, clothes, the idiosyncrasy, shape, and length of her shadow on the wall—the elements with which we'd constructed the imagined old maid, older lady, Swiss, blonde, skinny, and tall, full of strength and restrained brusqueness whenever she moved.

The summer burned, and the doors and curtains of the houses were kept closed from lunch until nightfall in order to separate patios and bedrooms from the sun and to build a tranquil coolness that always had as its center vases filled with jasmine in which the same brown tone of rotten fruit quickly grew.

We could no longer believe in a semidarkness that held the transitorily curved bust of the lady-writer, the lace blouse, the visible collarbones with the cameo held up by a black ribbon, the tired smile, the implacable nose. We didn't see any siesta darkness pierced by her coming and going from feeding the cats to the watering of plants, and it was impossible for us to place the zigzag or curve of streets resonant with roosters and birds she would trot along, touching her nose after each livid half-block with the hanky she kept in her sleeve.

We'd also lost faith—and this privation was more serious—in the existence of the muted chorus of girls that gathered, as was proven, in the house of Julita Bergner, Malabia's widow. The girls who went to have tea, laugh for false reasons and without conviction, spy into the corners of Julita's bedroom and into her hallucinated face, her secret revealed and hidden by her thick, low eyelids and by the obsessed, smooth joy that raised the ends of her mouth. Spying with the same dissimulated interest with which they spied the future, the eyes of the men, the ambiguous evening sky, the foliaceous and taciturn shape of their half-open sexes devoid of consequences seen in the mirrors they took down from the bathroom wall.

We no longer believed either in the old lady or the girls. The tone of the most recent anonymous letters, their remote, purified anathemas, their deliberate avoidance of personal attacks, the same vulgar, earthy, final request that copies be made and sent "to the souls that you know need this warning" impelled us to imagine that the letters fell from heaven into our mailboxes one hour before the mailman got on his bike. We imagined that a gigantic angel bent over to write them, brushing against the roof of the sacristy, flanked by the prayers of the priest Bergner (kneeling and ecstatic), illuminating the portrait of the pope on the wall with the gold of his round, fallen head, turning the body of the crucified dove into soft, warm silver.

Of that period, the final period, there remains an example that can confirm what we said or make it at least more comprehensible:

> The sinner with dirty hands must know that friendship with the devil means being an enemy of God. All we have to do is resist the devil to make him flee; so there are no excuses. Your laughter will become tears and your joy affliction because the face of the Lord is over those who do evil. If God condemned the cities of Sodom and Gomorrah to destruction, turning them into ash, he will know how to torment the sinners of Santa María.
>
> The Lord reproaches you. You should make three copies of this epistle and see that they reach the souls that you know need this warning.

And we discovered that some things always come in threes even if at times there aren't two or four; there are always three, we found out, to remember as brothers, to deform them until they are identical to us, three with whom we can be silent, smile, not explain things. Perhaps each one of us only wanted to bother three; perhaps we were only interested in imagining their faces leaning over the anonymous letters we copied and were going to slip into the mailbox at night, imagining what memories, what repentance we were going to evoke for them, for each one of the three we'd chosen.

Before anything happened that it might be important

to tell, that Sunday was premonitory, doubly marked by
the end of the jasmine invasion and by the absence in
the priest's sermon of any phrase that might allude to the
bordello on the coast. This last fact may be attributed to
the literary talent—this is the opinion of Sabatiello the
bookseller—or the tactics—this is the opinion of Dr. Díaz
Grey—of Father Bergner.

The sun rose on a city free of the barefoot little boys
who had held bouquets of jasmines wrapped in newspapers against their dirty shirts crisscrossed by suspend-
ers. A city free of women wearing useless aprons over
their poor dresses, who had arrived each morning from
the farms, dragged in by languid, hairy horses, or who
walked on foot, carrying on their heads, perched on a roll
of rags, the baskets that overflowed with the excessive
whiteness, the lunar perfume of the flowers.

With regard to Father Bergner: That suspicious Sunday he also omitted the impassivity which distanced him
so much from his disciples and which they suffered perhaps with more pain than his words of reproach and
threats. He omitted the melancholy, ostentatious pride
that made him stand in erect solitude three feet above
the silent multitude, distant, irrevocably resolved to bear
the guilt that his children tolerated and were incapable
of avoiding. As usual, he bent his wide body over the
pulpit, and raised it up laboriously, gradually, in order
to present to the huddled mass of fear and expectations
a recognizable, understanding, happy face, eyes and
mouth that distributed peace, thanks for having been
born, the conviction that life is good because it cannot
be discussed. Men and women felt that the reconquered,
amiable, frank, and rubicund head was the same as a
paternal pat on the back, as greetings in the church

atrium, or at the doors of houses in Colonia, as the disappeared questions about the birth of calves, plantings,
marriage plans, the irregularities of health.

Many of us believed that the evil had been vanquished
and leaned toward the pulpit to listen to the first news
and deduce from the confused forebodings and ambiguous biblical examples the specific details of the miracle
we supposed had taken place a few hours before, during
the always bewildering, always treacherous Saturday
night while we were going over our account books, gra-
tuitously playing cards, or fogging the lenses of our in-
frequently worn glasses as we found out about the
adventures of the relatives of the neighbor who'd just
arrived at the gathering.

A minority said later that they'd discovered in the
priest's wide, happy, friendly face promises of evils more
fearful than those in the distant, gloomy, indirectly disdainful expression he'd imposed on them over so many
previous Sundays, almost like a habit or a landscape,
almost by now like a ritual element. But perhaps only
old man Küttel—enormous, dressed in black, his beady,
light eyes barely separated by his ladylike nose and surrounded by his round, white beard, sucking his empty
pipe and hiding it out of respect—was aware of what the
indulgent sermon was serving as a prologue.

Erect, colloquial, sonorous, and wholesome, Father
Berguer rapidly said that Mass was over and brusquely
raised his head and one hand so that all of them would
stop and see him smile. It was then that his flock began,
slowly, awkwardly, and full of disgust to be sorry they'd
substituted their apprehension with forgetting.

They had just stood up, just begun the stiff walk to
the aisles, mixing the theme of the sermon with images

of vehicles parked around the plaza, with expectations about the power of the sun on the street and on the downhill road, with pardonable gluttony about pieces of boiled chicken. Above, in the pulpit, he maintained his joyful expression; it was the same expression of enthusiasm and excuse with which Father Bergner distributed his various kinds of help. They had seen it after dinner, in private consultations, at wakes and baptisms. But now they saw that the priest was deliberately showing them the goodness and the pleasure of humbling himself; that the smile—which barely raised his brows, which barely introduced his lips into his freckled, pink cheeks—alluded to diffuse martyrdoms and tenacities, to farewells that could be detailed but were summarized by modesty and another form of humility.

The girls from Action were already in the street forming into ranks of four on the side of the church in shadows, looking toward the plaza and the sign announcing ice cream flavors that stuck out of the sweetshop. The school principal, hobbling along, inspected the ranks, corrected distances, and evened out the shawls covering the girls' shoulders and their modest décolletés. The people slowly emerged from the church, blinking in the sunlight, advancing without impatience toward the horses and cars, toward the doors of the sweetshop and the hotel.

Some saw the calm column of women protected by the church wall, others saw the cloth banner they'd begun to unfurl, still others saw the town band gravely, martially, almost heroically approaching to place themselves at the head of the battalion of girls. Others might have seen the school principal's hat: round, as stiff as steel, incapable of bending or being flexible, as she finished her incessant, anguished to-ing and fro-ing alongside the immobile girls, who now raised their chins and their bosoms. The people all saw something of this and stopped, waiting. They were surprised by the slow, discreetly jubilant tolling of the bells swung over a blue sky, over wrinkled, scarce, and lazy clouds.

Her inspection over, the school principal took her place just to the side of the third platoon and unostentatiously took command. Her stockings were sagging and she tried to distance her bright red face from the embarrassment of her exasperated timidity by means of a reticent expression and severe eyes that were already looking toward the final meaning of the ceremony. Those of us in the plaza or peering into it knew that something unusual was finally going to happen in Santa María. At least we knew that the battalion of girls was going to start marching.

And nevertheless, when the generally moustached men in the band tried to unite the noise of their respective instruments in order to play "Oh Holy Mary," and the girls in the last rows—who could see neither the face nor the gestures of the principal—disconcertedly began to sing the first two lines, a clap of the principal's hands started the entire column on its way. Then we felt that we could not have guessed this, the only reasonable thing, the only one that could have been foreseen.

Now it's impossible to find out what we would have admitted without surprise, what would have seemed more normal to us than the parade of girls around the plaza. But the truth is that those of us in the plaza or spying from the doors of the shops and the tables at the hotel and the café, knew, purely and surprisingly, the extraordinary and surprising quality of what was taking place. The girls, now silent, dragged along by the band's slow, supplicating music and what was like a normal prolongation of it, began to walk along the side of the plaza where the sweetshop and the club are, where Alsina's store once stood. Young, vigorous, and awkward, they marched out of step, each one wearing the absent, challenging expression they seemed to have copied from the principal, which they thought sufficient to individualize them, to make them memorable for the multitude they were part of.

Two paces behind the music, Küttel's gigantic granddaughter and the baker's daughter were effortlessly holding up the banner where high, narrow, black letters sweetly blazed forth:

WE WANT CHASTE BOYFRIENDS
AND HEALTHY HUSBANDS

With their mouths shut, excessively erect, impatient and tolerant, holding hands, arms stretched as far as they could without dropping the missals they held in their armpits, they marched all the way around the plaza, with their heels kicking up the reddish gravel, silent under the slow roar of the band.

We saw them tall, blonde, and athletic; we supposed they were virgins, sweaty and conscious of both things, as we indolently and with critical intent compared legs, busts, hips, grace, and thinness of necks. When they finished their lap around the plaza and reached the church again, the principal reappeared at the head of the column waving her arms, stepping right into the greenish uniforms of the musicians, who quickly left, putting away their instruments, again aware that they were men and superfluous. All of Santa María silently stared from the four sidewalks.

Less than a minute later, we saw that the summer

dresses—stripes in vehement colors, impossible flowers, geometric repetitions—of the girls in Action were violently regrouping in order to march off instantly, to glide across the church's gray background in order to get to the automobiles and impassive beasts standing on the steaming manure and impose solitude on the atrium. The bells stopped ringing, and we then understood they had been ringing, grave and soft, ominously happy and contained, during the time it took the girls to march around the plaza. We were all silent, and we thought we'd guessed what the end of the midday would be.

Father Bergner, black and slow, with routine gestures, his hat pulled down on his head, appeared at the door of the church without brushing its half-closed panels, closing them effortlessly. He became solitary in order to look at us and count us, holding the huge padlock against his stomach. Then he slipped it through the loops and locked it. He came, visibly not toward us, but toward the bars on the door. He looked patiently at us, measuring and comparing us, thinking perhaps about used biblical groupings, about the appropriateness of speaking to us, about glossing for our benefit the slammed door and the gray lock. But all he did was look at us again, now sadly, pardoning us without reproaches.

We also knew that his final theatrical gesture, skillfully outlined by the silence, was and was meant to be an end for the opprobrious guilt that weighed down the citizens of Santa María and spread, in an unfair way, to the inhabitants of Colonia, Swiss, Catholic, and pure by definition. And if it is true that old Lanza or anyone else of our group was writing a chronicle based on the transcendental event of the death of one year and the beginning of another, the locking up of the church ordered by

Father Bergner also quashed all kinds of written truth and fantasy.

Enormous in her isolation and silence, Küttel's grand-daughter left her grandfather and went to look for the priest. Father Bergner smiled at her and dropped his head twice; with his hat in his hand, heavy, awkward, inde-cisive, humbling his stature, trying not to get ahead of the girl, he reached the coach and got in. Old man Küttel had been waiting in the driver's seat, the reins and the whip in his hands, leaning back, his white beard almost horizontal. He had only to say one word, and the animals trotted in front of the church, turned without any pressure at the corner and went moving along, fat and moist, under the sun, until they reached the road to Colonia.

CHAPTER XXXII

On the eve of carnival, Santa María was a complete city, the Berna's roof was garlanded, while a sad, fat man played a German melody on his accordion and some tables chorused it.

We were crowded into the reserved room, eating dessert, waiting until the imprecise moment when the train would arrive to pick up the plague sullying Santa María and return it to the capital. Governor's orders. Stubborn and astute, Father Bergner had won the short or long battle. We were waiting with laughter and silence, breathing the thick air, the smoke, and the insolent perfumes the women were wearing.

María Bonita sank her left hand into the bag of grapes and then removed it; her right hand was on the table, for me, so that I could caress it. I had Marcos's pistol in my belt. I accepted tolerance, but I distrusted all shades of mockery or patronizing attitudes. I thought about Julita and about my parents, about my furious desire to shed my belief in brief lives and farewells, about the foul vigor of apostasy. I still felt no remorse. I knew that I would, as soon as that ghostly train devoid of schedule would appear and I'd taken it to be alone.

There was, in the meanwhile, a bitter taste, a form of precaution and consolation in the challenge of publicly patting, in the Berna, the right hand of a prostitute old enough to be my mother, who smiled lovingly at me, who was trying to leave behind as a souvenir the image of a lady dressed in a severe, dark tailored suit.

I smoked, occasionally looking at Body Snatcher's face out of the corner of my eye: it had become fat since the bad news came; all the hair he had left was one single lock plastered down over one brow.

Dr. Díaz Grey was wearing a new blue suit, and he was the only one who seemed to be sincerely enjoying himself. He spoke little and smiled as if the story of the bordello and its last chapter—which he was contemplating—had been his creation. Medina was next to the curtain of the reserved room; as chief of police, he was responsible for seeing that the blot on our honor left Santa María.

"All I'm asking," insisted Larsen, rocking back in his chair, "is whether the thing was legal or not. Did we or did we not have a permit from the council? I can tell you the number of the bill. And it was never revoked, never."

"Bah," said Medina, "you and the pharmacist probably wrote it up together. There's an order from the governor, and as far as I'm concerned that's it."

Old Lanza came toward the table, limping worse than

ever, his hat on his head. He drank some wine and filled
his glass again.

"You, Larsen, repeat things until you bore everybody.
The ladies are getting tired. Council, permit, bill. Our
friend Medina here, who perhaps has put his shoulder
to the wheel, so to speak, more than once in noble causes,
is only following orders."

"I don't know what Irene and Nelly think," said María
Bonita, "but as far as I'm concerned, no one has to call
me lady. For my real friends, María Bonita is enough."

"Thanks," said Lanza, saluting her. "Even if we never
see each other again, thanks."

"As I was saying to Jorge," María Bonita went on as
she tousled my hair, "the priest—excuse me for saying
so—must have gone nuts. None of us ever offended God."

She rapidly made the sign of the cross.

"No reason to doubt you in that. So, just one more
chapter in the ancient struggle between obscurantism and
reason. Reason, of course, is represented here by our
friend Larsen. But I see him, I feel him tonight to be like
Churchill: He can lose all battles but the last."

Patient, allowing himself to be surrounded by the cli-
mate of jokes, disarmed and aged, Body Snatcher lifted
his shoulders and the hand that was feeling for an un-
necessary support on the table. For a moment, his bulging
eyes fixed on María Bonita and Díaz Grey.

"Why didn't the councilmen suspend their recess?"
he stammered.

"Ah," said old Lanza. "I swear to you that we'll all
remember this night. The losers, the winners, and the
curious neutrals. Larsen fought for liberty, civilization,
and honorable commerce. And now he's worried about

the proper respect for institutions. After all, we mustn't put all the blame on Father Bergner. In reality, it was Santa María that put an end to the unforgettable enterprise. Fortunate are they who go." Serious and lucky, he raised what was left of his wine in a toast. "This city. *Ave Maria, gratia plena, Dominus tecum, Benedicta . . .*"

With a slow laugh and a fit of coughing, Díaz Grey interrupted him.

"It's late," said Lanza. "I've got to go. It's unfortunate we can't print a few lines of hail and farewell in the *Travelers* column."

"Go to bed, Spaniard," grumbled Larsen, swaying again.

"To work, to sink into yards of lead and stupidity. But someday I'll publish the history of these hundred days that shook the earth. And perhaps . . . Just think: If one came back from Elba, another can escape from Saint Helena. Good night."

By common accord, the three women were putting on fresh lipstick. They used brushes, some strange little boxes that looked as if they held watercolors, saliva or ice water from the bowl.

"All right," said Medina. "At one, we leave for the station. Not much time left."

Larsen looked at him puzzled, still hating him. Díaz Grey turned to look at me.

"You going?"

"You just heard the man. At one."

"What are you thinking, doctor?" said María Bonita. "Think I'm a kidnapper?"

"Not at all, excuse me," answered Díaz Grey. "I think he's going because he wants to, that he's got more than enough reasons for leaving Santa María."

"I can't keep him or anyone else from getting on the train. Look: I'm a woman, and I'm thinking more about his mother than about him."

"There's his father too," whispered Medina.

I dug around in my pockets until I found my pipe. I didn't look at Medina.

"I can travel in another car. I can go tomorrow or whenever I like. Besides, doctor, I don't think any cop's going to tie me up." Now I did look for Medina's face. "No offense. I didn't say it because of you."

The man smiled and shook his bored head.

"Things were bad enough," grumbled Larsen once more. "Let him go any time, whenever he wants. But not with us. One more complication, as if we didn't have enough."

"He's a snotnose kid," affirmed Nelly, the fat one, as she angrily closed her purse. "This is just a whim and nothing else. The spoiled brat. Feels like giving us a headache and playing at being a man."

"You all heard him say it," said María Bonita. "He said it clearly. That he's not going because of María Bonita." She gives me her hand again so I can caress it and then tousles my hair. "What do you think, doctor? Sixteen, seventeen . . ."

I waited for them to forget me so I could think about Julita, vaguely recall my mother. Medina yawned and slowly made his way to the door of our private room. My watch said almost one o'clock; but I felt at that apathetic hour of the morning, when everything's been said, when we're sorry for having spoken and listened, that variable but punctual hour that comes back to convince us of the uselessness of the company and the words. Medina came back shortly:

"Ladies and gentlemen . . . Whenever you like."

Behind the curtain, I saw the boots of a couple of policemen. Here or at the station, I wondered, calculating, trying to guess, to intuit. We got up with difficulty, and Díaz Grey's face said nothing to me. He went on enjoying himself, needing to witness the final moment. I sat next to him in one of the cars, between Irene and him. In the front seat, the driver was annoyed by Nelly and a cop.

Then I had to address the doctor's immobile, thin profile, the incurable expression of vigilance under his thin hair, which was so blond it disguised the gray.

"I'm sure that you made all this up. It's absurd, I know it. I'm referring to everything, not only the end, which you're determined to watch more out of a mysterious (for me) sense of obligation than for the pleasure that you can get from being sure of a defeat. That is, your own failure. There's more: Of all the filth filling up these two cars, you're the filthiest. We don't know each other well, that's true, but I'm never wrong. Sometimes, when I think about you or look at you, I despise you. Other times, I'm sorry for you. I wanted to tell you, as a farewell."

The doctor remained calm without changing his expression. Irene didn't protest. We reached the station and were crossing the end of an autumn night, without hurrying or speaking. The two policemen brought up the rear. It would be there, in that case.

"By a miracle it's not late," said Medina.

There were very few people waiting for the red lights of the approaching train. I let them get on, I saw the old women bent down with their baggage, I saw a Body Snatcher diminished in his stature, downcast, his hands behind his back, held up by what was left of his strange pride. Medina got on behind him, and I decided to move.

But the two cops, flashing paternal smiles in the station's yellow light, in the unlimited night of Santa María and its silence, stood at attention in front of the steps to the train. It was to be here. I showed surprise and consternation, the weakness of my years, as I took out Marcos's pistol and took off the safety with my thumb.

"Out of the way or I'll fire." Now it was my turn to show my teeth. "Right now or there will be two sons of bitches less."

I was moving the pistol from one chest to the other, when someone softly touched me on the shoulder.

"Jorge. My son. Not tonight."

I recognized Father Bergner's voice. It was free of threats, orders, domination; free as well of supplication. The furious faces of the two cops barely nodded in greeting. I think that one, the one on the right, saluted.

The weight of the hand was identical to the voice, as sad as that voice. I lowered the arm holding the pistol while the priest poured over me the slow absurdity without tears:

"Julita died tonight. No one can know if she was waiting for you, no one can know if she was forgiven."

I handed him the pistol, and we left the station together.

CHAPTER XXXIII

Julita was dead. It was like one of so many Santa María traditions, false or not, inherited by all the survivors. Not much more than that. For such a long time, for an immeasurable time, since the death of my brother, we knew that Julita was dead.

It was absolutely necessary to pretend for the others, to feign ignorance and a mild grief. I did it, we did it over so many nights. There we were, the two of us, she and I, knowing and lying, resigned to waiting.

My father chatted with the judge. Impassive and sorrowful, a strong man destined for history if history were given time enough to recognize him. Surrounded by strong, solicitous matrons, my mother slavered, said no, and drank the cups of tea handed to her between sighs and bouts of weeping.

For us men, there was soda water, tall bottles, and fat

bottles. A long night, worthy of the fallen, of the first incursion of civilization in this place.

Out of respect, I put away my beret and stuck my tongue into the cognac to seek a memory prudently, to burn a memory and seek diverse, daily, and nocturnal deaths.

In Julita's words, I was a sweet little monster. I was a brother-in-law, I counted the floor tiles, I suffered without smiling. Helped by the irony of the dead woman, I bent over, lit my pipe, and returned to the cognac.

I heard so much crying, so many well-fashioned sighs that I came to feel myself separated again. I banged my pipe, but nothing could hide Marcos's exaggerated crying, the short spiritual yielding of a drunk mixing with the comic, measured rocking back and forth of feminine hysteria. The screams rose, begging to share her death, then fell to offer food and drinks.

I knew that no one loved her as I did, I remembered the knife and I calmed myself with the cold of its blade. I knew that no one loved her. I put a match to my lit pipe. I looked at the tiles on the floor, but it was much too late to count them.

It was all a dream, and I was in peace, bent over in the chair, ignorant of Julita, disloyal as usual, filling my-self up with love. But they didn't give me time. My father, the judge, the inevitable Díaz Grey, the officer, spoke rapidly in a strange language. They agreed. I understood what it was necessary for me to do and got up with the knife in my hand, made the blade pop out with a friendly snap. I was determined and tender, in no hurry.

"Sorry, I want to see her before you touch her."

I didn't say it for the poor invisible people who sur-rounded me in silence. I didn't say it to my disaster, to the unhappy son of the silver dove, betrayed, as usual, by his father. I began, simply, to chat with Julita. We were together again, and I needed a pure minute, my own, saved from the hours we'd lost. I went into the bedroom.

Then, deaf to so many different forms of stupidity, to the tide of voices, supplications, and whines, I raised my head to see her, almost immediately to look at her. I approached her shined, chestnut sandals without abandoning the useless ferocity of the knife, without diminishing the mocking smile that only she could have turned into weeping.

I looked at her. She barely swayed and seemed to do it as a whim. Hanging from a beam, possibly with a broken neck, her head twisted, the foam-covered tip of her tongue protruding. She'd shrouded herself in a white high-school girl's tunic, severe and stiff with starch. She'd tricked herself out with a big chignon tied up with a blue tie. Just for me, she'd put on black stockings stretched to reach the top of her calves. She knew what she was doing. No teacher could have reproached her, on earth as it is in heaven. She swung hanging from the beam, swinging out of respect for the wind that comes at the end of the night. Her thighs lengthened incongruously, something slowly poured out.

She didn't shock me for being dead. I'd seen her like that many times. Her sudden, growing age disgusted me, the immodesty of the face she presented, which after bouncing back to infancy progressed quickly toward the filth of old age, destruction.

But, in any case, obscenities invaded me, filthy, untimely ideas. Disgustingly dead, she was finally mine, a friend forever. We were understanding each other, an indestructible pact was being formed, a certain complicity in the joke. She moved, slow and bored, while I prayed an old song to her:

The puppets dance and then they play
They give three turns and go away.

The priest was sitting in the large armchair, so familiar, next to the fireplace without a fire in it. Smoking Marcos's cigarettes with his legs crossed, he rhythmically tapped the small valise next to him with a distracted foot. Stubborn, with his back turned to everything, muttering between his teeth. It occurred to me that he knew, that he'd been watching us since the first night.

The immediate future enraged me, the image of a long, stiff Julita in the bed, with her schoolgirl's disguise, with the definitive expression of gravity and respect it's necessary to offer as a farewell to a world made and run by imbecilic little men. The inherited phrases coming and going like flies from her mouth in peace, her sightless eyes, her cynical nose now without a motive pained me.

Before leaving, I put away the knife, put on my beret, and went back to greet the mourners.

"Shit," I said with a sweetness, a piety, a joy that only she, rotting away hanging from the beam, could have understood.

Only she could see how I went away in order to go down, fatally, toward a normal, astute world whose drivel never reached us. Julita and I, from now on only me, enduring her, finally, really, honorably.

ABOUT THE AUTHOR AND THE TRANSLATOR

Juan Carlos Onetti lives in Spain.

Alfred MacAdam has translated works by Mario Vargas Llosa, Carlos Fuentes, Octavio Paz, Guillermo Cabrera Infante, and Alejo Carpentier, among other Latin American writers.